Commando

Book 1 in the Combined Operations Series

By

Griff Hosker

Commando

Published by Sword Books Ltd 2015

A CIP catalogue record for this title is available from the British Library.
Cover by Design for Writers

Commando

Dedicated to my little sister Barb, and in memory of my Dad who served in Combined Operations from 1941-1945

Contents

Part 1- Prelude to War

Chapter 1

My father was a war hero. I had grown up in awe of the British Ace who had both a Victoria and a Military Cross. He was my hero. Wing Commander Bill Harsker was famous. Mum and Auntie Alice both had many cuttings and clippings from newspapers. My Gran and Grandad still spoke of the pride in their son having been given his medals by the King himself. Even more remarkable was the fact that he came from humble beginnings; he had been born the son of a groom and, until the Great War, had been destined to end his life as a servant. The war had changed all that.

As a senior officer in the new Royal Air Force, we had travelled around in the early twenties. My childhood had been spent on various airfields and postings but each one had something in common, apart from the uniforms, the barracks and the food; my father was revered by the men in every one of them. Unusually, it was not just the officers who held him in high regard, the warrant officers and lower ranks all seemed to view him as something special. His fame was always there; like his medals, it was part of him. He had never sought the fame and he handled it well but it hung over his shoulders like an albatross.

They had called it the Great War but I knew that it was anything but great. When my Uncles Gordy and Ted came to visit and I would ask them about it, they told me of great deeds and heroism but there was bitterness in their words for they had all lost close friends. They told me of the slaughter they had witnessed from the air and the futile fight for a few feet of land. Neither of them had stayed in the Royal Air Force after the war had ended, but each year they made a pilgrimage to meet my father and to remember those who had fallen. The annual event was both joyous and sad. No matter where we were in the world we always came together for that anniversary. I grew up watching the three of them grow old and, on that one day, look so sad it always brought my mother to tears. My favourite Aunt, Alice, also came on that day and she too always shed tears. She would ruffle my hair and hug me with tears coursing down her cheeks. She was a successful dress designer, but my mother always said she would have traded all of her success for the love of her life, Charlie, to be alive. Victory had been bought at a high price. It had not just been the soldiers, sailors and airmen who had paid. That day was always a sad one.

The rest of my life, as I grew up, was joyous. My father and my mother were great fun to be around. They enjoyed life and they enjoyed being together. Our family holidays to France were the highlight of my time growing up. Before we had been born, Dad had gone to France and bought a dilapidated farmhouse not far from the Belgian border. By the time I was old enough to understand such things and, after my sister, Mary, was born, I discovered that he had been rebuilding it. He had been helped by my Uncle Lumpy as well as Uncles Gordy and Ted. Uncle Lumpy was another of my Dad's former comrades and, of all of them, he was the most fun. He had lost a hand in the war but it did not deter him. He did not simply enjoy life, he loved it. He lived in the northeast where he had married the widow of a former comrade and they had a houseful of children. By the time I was five the house had almost been rebuilt. Uncle Lumpy was there the year we finished it off. They named the house ***'Albert'*** for some reason. At first, I thought it was named after my Dad's brother, Bert, who had died in the war but Uncle Lumpy told me when I became older and was able to comprehend the complexities of war, how a farmer called Albert had saved their lives and died in the farmhouse which had once stood there. It was Dad's tribute to an old comrade. He was loyal to all those with whom he had served.

We spent every summer there. Sometimes Dad would not be with us. He was often kept busy in some part of the world. In those days he had just been a squadron leader. Often, he would be called away and disappear for weeks at a time. Now that I am older, I think I had a better idea of what he was involved in, but back then I just missed my Dad. Mum told us not to question him when he returned. She would have to be Mum and Dad for us. We would go, the three of us, Mum, me and my sister, Mary, on holiday for the summer. Just getting there was an adventure. We would travel by train, then ferry, a train again and then a wonderful country bus filled with chickens and ducks going to market and Frenchmen smoking Gauloise and Citanes. We never minded the smoke. The French always made a great fuss of us; I suspect it was because of my pretty mother but I may be doing the French a disservice.

As the farm had fields, woods and streams nearby, Mary and I thoroughly enjoyed ourselves just exploring. The woods were our hunting ground where we would build dens and play cowboys and Indians. We would be Wendy and Peter Pan! The farm was so isolated that we had complete freedom to play where we wanted. It was during those holidays that Mary and I became totally fluent in French. Mum got better but we took to it like ducks to water and could speak it better than she could. On shopping trips to the local villages, we were encouraged to mix with the French children. There was no point in speaking English for they understood not a word. It helped us learn the words that they do not teach you in school. I remember how we were always treated with great respect; we were English and had helped their fathers fight the Boche. When it slipped out who my father was, then we became almost celebrities. Eggs and milk would miraculously appear on our doorstep. When we went into the local village to shop, men would doff their hats to my mother and we would be given generous measures of cheese and the local hams. The French and the Belgians remembered the sacrifices that had been made. It was an idyllic time to be young and carefree.

Dad would come whenever he could. Sometimes we would travel to France at Easter if his leave coincided with the school holidays. I loved it when he was with us. I would sit, in the bars and cafes, and listen to the stories that would be told. It was never Dad who told the stories, it was the locals. They all knew of the British Ace who had flown the Sopwith Camel and had even fought the Red Baron. Dad rarely talked about the war to us; I gathered my information from my uncles, Lumpy, Ted and Gordy. For some reason, Dad seemed happy talking to the French and the Belgians.

School was less fun. Dad soon realised that I did not like academic studies although I was constantly at the top end of my classes. I don't know if it was his idea or Mum's but when they suggested flying lessons from Dad if I improved my attitude I jumped at the chance. I learned in an old Sopwith Dolphin. There were plenty of old Great War aeroplanes and Dad liked the Sopwith. By the time I was thirteen, I could fly solo. My friends were green with envy, and I loved it. My marks did improve. I always kept my word. I had said I would improve, and I had. I pushed my luck and asked for an aeroplane of my own but Dad was too clever for that. He told me that when I achieved a place at University then I could have an aeroplane. It worked- as I did!

I never found school work hard, rather the opposite, it was easy but I did not like it. I preferred being off with Uncle Ted when he came to see us. He was single and seemed to regard me as the son he never had. He taught me to hunt and to fish. Uncle Gordy taught me about engines. He was a wizard with engines, and I could strip an engine and reassemble it by the time I was sixteen. I had learned to drive just after I flew solo. They were the kinds of things I enjoyed. I read books but I preferred working with my hands and building things. I knew that I wanted to be an Engineer.

With Dad being away so much I found myself with Mum and Mary quite a lot. Most boys had a Dad around, even on the airfields where we were stationed. Mum was aware of that and she took to giving the two of us adventures with her. When we weren't in France, she would take us sailing and canoeing. She loved both activities. I found I enjoyed sailing. It was not the same as flying or driving. It was too slow. But I was competent. Dad told me how he and Uncle Lumpy had once escaped from France in a sailing boat and he had nearly drowned the two of them. The two other things Mum taught us were first aid; she had been a nurse and cooking. Just because I was a boy didn't mean I couldn't learn how to cook. When I went hunting with Uncle Ted, I combined the two. I shot the rabbits, skinned and gutted them and then cooked them. Those were wonderful days.

It was 1937 when our lives were touched by tragedy. Grandad died in January. He had been ill for some time but he always managed to recover by the time we had been summoned to his bedside. I liked Dad's dad. He was my only Grandad as Mum's dad had died before I was born. I loved the smell of his pipe and the fact that he always smelled of horses. He always had a mint in his pocket for me. We didn't see him often; just two or three times a year but I loved going up to his house. That would be when I saw my Auntie Sarah and my cousins. My eldest, Billy, had been named after my dad. I loved the Big House, as they called it. Lady Mary was a kind lady and she was always good to me. Burscough was always somewhere I loved: I would be given a mint from my Grandad and Lady Mary would slip a sixpence into my hand when I saw her. We saw more of them in the last year of his life for Mum took us whenever Auntie Sarah wrote to tell us he was ill again.

When we went to my Grandad's funeral, I was sixteen years old. Mother Harsker, my grandmother, couldn't stop crying and wringing her hands. They had been married for almost sixty years. I hadn't cried when I had heard my Grandad had died, it had been expected, but I did cry when my grandmother threw her arms around my Dad and wept, uncontrollably, "Billy, our Billy! Whatever will I do without him?"

Everyone cried, and I did not feel foolish when I wept too. One highlight of the funeral was meeting up with John again. John had been my father's batman during the war. He was a lovely gentle man and he had been fond of my grandparents. He was as upset as any but he was a dignified man and he did not weep. He had confided in me, "I shall mourn in my own way and my own time, Master Thomas. Both of your grandparents were kind to me and welcomed me into their home. Your grandfather was a good man." John now managed a fine hotel in London. Dad said he was born for such a job. My father was very close to his old servant who, he said, had made him into a gentleman.

When John saw me, he appraised me and tutted. He walked over and touched the hair over my ears. "Master Thomas, you need a haircut. You are a gentleman and there are standards."

"Sorry, John. If I had known you were coming for the funeral, I would have visited the barbers!"

He laughed, "We will let it go for today. And as for being here for the funeral; wild horses would not have kept me from it. Your grandfather and grandmother made me part of their family and I will be eternally grateful to them. You come from good stock, you know. Never let anyone tell you differently. And I am pleased to see that you are growing into a fine young gentleman."

I saw him again all too soon. Poor Mother Harsker outlived my Grandad by only a month. My Auntie Sarah said that she had just faded away after the death of her husband. She gave up on life. When we buried her, in the graveyard near the estate in the village, it was a change in our lives. We would come to Burscough no longer. Our world had changed.

When we had the Munich crisis, the next year, and we only saw Dad for a few weeks in total, it seemed that the whole world was changing. After Mr Chamberlain returned to tell us that we had peace in our time, so did my Dad, and he opened the whisky when he did. That was not like him. He drank but not until late in the evening. While Mum and Mary did the dishes, he sat with me and smoked his pipe. I liked the smell for it reminded me of Grandad. That was the night he put a glass of whisky in my hand for the first time.

It was not my first drink. I had been out, with some of the other children of the officers, and enjoyed a couple of illegal pints in a local pub. I know the landlady had known our age but we had not pushed our luck and we had behaved. That night was, however, the first time I had drunk spirits. Dad had downed his in one and filled it up again before I had even sniffed mine.

"Tom, there are some dozy buggers running this country! Everyone can see this Hitler chap wants to rule the world. We need a man with the backbone to stand up to him!"

I did not know what to say. I was being treated like a man and it felt strange. "Perhaps it will turn out for the best," was the best that I could manage. It sounded empty and vacuous to me. I covered my embarrassment by knocking back the whisky as my Dad had done.

He laughed as I coughed and spluttered, "Steady on, old son! Old Archie would have a fit if he saw you wasting Laguvalin like that. Sip it."

"Sorry, Dad."

He shook his head, "You have nothing to be sorry about. I am just sorry that war is coming again." He poured me another whisky and cocked an eyebrow as I sipped it. Then he nodded and smiled.

"But I thought Mr Chamberlain said we would have peace in our time."

"Mr Chamberlain doesn't know his... well, let us just say that I didn't vote for him. We need someone like that Winston Churchill. He is a good chap. I know he made a mess of Gallipoli but I like what he is saying."

"If there is a war then we can do what we did in the Great War, we can send the Germans packing."

"I am afraid, son, that we are not prepared. We don't have enough fighters and our bombers are... well, the Germans are streets ahead of us there. They have been practising the art of war in Spain. We have been drilling and looking smart for royal weddings. There is a world of difference. We had the best aeroplanes and the best tanks in nineteen eighteen. That is true no longer. The Spitfire is a fine aeroplane but the Germans have ten times the number of ME 109's. I am afraid we would lose the war in the air if the Germans attacked us now."

"We have the Navy."

"Yes, you are right there. We have the Navy, but I fear the modern war will be fought by tanks and aeroplanes. The Germans have better ones than we have."

I was enjoying the conversation but the reappearance of Mum and Mary ended it. She glared at the whisky in my hand. Dad shrugged, "It's about time he learned how to drink. Next year he will be going to University and he will be away from our control."

"Dad, University is too expensive. I can just get a job. That would be fine."

He leaned forward, "Tom, too many bright and clever officers died fighting alongside me in the Great War. Your mother watched a lot more die in hospital. We owe it to the next generation to have the brightest and best minds running this country. That will be you. We can afford it, can't we, Beattie?"

Mum smiled and put her hand on mine, "I will be as pleased as can be when you get to go to University. None of my family or your father's ever went to University. You will love it."

In the end, they were wrong. I hated it. But it did one thing, it changed my life forever.

My schools had been those schools that were close to the airfields where Dad had worked. For a while, he had been based in London and there I managed to go to a fine old grammar school. Most boys paid fees but the head had served with my father and I had my education there free for a year. That was my best school. The problem was I only knew the children of the airmen and officers of my father's squadrons. They weren't always posted to the same field. The result was that I had no close friends. Mum told me that Dad had had the same problem but for different reasons. It did not make me lonely but excluded me from the close friendships of children who had grown up together.

I passed the entrance examinations for Manchester University. It specialised in Science and Engineering and those were the subjects which appealed to me. I was due to go there at the end of September but I had enrolled in the Officer Training Corps at the University and I would be there in July of 1939 for a month-long indoctrination and training session. The peace of 1938 was a distant memory. The Germans had annexed Austria and taken over Czechoslovakia. It was rumoured that Poland was next. Certainly, there was an air of tension throughout the country. The ranks of the Territorials were being filled. Dad had thought the OTC was a good idea.

At the end of June, I came home from school and found him packing. "Off again, Dad?"

He stopped packing and pulled out his pipe. It was always a sure sign that he wanted to speak with me. "I have been seconded to the Air Ministry. Between you and me, Tom, Herr Hitler looks like he is planning to invade Poland. Even Chamberlain can't allow that to happen. There will be a war." He got the pipe going. "So, you work hard at University. I am even happier now that you are going to be involved in the OTC programme. I was promoted from the ranks and it wasn't easy. When you have your degree then you can join up." He smiled, "The Air Force, eh?"

I grinned, "Rather. But shouldn't I join up now? I can always continue my education when the war is over."

He shook his head, "When it does start, we have no idea how long it will last. They thought the last one would be over by Christmas that first year and look what happened there."

I nodded. "Still, I will find it hard to study knowing that others, like you, will be fighting."

"I don't think they will let old codgers like me take to the air. The reflexes aren't the same. My war, if it comes, will be behind a desk. I just hope I don't make the same mistakes as the desk wallahs did in the Great War!"

"You couldn't."

He shrugged, "I will never judge a man until I have walked a mile in his shoes. That was one of my dad's sayings and it is apposite now." He closed the fastenings on his case. Holding out his hand he said, "You take care, old son, and keep an eye on your mother for me."

"Of course." I felt guilty, later, about the fact that I did neither of the things I had promised him. I followed him downstairs. He kissed Mum and Mary goodbye, and I watched as his drophead Alvis roared off towards the main road.

The next fortnight was a hectic rush for me as Mum helped me choose what I would need for University. She was a very practical woman. She had been a nurse in the war and knew what was necessary and what was not. The night before I left, we had a quiet supper and then Mum sent Mary to do the dishes alone. My little sister sulked. "How come Tom never has to do them?"

"He is a man now, and besides, I need to talk with him. Off you go, young lady, and don't answer back!"

"Sorry, Mum." She couldn't resist sticking her tongue out at me as she did so.

"I don't know what I shall do with her now that you and your Dad will be away."

"You'll manage. Besides, it will be nice and quiet, won't it, without two blokes making a mess of the house and leaving the toilet seat up!"

She laughed. My Mum had a lovely laugh and it made her look like a young girl. She never looked her age. Most of the other mums looked dowdy and dull. Mum was never that. I know your Dad talked to you about being away from home but I am going to give my two penn'orth too. You are a good lad and I couldn't be prouder of you. But you know that. You are more down to earth than you have a right to be and that is all good. You are good with languages, you are clever, you are practical, and you are witty."

"Stop it; I will be getting a big head soon."

"The thing is, you will be mixing with those who have been to private schools. There will the sons of rich men and, well, sometimes they aren't very nice."

"Dad said much the same."

"We both met people like that. They are snobs. They think they are better than everyone else. Thank God that Lady Mary and Lord Burscough weren't like that when his lordship was still alive."

"There you are, there might be a lot of men like Lord Burscough."

She shook her head, "I am afraid that most of the good ones died in the Great War; I watched them die. The world changed in 1914. All I am saying is to remember who you are and be true to yourself. Your Dad and I can't be there to guide you anymore; it isn't right in any case. You are old enough now to make up your mind and to make your own decisions. We trust you to do the right thing and I know that you will never let us down." She began to cry. When she did that it would normally be Dad who would comfort her. He wasn't there and so I stood and put my arm around her. She buried her head in my chest and sobbed. I still don't know why. I let her cry herself out and then she stood. "Fancy making a fool of myself like that. You be careful."

"I will, Mum. I promise, and it isn't as if I won't be back. You will see me again at Christmas." Sometimes we make promises we intend to keep and that was one. I did not keep it. I would not see Mum and Mary for over a year. By then we were a world at war once more.

Chapter 2

I took the train to Manchester. Normally we went to Liverpool Lime Street to visit Burscough and this was a new experience. As the University term had not started and there were so few of us, we were accommodated in the University Halls of Residence. We even had the luxury of a room to ourselves. When I arrived I saw no one. After unpacking, I walked around the old buildings to familiarise myself with them.

Dad had always said that reconnaissance was never wasted. In the next few years, I would discover the accuracy of that statement. I left the University and Oxford Road. I headed to the magnificent Town Hall in St. Anne's Square. My Dad had told me how he had been called upon to put down a riot not far from here. What I noticed was the tension on the streets. This was not a populace ready for riot but there were Black Shirts who followed Mosley, the English fascist, and the Communists with their red banners. They circled each other like packs of wild animals and were only kept in their place by a couple of bobbies armed with nothing more than a truncheon.

After making sure I knew where the important buildings were and that I could find my way around the city, I headed back to the University. We had been given a detailed programme before we arrived and I knew that there was a formal dinner to be held in the main hall that night. Dad had ensured that I knew how to conduct myself and I had a good dinner suit, shirt and silk tie. I also knew the correct order for both food and cutlery. He had had to learn the hard way. I had been taught from birth. I made sure that I was ready in plenty of time. As I descended the stairs, I was nervous. I was used to meeting strangers; after all, moving around with Dad so much meant I constantly met new people. The difference here was that I would be with them for three years. Mistakes I made now would live with me for my whole time here. I was determined to make a good impression.

I was not the first one there. There were two or three huddles of young men attired much as I was. As I entered the hall, I was given a glass of sparkling wine. I knew, from the wine we had drunk in France, that this was not Champagne but it was dry, bubbly and pleasant enough. I was pleased that Dad had insisted that I have a well-tailored dinner suit for I soon saw that the others had equally fine suits too. I saw that the majority of the people in the room were students but one, with slightly greying temples, was obviously not. I took him to be a professor. I hovered on the periphery for I was still a little shy in those days, and I listened.

It was one of the students who was speaking, "My father, General Hughes-Graham, told me that if it were not for the officers' fine example in the Great War we would have lost the war. They were steadfast, noble and brave. What do you think, sir?"

I saw that the older man found the question a difficult one. I had learned, from receptions hosted by my parents, how to watch people. This man, I took him to be an officer from the Great War, cleared his throat and took a sip of his wine. He wrinkled his nose and then gave a considered answer. He was being diplomatic and the answer he gave would reflect that. He did not wish to upset this young man.

"Well, Robert, there were some fine officers. I myself served under what I consider to have been the finest officer on the whole Western Front, however, the ordinary Tommy was a remarkable chap. He could endure the most frightful of experiences and still not only be cheerful but go over the top in machine gunfire which, quite frankly, was suicide."

The young man identified as Robert Hughes-Graham nodded and smirked, "Of course, you served in the Royal Flying Corps, sir. They had all of the glory and none of the discomfort. I can understand your misguided view."

I saw the older man colour and he was about to say something when one of the college servants entered and said, "Dinner is served, gentlemen!"

We seated ourselves and then said grace. I found myself between two young men whose suits showed they had not had the good advice I had enjoyed. They appeared to have self-tie bows which always looked as though the wearer was being attacked by a bat. Both appeared more than a little nervous and they answered my questions and attempts at conversation with desultory answers. I ate the meal and sipped the wine. If this was University life then I would find it boring.

After the meal, the older man stood, "Gentlemen, you may loosen your ties and you may smoke if you wish."

I saw that those seated around Robert Hughes-Graham all took advantage of the offer and not only loosened their ties but all lit up cigars. The frown from our host spoke volumes. I did neither. I didn't smoke and Dad had told me that a real gentleman kept his tie on until he returned home. I smiled when I saw that two of those around the General's son had bow ties which were self-ties like my two companions; they had not learned how to tie a tie.

Our host took his glass of whisky and held it up, "I will give you all a toast. To those who went to war in nineteen fourteen and did not return home. Let us remember them!"

We all stood and I know that I for one felt my voice thick with emotion as I repeated the toast. My uncles had all told me of those who had fallen in the war. This was a ceremony I had witnessed every year since I could remember. Once in the summer and then again in November. The moment was spoiled by a laugh from Robert Hughes-Graham and those who were sat next to him.

The host frowned again. I wondered when he would say something. He did not. Instead, he put his glass down and smiled as he began his speech. "Gentlemen, my name is Captain Carrick. I am a professor here at the University. I teach Physics. However, for my sins, I am also in charge of the officer training here. In these uncertain times, I believe it is vital that we have bright and well-trained leaders. You have three years of study ahead of you but, unless I miss my guess, war will be coming soon. All of you may have to lead men into battle and that is a grave responsibility."

He stopped speaking and scanned the room. When he looked at me, he paused as though he recognised me and then carried on with his examination.

"Over the next month or so you will learn how to be officers and how to be soldiers. There are sergeants and corporals from the local regiments who will be drilling and training you all." There was a snort from the young man next to Robert Hughes-Graham. "Learn from them. All of them are veterans of the Great War and have forgotten more about leadership than you are likely to learn in a world of peace. That comes when you are hardened by war. Tonight will be the last night such as this for we will be working from dawn until dusk. Make the most of it!"

Many cheered and whooped but I did not. He was right. This was serious work. We all stood. I said goodbye to my silent neighbours and was about to leave for my room when Professor Carrick arrested me. "Don't I know you?"

"I doubt it, sir." I hesitated, I did not wish to come over as a sycophant but I felt I had to speak, "I thought you made a fine speech, sir. It moved me."

"I am pleased but I meant every word I said. If I thought the RAF would have me, I would rejoin in a flash." I nodded. "What is your name then and what are you studying?"

"I am studying physics and I am Thomas Harsker."

He stared at me, "Not Squadron Leader Bill Harsker's lad?"
"Actually, sir, it is Wing Commander now but, yes, I am Bill's son. Did you know him?"
"I am Freddie Carrick and I served with him. Your father was the officer I was referring to. I would not have survived the war but for your father." I know he meant well with his next words but they proved to be a disastrous mistake. He suddenly shouted, "Everyone! Listen! We have the son of a real hero here. Young Thomas' father won the VC, the MC and was one of only a handful of British pilots to shoot down more than fifty Germans." He began to applaud. Gradually everyone joined in; every one that is, except for Robert Hughes-Graham and his cronies. Captain Carrick put his arm around me and waved a waiter over, "Two whiskies!" When the waiter nodded and scurried off, he continued, "I am surprised you haven't joined the Royal Air Force."
"Dad wanted me to get my degree first."
He nodded, "Still, you would make a wonderful pilot. You can fly, can't you?"
I nodded, "Dad taught me almost as soon as I could walk."
"There you go. You would be a natural. How is your father?"
"He is fine. He is at the Air Ministry."
"Good, and your mother?"
"She is well."
"She is a wonderful lady. Your Dad is lucky." I saw that a small crowd had gathered around us and Professor Carrick regaled us with tales of my father and the other pilots. I found it embarrassing but the others seemed to enjoy it. The exceptions were Hughes-Graham and his coterie. They soon left.
When the professor began to speak more of the family rather than the war, the rest drifted off too and we were left alone. "Come, let's go outside. It is quite a pleasant evening I believe."
There were some benches outside the hall. I supposed that they would be a good place to sit on a sunny summer's afternoon. "What made you choose Manchester, Tom?"
I shrugged, "The course seemed like one I would like and, well, it is close to Burscough. That was where Dad grew up. I can't think of anywhere that I would call home. I like to think of myself coming from the north."
He laughed, "Even though you don't sound like it."
I laughed too, "No, you are right. It isn't much of a reason but there it is."

"It's as good a reason as any, and you have made a good choice. It is a good course." He looked up at the sky. "If the Germans decide that they want war, however, that may all change." He shook his head. "I thought we had ended it all in 1918. Good God, we made enough sacrifices. Look at your Auntie Alice, poor Charlie and she were meant to be together. He was killed and her life, well, it isn't the life she hoped for. We came back to a land filled with women dressed in black." He smiled at me, "I have lost touch with your father, your Aunt and the others. I travelled after University. I only came back when this latest trouble started. It seemed the right time to return to England, eh?" He stood, "Anyway, tomorrow we start the work." He held out his hand. "It has made my day to find my old commanding officer's son here. I look forward to the training."

I made my way back to my room. The corridors appeared silent. Although I fell asleep quickly, I was woken by the noise of some of my new acquaintances as they returned, drunk as lords. They were very loud. I could not make out much but I did recognise the slurred voice of Robert Hughes-Graham. "Any of you chaps know which is the room of that oik, Harsker?"

There were mumbled and indistinct replies.

"No matter, I have three years to find out, what?"

It took me some time to get to sleep after that. I had been here for less than a day and already I seemed to have made enemies through no fault of my own.

I was one of the few down for the cooked breakfast. I managed to leave the hall before the others were up and I went to the bursar's office to find out where we ought to be. Professor Carrick was there already and he was wearing his air force uniform. I recognised some of the medals. There were some soldiers there too. They were all in khaki and bore sergeant's stripes. When they turned, I had a shock for two of them had badly disfigured faces. It was fortunate that I had met such men before when my father had visited old comrades. I steeled myself.

"Good lad. I knew you would be the first. Gentlemen, this is Tom Harsker, and his father won the VC and the MC."

I wished he had not said that. The four sergeants' faces broke into smiles. "And you will be just like your old man, eh, son? I am Sergeant Greely. I served in the 1st Loyal Lancashire Regiment." He looked to be slightly younger than the others who all had grey hair. I learned later that he was still a serving soldier and his participation with the cadets would only be for a month.

One of those with a disfigured face said, "Would your Dad be Squadron Leader Bill Harsker?"

"Yes, he would, sergeant."

He shook my hand, "I served with his brother, your uncle, Bert, in the tanks. He was a good lad was your uncle." He held his hand up to his damaged face, "I got this the day he died. He was a proper hero, just like your Dad. It must run in the family, eh? Proud to meet you. I am Sergeant Harrison."

I discovered that the other two were Sergeant Ashcroft and Sergeant Williams. It was amazing that two of the men who would be training me knew my family. I had just wanted to be me but now I found I was tainted with the brush of a hero's son and nephew.

"If you chaps would take Tom here and get him kitted out, I will send the others over just as soon as they arrive."

I hesitated, "Er, sir, I think some of them may be a little delicate this morning. Many of them spent the night bringing back last night's dinner."

Sergeant Greely laughed, "Don't you worry, Cadet Harsker, by the time we have finished with them they will know what the word delicate really means."

The four of them led me to a large wooden hut that had been recently erected in a quiet corner of the University grounds. There was a smartly stencilled sign which said, ***'OTC Headquarters, Manchester University***'. Inside there were trestle tables and various pieces of equipment and uniform. The four of them each went behind one of the tables.

Sergeant Greely rubbed his hands together, "You are lucky, son, we have uniforms for the twenty-five of you but the first ones will get the uniforms which fit the best. Let's get you kitted out!"

Apart from the battle dress, helmet, rifle, boots and cap we also had our webbing, blanket, mess kit, respirator, anti-gas cape, entrenching tool, haversack and knapsack. I almost disappeared under the mountain I carried. Sergeant Harrison laughed. He came from behind his trestle table and steered me behind a screen. "We thought you lads might like privacy while you change. There are supposed to be some lockers delivered but they haven't arrived yet so put your clothes in a pile yonder, sir."

I was halfway through dressing and working my way through the myriad of buttons and straps which appeared to serve no useful purpose when the rest arrived in dribs and drabs. I had just finished when the two lads who had sat near to me at dinner came behind the screen. They actually smiled this time. "I say, you were jolly quick."

"It is the early bird and all that. I'll get out of your way."

I picked up my clothes and went to where the sergeant had pointed. I laid the clothes in neat piles, carefully folded and with my shoes before them. It was the way I had been brought up. My Dad had served since he was fifteen and neatness was drilled into me. I could polish shoes so brightly that you could shave in the reflection from the toe caps. That had been the mantra of both my Dad and my Grandad. They both put great store by highly polished boots and shoes. My father's old batman, John, had given me the trick of keeping them shiny as well as how to have the sharpest creases in my trousers. I looked at the boots as supplied; they still had the hard varnish which I would have to remove with the back of a spoon. There would be many hours of work before they would pass muster.

I closely examined the Lee Enfield .303. I was more than familiar with it. I had been brought up with guns. I could strip a Lee Enfield down blindfold. I also knew how to strip down a Luger and a Webley service revolver. Both had been the handguns my Dad had taken into the air with him. He had also taught me to shoot. Talking to my uncles, I knew that he had been a very good shot. In fact, they said that he seemed to be able to hit the enemy without even appearing to aim- a rare skill.

The hut filled with a cacophony of noise as the rest of the cadets arrived. Everyone was trying on the various bits of uniform and equipment. It was all very leisurely; a little like a schoolboys' outing. Suddenly Sergeant Greely's voice boomed out. "On parade outside with your rifles now!"

I heard one voice say, "I shan't be long, I just..."

The unfortunate cadet got no further, "If you aren't out of here by the time I count to five, then you will get my size nine right up your delicate little arse, my son!"

Everyone scurried out like woodlice when a plant pot is moved.

I knew marching and I knew attention. I stood with my feet slightly apart with my rifle butt touching my right foot. I had an impassive face. I knew you didn't smile. It invited punishment. I risked a glance down the line. The ones who had just erupted from the wooden hut were hurriedly dressing and their end of the line was a little wavy. I saw Professor Carrick and his wry smile. He caught my eye and winked. It was reassuring.

Sergeant Greely shouted, "Atten……shun!" I snapped my feet together and kept my rifle straight. Some of the others managed to do the same. The far end of the line, however, had failed to do so and Sergeant Greely leapt down to that end. "You are a shambles! You are a shower! I have seen Girl Guides with more about them! You, feet together! Back straight! Keep that bloody rifle straight too!"

He strode down the line glaring at everyone. He reached me and gave the slightest of nods before going to stand in front of Professor Carrick. The sergeant smacked his swagger stick into the palm of his left hand as he punctuated each of his sentences. "This was not a good start, gentlemen. There are only two of you who managed to stow their clothes correctly. When Captain Carrick has finished with you, then you will go back in and make yours look like Mr Harsker's and Mr White's! That is how you leave your equipment. We have two months to make you into what might, in the fullness of time, become British Officers. From what I have seen this morning, that is, with one or two exceptions, a vain hope!" He glared at the ones at the far end of the line. "Captain Carrick, sir!"

"Right chaps, the sergeant was right. This has not been a good start. I expect you all here tomorrow morning at seven a.m. No excuses. If you have a skinful, then you deal with it. My advice would be not to have a skinful but you are all men now and you make your own decisions. We will begin this morning with some marching. Then we will have a full five-mile run with all your equipment, including your rifle, before we finish, just before lunch, with a session at the rifle range."

The marching proved to be less of a disaster than I had imagined. The sergeants cleverly put those of us who had stood to attention best at the front. It meant the rest could follow us. We had an hour of drilling up and down. None of it was hard but some of those at the back received blows when they mixed up their left from their right. The five-mile run proved more challenging for some. I enjoyed running. Some of them did not. It was not helped by the fact that we ran through the streets around Oxford Road. There were many children on the streets and they took great delight in running next to us and mocking us. The sergeants all seemed to enjoy our humiliation. I saw some of the cadets flushing and it was not with the effort of running, it was an embarrassment.

Captain Carrick awaited us at the firing range. While we took off our packs and tried to regain our breath, Sergeant Harrison stepped forward. He held up the Lee Enfield. "Now, I know that you will all be officers and that this rifle will be beneath you but you will learn to fire it and fire it well. You will learn to strip it down and reassemble it. You will, by the time we have finished with you, be able to fire five rapid rounds and hit the target with every shot! You should be able to do what the men you will command do."

He took us through the component parts and then Sergeant Williams issued us with our ammunition. It was not a large firing range and it could only accommodate five rifles at a time. I was selected to be in the first five. I lay down and licked my finger to sharpen the sight.

"Whenever you gentlemen are ready. We will try five rapid shots just so that you can get the feel for the weapon and so that we can assess your abilities. Shout ***'clear'*** when you have emptied your magazine."

I squeezed off my five shots. "Clear!"

It seemed an age before the other four shouted ***'clear'***. I heard a snort of derision from behind me and recognised Robert Hughes-Graham's voice. "Damned fool fired too fast. I bet he hasn't hit the target once."

"Quiet in the ranks!"

The targets were on a pulley system, "Right, gentlemen, retrieve your targets and let us see the damage."

As mine came towards me I could see that all five had found the target. Three had made the inner but two were in the outer. I frowned. From the grouping, the rifle pulled a little to the right. I would have to correct that. Sergeant Harrison said, "If you will give me that, Mr Harsker." He went along the line collecting the others. One by one he held them up. "Two hit the target, just. Two in the outer, not bad. Three hit the target. Three hit the target one inner, well done." He dropped them to the ground and held mine in both hands. "Mr Harsker, on the other hand, not only hit the target with every shot; he even managed to get three inners. He has achieved his target on the first day. Well done, Mr Harsker. The sights look to be off."

"Yes Sergeant, it pulls to the right."

After a short break for lunch, we repeated the morning's activities again. By the end of the run, I began to realise that I was fitter than most of the others. It came as a surprise to me for I hadn't thought that I had done anything special to prepare. We picked up our clothes and headed back for our dormitories. One or two of the lads had quite warmed to me but I could feel the daggers in my back from the General's son and his cronies. There were just six baths and we all had to queue. I didn't mind for I took the opportunity to write a letter to Dad and another one to Mum. Both would be interested in the presence, at the University, of Captain Carrick. It certainly made me feel better. I also mentioned, to Dad, about Sergeant Harrison. I knew from John that Dad had seen his own brother die. He would never talk about it. Perhaps he would have solace from the knowledge that his brother had been held in high regard too.

When I had finished, I was able to enjoy a bath; however, the chap who had used it before me had shaved and he had not removed the hairs from the bath. I had to clean it out before I could fill it. The result was that I was one of the last to reach the dining hall. Captain Carrick was seated at the head of the table and, this time, a place had been left for me next to him. I didn't know if that was his choice or the fact that none of my fellows wished to sit so close to him. I didn't mind and I enjoyed a pleasant dinner. It seemed that I had impressed the sergeants not only with my marksmanship but also my general demeanour and attitude.

"You see, Tom, all of those sergeants were like your father, they began in the ranks. Some of the officers they served under weren't very good. They are keen to make better officers for the next war; whenever that comes. They see great potential in you."

I did not drink to excess and I noticed that the majority of my peers restrained themselves too. I left with Captain Carrick and most of the cadets. I had washed and was ready for bed when the drunks returned. I heard them coming down the corridor. They were incredibly loud. They reached my door and it was thrown open and a drunken Robert Hughes-Graham stood there swaying.

"If it isn't the teacher's pet! I felt positively sick all day watching you sucking up to those moronic sergeants."

I saw heads appear from the other rooms along the dormitories.

"Perhaps it was the drink you had. And you are drunk again tonight so goodnight." I went to close the door but he put his foot in the way. He was with three of his inner circle and they blocked my door.

"You never went to public school I can tell! Not a surprise from someone whose father is obviously not a gentleman born but we will introduce you to a little tradition called scragging! Get him, boys!"

I had met bullies before and I was not intimidated. Dad had taught me to go on the offensive straight away and I did. I punched the General's son hard in the stomach with my best shot. He reeled backwards into the corridor and began to vomit.

Alfred, his best friend, shouted, "Why you…"

He got no further as I pulled his outstretched fist towards me and rammed his head into the edge of the door. He slumped to the ground with glazed eyes. The other two stood there with fists at the ready but doubt in their eyes. The doors down the corridor opened wider and the other cadets came out of their rooms to look down at the scene. "Now then you two, you are drunk and I take no pleasure in giving a drubbing to a drunk. But if you don't take your two friends away and clean up the corridor then I shall give the two of you a damned good hiding."

Their fists lowered and they did as I asked. When the corridor was empty and they had made a half-hearted attempt to clean up the corridor, I went to the cleaner's cupboard, found a mop and bucket and finished off the job. I was just finishing when the night porter arrived. He nodded, "You been ill then, sir?"

"No, Jenkins, it was one of the other chaps."

He held out his hand, "Thank you for doing that, sir. I'll put it away for you. Good night."

When I went into my room, I jammed a chair behind the door. I wanted no more surprises.

Chapter 3

The next morning, when I went down to breakfast, I received scowls from half of my fellows. Surprisingly, three came to sit next to me. Alfred, the friend of the son of the General, had a blackened and swollen nose. He looked positively apoplectic with rage. I sighed. I could do nothing about it.

The young man next to me held out his hand, "My name is Roger Pearson. I saw it all last night. It was terribly brave of you to take four of them on, don't you know."

"Oh, it wasn't that brave. They were drunk and, like all bullies, they thought they could frighten me."

"They terrify me! I was badly bullied at Harrow. I came up here because I thought there wouldn't be bullies." I looked at one of the quiet lads who had sat next to me on the first night. I felt guilty now. He had been quiet and reserved because he was terrified. He shook his head as he held out his hand, "Phillip Cowley."

I shook his hand, "Pleased to meet you."

We were all on parade on time. I noticed wry grins on the faces of the sergeants and Captain Carrick.

Sergeant Greely stood with legs apart and his swagger stick held behind his back. He rolled up and down on the balls of his feet as he spoke. "You will be pleased to know that today, we will not be marching, running or shooting." There were audible sighs of relief. "Today we are going to teach you how to fight without a gun; unarmed combat." He openly grinned at Alfred. "I think some of you, from what I hear, may well need it."

Inside I groaned. I did not need this.

We were taken to the University rugby field where the sergeants showed us moves designed to defeat an enemy by using his own strength and weight against him. I had been taught some of the moves many years earlier by Warrant Officer Ted Taylor who had been an expert himself. Once again, I was praised for my success. I did not want notoriety I wanted anonymity. Things went from bad to worse. I was not threatened again; I think they all knew they would come worse off but their snide comments and mockery wore me down.

It came to a head when we were issued a Webley revolver and taken to the ranges. I deliberately missed with my first six shots. Sergeant Greely's face became crimson and he hauled me by the ear from the firing line. Out of the hearing of the others, he said, "What is your game, young man? Why did you deliberately miss?" My eyes involuntarily flickered to my tormentors. The sergeant smiled and put his arm around my shoulders, "I thought as much. Listen, son, we all heard what happened when they tried to rough you up and you did the right thing. There are tosspots like that in every walk of life. You behaved as I would expect a gentleman to behave. They did not. Now get back there and show me what you can do. Losing is a bad habit to get into. I prefer it when you are winning because that is what you are, Mr Harsker, a winner."

"Right Sarge, sorry."

I reloaded and this time hit five bulls and one which clipped the edge of the bull. The sergeants all clapped and Sergeant Greely said, "Now that is how you shoot."

That proved a turning point and the bullies, with an increasing number of allies, began to pick on those who had befriended me. One by one they stopped sitting with me. The last two to leave were Phillip and Roger. It took a bloody nose for Phillip to switch allegiances and I did not blame either of them. In fact, I felt happier when they were away from me for that way they were safe. I made sure that my letters home did not give a hint of my troubles. Both my parents had enough to worry about without me adding to them. I would deal with it.

As July drew to a close, I found myself alone in the small park just down the road from the University. I have always had this ability to think things through. As I watched the urchins and street children playing games together, I worked out what I ought to do. If I stayed at University, I would be alone. Robert Hughes-Graham had too much influence. I did not mind being alone but what was the point of being at University if I could not socialise. In addition, I would be with them all for the officer training for the next three years. I would be with them for twenty-four hours a day and that idea did not appeal to me.

It was the officer training element that decided me. I thoroughly enjoyed all of the training we had been given. I felt alive and I knew that I enjoyed the military life. However, I preferred the company of the sergeants to my peers. I did not want to be an officer. That decided, my future became easy. I would join up.

I was no coward and I steeled myself, the next morning, to face Captain Carrick. As soon as we were dismissed from the parade and before we were marched off to our rifle practice I said, "Permission to speak with the Captain privately, sir."

I knew what they all thought. They believed that I had been broken and that I would be telling tales about the bullying. I saw it in the faces of my tormentors. Nothing could be further from the truth. I could handle being sent to Coventry. I could face the bullies. I could endure the isolation. I was making my decision because it was something I wanted to do. The only thing their action had done was to focus my mind and, for that, I ought to have been grateful to them.

"Permission granted."

Every eye was on the two of us as I followed Captain Carrick to his office. I stood to attention and he waved me to a seat. "What's this about then, Tom?"

"I'd like to leave, sir."

His mouth opened and closed like a fish. I smiled as he reached for his pipe. He had learned that from my Dad. He used the pipe to give himself thinking time, "Is this about the bullying if it…"

"No sir, it isn't. I can handle that."

"But you are doing so well. The sergeants can't sing your praises highly enough. They are excited to be training such an accomplished officer. Your parents won't be happy if they think you are giving up."

I felt myself colouring, "With respect, sir, I find that remark offensive. I am not giving up!"

"That is what it looks like from this side of the chair."

"No sir, you are wrong. Look, may I speak candidly?"

"Of course."

"There is a war coming and we both know it. I want to be part of it and not stuck in a university. You went to war when you were my age, didn't you?"

He smiled, "I was younger, actually. I did my degrees after the war."

"Exactly, sir, and that is what I want to do. Could you have a word with the Chancellor and see if my place can be kept open for me until after the war?"

"I am not…"

"I know you could do it, sir. I have come to realise that you are held in high regard here."

"Well I suppose I could but what would you do then? Go to Officer Training School?"

"No sir, enlist."

"But you wouldn't be an officer."

"Nor was my father when he joined up. I am happy about that."

He tapped out his pipe which had gone out. "I suppose that would be an interesting idea. Which branch of the air force; fighters, bombers…?"

"Not the air force."

"What!" This time I had truly surprised him.

"I know what it would be like. Every officer I met would have heard of my Dad and what he did in the war. They would all expect me to be the same and I'm not. People would make allowances for me and treat me differently. I am sorry, sir, but it has happened here. You couldn't help telling everyone what a hero my Dad was, and I agree with you; he is my hero too. That is a huge cross to carry. I am not certain that I could."

I could see that I had stunned him. "Then what would you do?"

"I have enjoyed what I have done here already, sir, and I think I would join the army. I'd like to be ready when war is declared."

"But you have so many skills. They would be wasted as a squaddy!"

I laughed, "Dad joined the army as a cavalryman and the Royal Flying Corps because he could mend cars. He became a pilot. I don't know what I will be good at yet. It might be nothing but I am an optimist and I believe that there is something out there that needs me to do it. It isn't sitting in Manchester University for three years while good men die."

He fiddled with his pipe and then he grinned and stood up. He held out his hand, "I'll tell you this, you are your father's son! I'll do what I can."

"Thank you, sir. Do you mind if I change into civvies? I'd like to go into Manchester and get things started."

"Yes, of course." He shook his head, "When you make up your mind there is no stopping you, is there?"

"No sir, it is a family trait."

I got changed and went into Manchester. There were offices to recruit into all the services but, annoyingly, the one for the Army was closed until the afternoon. I visited the others just to get a feel for the questions I might be asked; reconnaissance again. I was flattered that they all wanted me to sign up there and then. The other volunteers, who were in the offices, looked a little unhealthy and perhaps I was seen as a healthy specimen. I felt better about my decision.

I walked the streets until it was time for the office to open. I waited outside. I was keen and I didn't mind if they knew it. A sergeant and a private strode up two minutes before the opening time and unlocked the door. They waved me in. The questions I was asked were almost the same as in the other offices and I answered them well. I had had practice. However, when I said I wanted to sign up they asked me an extra one I hadn't been asked earlier.

"Right then, Thomas, do you have your parents' permission to join up?"

"Pardon?"

He tapped the form and pointed to my birth date. "You aren't twenty-one."

"I thought that was just to vote. Besides, they said I could do what I wanted." I heard the door open behind me and the sergeant glanced up. I assumed it was another recruit and he would soon hurry me out. I would have to go home and get permission and I was certain they would not give it, either of them.

"I am sorry, son. I would love to sign you up but I wouldn't want your parents to come down on me like a ton of bricks."

The voice behind said, "Jack, that would be a mistake. This young lad is just what the 1st Loyal Lancashire regiment needs."

I turned around and saw Sergeant Greely standing there. "But he isn't twenty-one, Harry!"

"And neither were we when we joined up. Let him sign the papers. I'll put my name on it if you like."

The sergeant shook his head, "You are joking. I am not letting you have the bonus. You are already on a nice little number at the OTC. Here you are son, sign here!" I signed. "All you need to decide now is three years or twenty-five years."

"What?"

"How many years do you want to enlist for?"

"Three years."

"You get more money if you sign for twenty-five."

"Three years is fine or the duration of the war."

"What war?"

"Trust me, Sergeant, there is a war coming."

Sergeant Greely waited while I signed everything. As we walked back towards the university he asked, "Are you sure about this, Mr Harsker? I mean, you could be an officer. You have more military sense than the rest of that shower put together."

"I know what I am doing, Sarge, and thanks for your help back there."

"It was Captain Carrick who sent me; he thought you might have a problem." He smiled, "Well, tonight is your last night as a civilian. Come on, let's go to the Red Lion and we'll have a pint. Tomorrow I will be shouting at you and chasing you from haircut to breakfast time!" The Red Lion was just off St Peter's Square and was a quiet little pub.

"But I thought you were based at the university?"

"I have to go back to the regiment. Things are hotting up. It seems you have joined at the right time, old son."

I spent some time talking with Sergeant Greely. It seems he had joined up in 1917 and stayed on after the war. The other sergeants were all due to be retired within the next year but the sergeant was in for another three years. I found out as much as I could about the 1st Loyal Lancashire Regiment. I knew that I was taking a huge step. We only had two pints and then we marched down to the University.

"With talents like yours, you will soon be made up to non-com."

"But what if I just want to stay a private?"

"I know you don't want your Dad bringing up but he is a good example. He was promoted because he could lead when others couldn't. You are a leader. You know how to make hard decisions and you are not afraid to upset people. If there is a war then the last thing you need is someone dithering when a decision has to be made. Anyway, that is some time off. I'll see Captain Carrick. I daresay he will want to see you off tomorrow."

"Won't he be at dinner tonight?"

"No, he has to go to the Chancellor's dinner. He will see you in the morning. Last night for the monkey suit, eh?" I nodded. "I should just take one suit of clothes with you. The other recruits will have just what they are wearing and, from now on, it will be khaki for you." He tapped his nose.

"But won't they have a change of trousers and the like?"

He shook his head, "The lads who join will have one pair of shoes, one jacket and a couple of shirts at best. You'll see." He smiled. "The first proper boots I ever had were the ones the army gave me. I wore clogs until then." It was sage advice.

The cadets were still out. I went to the porter's lodge and explained that I would be leaving the next day. The old porter just gave me a sad smile and nodded, "A shame, young sir, still you are doing your duty and that is always for the best."

I wondered as I went to my room, how he knew. Then I realised that with so few students in the dormitories there would be no such thing as a secret.

I began to pack. Mum had chosen some really fine clothes for me to wear. She had not wanted me to look in any way down at heel. Now I would have to send my case home. I looked at the leather-bound shaving kit. That would have to go. From now on, it would be army issue. I put the razor to one side and the brush. The rest could go back but I would retain those. They were both small and would be a reminder of my Mum's thoughtfulness. I packed a small bag with my essentials.

The word must have spread for I did not receive the normal cold shoulder the following morning at breakfast. Only Hughes-Graham and his inner circle seemed to take any pleasure in my departure. Phillip sat next to me, "I am sorry those beasts won, Tom. I should have stood by you."

"No, Phillip, and they didn't do this. I could have taken all that they had to offer. When the war comes, I want to be there from the start."

"You are so keen to fight?"

I shook my head, "If I am honest, I am scared stiff but I feel I ought to do as my Dad did and do my duty."

He said quietly, "My father was gassed. He spends most days staring at the walls. My mother cries a lot."

I had my case ready the next morning and I had deliberately chosen the clothes which would, I hoped, help me to blend in. I left my case in the porter's lodge and went over to Captain Carrick's office. His car was outside. As soon as I entered, Sergeant Williams barked, "He's here sir." He smiled at me and said, "Good luck, Mr Harsker. I admire what you are doing." He held his hand out and shook my mine warmly.

"Ah Tom, come along, I'll pop you along to the barracks. Save you walking, eh?"

We picked up my bag which was then jammed in the jump seat of his MG. As we drove, I shouted, above the noise of the engine, "Sir, is there any way you could look after my case until I get some leave?"

He shook his head, "You won't get leave for some time, but I will look after your case." He glanced at me. "I intend to drive down to your place this weekend. I can drop it off then, eh? I daresay you haven't told them yet?"

"I have had no time," I said weakly.

"Write to them today and I will explain to them what happened. They need to know. I know your Dad and, I think, I understand your mother. Both will see the reasons behind what you have done but not the fact that you were scared to tell them."

I took the letter from my jacket, "I wrote it last night, sir."

His face broke into a grin, "Then I apologise for misjudging you. If you give it to me, I shall post it directly."

As I handed it to him, I felt a great sense of relief. He was right, they deserved to know and they would understand.

Part Two- The War

Chapter 4

My training at OTC stood me in good stead. When I arrived at the barracks, I was ready for the barking sergeants and the ill-fitting uniforms. The first two weeks in August I was drilled to within an inch of my life. The difference, this time, was that I was anonymous. My name meant nothing. Most of the lads I bunked with came from Manchester and South Lancashire. There were even a few lads from Ormskirk, Wigan and St. Helens; they weren't far from Burscough. The accents reminded me of my Grandad and I felt at home.

Twenty of us had joined up. Most of the other lads had been unemployed and saw the army as a way of earning a few bob. I was vague when quizzed about my background. It was easier that way. It meant I kept quiet and listened. I made sure that I joined in with the rest of the recruits and didn't act in any way differently. They just took me as being quiet. The rest of the battalion were kept away from us. They were on exercises and there were only the headquarters staff around. We became quite close. We were trained by Sergeant Hope and Corporal Garthwaite. Sergeant Hope belied his name; there was no hope with him. He was a martinet. He had a pencil slim moustache and a swagger stick which he employed in a variety of ways. It was a pointer, a weapon, a backscratcher. It was always in his hand. One of the wags, Willy Holden, remarked, "I wonder if he eats with it?"

He did everything by the book. When we discovered he was married, Willy enjoyed mimicking him in the barracks. "I can just picture him with his wife. He'll have his swagger stick in his hand and his wife, I bet her name is Doris, will be standing there. *'Stand by your bed, Doris! Hands on dress. Wait for it! Wait for it! Remove your frock! Hands on knickers! Off! On the command, you will lie on the bed and prepare to receive boarders! Lie*!'"

We all laughed until we cried and when he came into the barracks the next day, we all had to endure an hour of spud bashing for our inappropriate grins.

Our training included a great many things which were not on the curriculum of the OTC. The sergeants were thorough. We were taught how to eat with a knife and fork, instructed in the art of saluting, the how and the who: always officers and never non-commissioned officers. We learned to locate the enemy by the clock. Nine o'clock was to our left while three o'clock was to our right. We learned the difference between stand easy and stand at ease. We learned how to look after our equipment. As soon as I was able, I worked on my new black boots which gleamed. I was in great demand from my fellow recruits as they asked for advice on achieving the same effect. It was a contrast to my reception by the Hughes-Grahams of this world.

We learned how to improvise bombs and explosives; how to make tripwires. Most importantly, we were taught how to fire the Bren gun, Lewis gun and Vickers machine gun. It was when we were firing the Lewis that I came to the attention of Corporal Garthwaite. The Lewis gun I was firing jammed. Dad had told me of the gun for he had used one in the Gunbus when he had been a gunner. Almost without thinking I took out the magazine banged it with the palm of my hand sharply and then replaced it. It fired straight away. Corporal Garthwaite screwed up his face, "Have you served before, Harsker?"

"No, Corporal."

"Then how did you know how to do that?"

"My Dad served as a gunner in the RFC. He told me." It was not a lie and it masked my father's identity.

He seemed satisfied with my answer, "That was smartly done."

We were four weeks into the training when we were told that the whole of the army had been mobilised. The German Army was massing on the borders of Poland. Sergeant Greely returned and he and Sergeant Hope addressed us.

"Right lads. You have two week's training left but the Boche, it seems, has decided that we do not have the luxury of time. The rest of the battalion is returning today. What you haven't learned so far you will have to pick up as we go. Your squad assignments will be pinned up in the HQ building later on. Make sure you have all your kit and that your rifle is ready. We are on standby to move."

We were going to war. Sergeant Greely came over to me, "I hear you have done well, Tom. I knew you would. How has it been?"

"Better than the University."

He laughed, "Aye, well you might as well have stayed. A few days after you left so did that Hughes-Graham. It seems he didn't like the fact that he was unpopular amongst the others. They resented the fact that you had left because of him. Mind you, he was not ready to do mundane tasks. I am guessing his daddy had not prepared him as well as yours."

"Where did he go, Sarge?"

He shrugged, "No idea. A staff car arrived with a Red Tab inside. I think his daddy sent it for him."

"And where are we off to?"

He tapped his nose, "I told you, son, things are different here. You will just have to make an informed guess."

In our hut, there were divided opinions. "Norway! I have heard we are off to Norway."

"Nah, it'll be France or Belgium. The Hun likes that way. They are soft as, over there."

"Why not Poland?"

"It is a bloody long way to Poland!"

I kept quiet. We would be told when they were good and ready. Reg Dwyer ran in. "The new squads are here. The duty clerk gave me a copy."

He began to shout out the squads and platoons we would be part of. Willy Holden and I were to be in the same squad. Willy clapped me on the back, "I am sorted here, lads, I have the professor with me!"

"Professor?"

Willy lit a cigarette and we walked over to our bunks, "Aye, well you are a clever bugger, aren't you? There's nowt you don't know."

I was about to correct him on his double negative when I realised that was the reason they thought of me as they did. I smiled, "Well, I am glad that I am with you too, Willy." We shook hands and became close friends from that moment.

Sergeant Hope came in. "Right lads, get your gear shifted into your new barracks. This hut is first squad. If you are in first squad then you stay here."

We weren't and we gathered all of our gear. We learned rapidly how to pack and unpack our kitbags to make transporting our equipment easier. When we entered the new hut, we saw that there would be two squads in there. Sergeant Greely had told me which were the most sought after bunks. They were the ones closest to the stove. We wisely took the two closest to the door and the draughts. We heard the squealing of brakes and then a cacophony of noise as the lorries arrived and disgorged the rest of the battalion. They flooded in full of the buzz of conversation and freshly lit cigarettes.

They glanced at us and then began to unpack their equipment. A stocky sergeant and corporal marched up to us. We leapt to our feet and stood to attention. The sergeant looked us up and down. "I am Sergeant Jennings and this is Corporal Higgins. Which of you is Holden?"

"Me, Sarge."

"That is Sergeant Jennings! We do things right in this squad. You are the joker I understand." There was no answer Willy could give and he just smiled. "Well, you can take that grin off your face. I have no sense of humour and Sergeant Hope is a good friend of mine. Understand?"

"Yes, Sergeant Jennings."

"Then you will be Harsker?"

"Yes, Sergeant Jennings."

He smiled at the Corporal. "Harry Greely told me about this one. We have a clever clogs here. Could have been an officer." He turned back to me and there was no smile on his face. "Being clever cuts no ice with me, Sonny Jim. I'll chase you from haircut to breakfast if you don't jump when I bark. Right?"

"Right, Sergeant Jennings."

He walked away to shout at another of the squad. Corporal Higgins grinned, "His bark is worse than his bite. My name is Alf. Sergeant Greely did speak highly of you, as did Corporal Garthwaite. You are a good shot, you are fit and you are handy at unarmed combat. Keep your nose clean, son, and you'll do alright." He turned to walk away and then said, over his shoulder "And Holden, Sergeant Hope's wife wears khaki knickers; he salutes them before bed!"

We learned that the two non-coms were like a music hall act. They worked well as a team. The sergeant tore us down and the corporal built us up.

We had, however, little time to get used to life in the barracks for the next day, September the 3rd, we had a battalion parade and the Colonel, Lieutenant Colonel Grainger, addressed us all.

"Men of the 1st Loyal Lancashires, I have to tell you that we are now at war with Germany." I kept my eyes facing forward ahead but I heard a hum of noise until Sergeant Major Campbell roared out, "Silence in the ranks!"

"We have the honour of being selected to join the British Expeditionary Force which is to go to France and Belgium. Our transport will be here by noon. Sergeants, make sure your men have all the equipment they need. I fear there will be none for us in France." His face betrayed the fact that he had served in the Great War. We were going back and it would not be Norway or Iceland; we would be in France.

The first part of our journey was by train. It took eight hours to reach Dover where we boarded a requisitioned ferry. We were not the only ones. However, we were one of the few purely infantry battalions and that meant that we were able to embark and disembark far quicker than the artillery and mechanized forces. We were boarded, like cattle, aboard the French trains and headed east, into the night, before any of the other units. All of us were exhausted and we slept where we could. Our squad stayed together. We were jammed in a small compartment which would normally accommodate six passengers. There were nine of us and all of our bags. We were crowded. It did enable me to find out a little more about my new comrades. I listened as Willy made them laugh.

Our sergeant had found a berth with the other sergeants but Alf Higgins joined us. He sat opposite me and, like me, watched and listened. Jack Jones had been a taxi driver in Manchester but the recession in the early thirties meant he had been unemployed. The army had given him an occupation. He was the oldest of the squad with a wife and three children to support. Pete Smith had joined as soon as he had been old enough. His dad had been a regular who had been gassed and Pete was carrying on the family tradition. George Hogan came from St. Helens, not far from where my dad had been born. He was, like me, quiet. The rest of his brothers either worked in the glassworks or the chemical works but George liked the outdoors. He was also only a little older than me; he was just twenty. He was quiet and missed his best friend, Bill, who also happened to be his cousin.

Bert Williams and Mike Carr were best friends. They had joined in the recession and the army was their only job. They, along with Jack, were the original members of the squad. They were the old hands to whom we all deferred. I learned, from Alf Higgins, that none of them had any ambition. They enjoyed just following orders. He had joined later than they had but he wanted to be a sergeant.

The last member of the squad was the most enigmatic. Nev Wilkinson was well educated. I could tell that from the way he spoke. He had fought in Spain against the Fascists and joined up when he returned. He hated the Germans with a terrifying passion. He was, however, fairly solitary and his politics did not sit well with the working-class lads who made up the rest of the platoon. They liked the middle ground. The Communists and the Fascists were just too extreme for their politics. We had few arguments about politics. The most serious arguments were over football. Being a Manchester regiment meant that there were divided loyalties between the two Manchester teams. I fell asleep during one such debate.

When I awoke the train was stationary and we were in the middle of nowhere. Alf was awake and I spied the glow from his cigarette. The lights in the carriage had been turned down. "Where are we, Corp?"

"By my reckoning somewhere in Belgium. It is hard to tell. It looks like they have taken the station signs away; always a sure sign that war is coming." He stubbed his cigarette out. It won't make much difference where we are. We will be in a field and living under canvas. We will have to get used to that for quite a while, I reckon."

It did make a difference to me. We had a home somewhere close to the French and Belgian border. I knew the area, not well, for I had always been a passenger but when Mum had brought us, we had used the local buses and I had travelled the roads.

"Sergeant Greely says you can speak French." I nodded. "That might come in handy then."

"The trouble is the language in Belgium is probably Flemish. I only speak a little of that."

"Really? I thought they all spoke Frog over here."

"Oh, don't get me wrong, if they don't speak French then they will understand it."

"You been over here then?"

"Yes Corp, we had a few holidays."

He laughed, "I knew you were posh." He waved a hand around the others, "To these lads, a holiday is a day out in Blackpool!"

I looked around them, "What about Neville? He has been to Spain."

"You can't call that a holiday. The poor bugger was fighting German dive bombers. I might not like his politics but he has balls I'll say that for him."

Suddenly the train lurched as it began to move again. The motion brought the others to life. Willy's head had been on my shoulder. He rubbed the side of it. "You're a bony bugger, Tom. You need a bit of fat on you." He looked over to the Corporal. "When are we going to get a cup of chah? My mouth feels like the inside of a Turkish tram driver's jockstrap!"

"I won't ask how you know what that tastes like, Holden!"

Dawn began to break and I could see that we were approaching civilisation. The train began to slow down as we approached a station. "Better wake the other lads up."

"Why Corp?"

"Because, Private Holden, we are stopping and there are military police on the platform so I am guessing that this is our stop!"

He was right and we heard the cry to disembark. The tiny platform was soon covered with six hundred khaki uniforms. The British Army is a remarkable organisation. The Colonel spoke to the adjutant who summoned the Sergeant Major. When his wishes were passed on to the sergeants, we began to march from the station with kit bags over our shoulders. As was the norm we were soon marching to the songs from the Great War. The rhythm helped us to march. As we marched, I reflected that this was almost exactly the same country over which my dad had flown. It was still flat but twenty-one years of nature's hard work had eradicated all signs of the war. The trees were a little less tall, that was all.

Once again it was the sergeants and non-commissioned officers who came to the fore as we reached the fields which would be our home for the next few months. As soon as we arrived, we were given an area and we laid out our tents. We would be sleeping as eight-man squads and our tents would be gathered in platoons. The old hands quickly ensured that we had the flattest pitch which was possible.

"If you have any slope at all," commented Jack Jones, "you end up sliding to the bottom of the tent. That is no fun, believe me."

The chaos of hammering tent poles and guy ropes was soon replaced by the order of neat, straight lines. We were chosen to erect the field kitchen. That was not a bad chore. The cooks would remember if we did the job well and there might be extra portions. It was certainly better than putting up the HQ tent or the Quartermaster's stores and we avoided the task of digging the latrines- that most dreaded of duties would arrive one day.

After our meal, we were able to lounge around. We had not drawn sentry duty. Sergeant Jennings did gather the platoon around to give us his warning. "We are at war now, my lucky lads, and that means that the Hun could come down that lane at any moment. He did in fourteen and there is no reason to think he won't do so again. Like in the Great War we have Belgians and French on either side of us. Keep a good watch. You see grey when you are on duty and you shout! The colonel has forbidden any visits to the local village. If it is any consolation there is bugger all there. They don't even have a bar and you won't be able to distinguish the women from the pigs so you aren't missing anything there." We all laughed; not because it was funny but because it was rare for the sergeant to crack a joke. "Get a goodnight's sleep. Tomorrow we start patrols."

We went out the following day in a platoon strength patrol led by Lieutenant Ashcroft. Although not a brand new lieutenant he had only been with the battalion for three months. I breathed a sigh of relief when I saw him defer to Sergeant Jennings. I recognised a soldier beneath the martinet. The Luxembourg border was less than ten miles away. We were not at an official border crossing but close to one of the many minor roads which crisscrossed the land. The Ardennes was hilly and heavily forested. I hoped that it would prove a good barrier against the Germans. The German border was also close to us. Just twenty miles north of our position. We had the bulk of our troops there. We were, we discovered, the southern end of our line.

We returned slightly disappointed with the lack of incident. It was to be the start of many such days as, what they termed in England, the Phoney War got underway. To us it was not phoney; it was just days filled with the same activities. There were alternate days of patrolling and digging latrines. We slept in a field and bathed in cold water. I began to worry that I had made a mistake.

Chapter 5

We endured a winter in the field. It was only punctuated by a delivery of letters in November. It had taken all of this time for them to reach us. I had fretted more than most over the lack of mail for I did not know how my parents had reacted to my decision. There was a bundle of letters. Most were from my Mum but one was from my Dad. I read them in order. It suited my organised mind.

2nd September 1939

Manston

Dear Tom,

I was surprised by your letter. You are your father's son. I know you are a sensible boy and that you had your reasons for doing what you have done but I cannot see what they are. Your father was upset too but for different reasons. He does not mind you joining up but he wishes that you had spoken with him first.

You must write and tell me where you are stationed. You say you are enlisting in Manchester I suppose that you will be based up there. Your father is using his influence to find out. You have put the cat amongst the pigeons and that is no error.

You know that we all love you and we are thinking of you. I never thought, on the day that you were born, that I would have to endure this again. I thought when your father returned from the war then this would be a thing of the past. I was wrong.

Mary sends her love.

Much love,

Your mother

xxx

I had forgotten, selfishly, that my Mum and Dad had been separated by the war too. The letter made me feel guilty again about leaving without speaking to her. She deserved better than that. I regretted my impetuous nature. There were three letters for me and the second letter was also from my Mum.

5th September 1939

Manston,

Dearest Tom,

Freddie Carrick drove down yesterday with your things. He explained everything. I suppose I can understand your actions now. From what Freddie said you have thought this through. I pray so. I was just surprised that you had joined the army. Now that war has

been declared I am even more worried than I was. Freddie intimated that you had been sent overseas. He is too much of a gentleman to tell me where so I will just have to worry about that. I thought I had ended worrying and writing letters at the end of the Great War.

I have hung your clothes in Mary's old room with mothballs. I daresay you will have outgrown them by the time this war is over. The newspapers make depressing reading.

There is a call for nurses such as myself to volunteer again but your father is unhappy about that. For some reason, he does not want me close to London. Mary is also becoming annoying for she wants to do her bit.

I will close now. Your father is coming home later and we can have a long chat about this. I need to get this in the post.

All my love,

Mum

xxx

As I carefully folded it back into the envelope, I saw that the next one was from Dad. It was on official paper with a war office frank on the envelope. For some reason I became scared and I hesitated before slipping the bayonet into the corner to open it.

6th September 1939

Manston

Dear Son,

Well, you have gone and done it eh? Why am I not surprised? Freddie told us about this Hughes-Graham. There are many like him in the services and I am proud of the way you dealt with him.

I cannot deny that I am disappointed you did not join the Royal Air Force although speaking to Freddie on the telephone I think I understand the reasons. Sorry, son; I can't do anything about who I am and you know I would have preferred anonymity. Nor will I deny that am afraid for you. When your Uncle Bert was in the Army I fretted about him too. I can't help it. I know that you will do your best and do your duty. You are a son in whom I am inordinately proud.

I hope this war will be over soon although I doubt it somehow. Please write as often as you can although I know that you will have your letters censored. Any news will be welcome for that way we will know you are still well.

I have been where you are- I understand.

Keep your chin up,

Dad

I actually felt better when I put down Dad's letter. He had taken it far better than I could have dreamed. I read the rest and then re-read them from the beginning. I had a picture of home. Mary had even sent me a letter in with Mum's. In hers, she told me of my mother sobbing when she had read my letter. That made me feel worse for Mum's letters had hidden her pain. That was Mum for you. She kept it all inside.

By the end of April, we knew something was up. Patrols further north reported a build-up of German forces. Our platoon was selected for a special patrol in the first week in May. Lieutenant Ashcroft gathered us around him. I watched with some amusement as Sergeant Greely and Sergeant Jennings observed him carefully and listened to all that he said. They were preparing to intervene if he said the wrong thing.

"Colonel Grainger has given us the honour of a special mission." I saw Sergeant Jennings roll his eyes, "We are going over the border into Luxembourg to see if there are any signs of German soldiers."

There was a hum of comments until Sergeant Jennings shouted, "Stow that! Pay attention or you will be on a fizzer!"

"Thank you, Sarn't Jennings. Needless to say, we will have to tread carefully. The German border is less than five miles from the area we will be patrolling. The Germans may have their own patrols out too. I want to stress that although we will be taking loaded weapons we will not fire unless fired upon. We do not want another Norway here do we?" He turned to the two sergeants, "Have I missed anything?"

Sergeant Greely shook his head and growled, "You take rifles, Mills Bombs and bayonets only. We are not going to a picnic. And keep your eyes and ears open."

We marched from the camp towards the forest some two miles away. Sergeant Greely led. When we reached the forest, he halted. "Harsker, to me." I trotted up to him. "You have sharp eyes and quick reflexes I want you fifty yards ahead of us. You hear anything you stop and wave me forward. All right?"

"Yes, Sarge." I had no idea why I had been chosen but I was determined to do the best I could. I held my rifle across my waist. It was an easy way to carry it and I could swing it around quickly if I needed to. I had a bullet *'up the spout'*. Although frowned upon it meant I could fire faster if I had to.

I knew how to stalk. I had hunted with Dad and Uncle Ted many times. This was hunting but the prey was man. I scanned the ground before I moved forward and then I scanned from nine o'clock to three o'clock. I moved steadily up the slope. Suddenly I heard voices ahead. Not surprisingly they were speaking in a foreign language. I dropped to one knee and, without taking my eyes off the ground ahead waved my left arm. While I waited for Sergeant Greely I concentrated on the voices.

He dropped next to me. "What is it?"

"Voices Sarge." I pointed to the right.

He nodded and listened, "German?"

"I think they are Luxembourgers."

"You had better be sure. There are twenty men's lives depending upon it."

I listened again. "They are not German."

"Good lad. We had better avoid them; head further to the left."

"That is the German border, Sarge. What about the Lieutenant?"

"Just head to the left and take it carefully, eh?"

As I headed left, I began to feel how uncomfortable the helmet was. It also stopped you hearing as well as you might. I kept heading to the left. Suddenly I smelled smoke. It was pipe tobacco. The ground dropped away just ahead of me and there was a path of sorts. I dropped to one knee and took off my helmet so that I could hear a little better. This time I recognised the words which came from below me. It was German. I turned and waved my left hand down. The rest of the platoon dropped to their knees and the two sergeants ran towards me followed by the Lieutenant. The two sergeants looked at me. I mouthed, "Germans."

They looked at each other. The Lieutenant mouthed, "Where?"

I pointed down and Sergeant Greely took my helmet and gave me the signal to have a look-see. I laid my rifle on the ground and began to belly towards the edge of the slope. I picked up some soil and wiped it across my face. I slowly moved myself to the edge and peered over. There, below me, were four Germans. They were smoking. I recognised that one of them was a German non commissioned officer. I saw that they had a map and one of them was busy annotating it. they were a scouting party. After checking that they were alone and not part of a larger patrol I slithered back to the sergeants and the Lieutenant. I held up four fingers.

"Germans?" He mouthed.

I nodded. The Lieutenant chewed his finger. Sergeant Greely mimed slitting a throat. The Lieutenant shook his head and pointed back to the camp. The two sergeants did not look happy about that but they obeyed. I picked up my helmet and my gun and followed. When we reached the road again, they halted.

"Good work, Harsker. What did you see?"

"Four Germans with a non-com in command. They were map making. They had one submachine gun and three rifles. I couldn't see any unit badge, sir."

"Good."

"Did you hear them say anything?"

The Lieutenant shot me a surprised look, "You speak German?"

"A little, sir. My Dad said it would come in handy. My French is better but I understood them. They were talking about what they hoped was being cooked for their supper. One of them hoped it was sausage."

The Lieutenant looked disappointed. "I thought it might be important intelligence. What they are having for dinner and a little mapmaking is hardly earth-shattering."

"It is sir. They are scouting in Luxembourg and their camp is nearby. They could be preparing for an attack."

"You might be right, Sergeant Jennings. Right, let's get back and report to the Colonel."

When we returned to the camp I went to the washroom to clean the dirt from my face. I didn’t want to incur the wrath of the Sergeant Major. I had just dressed when Corporal Higgins appeared. "Captain Foster wants to see you. Get a move on."

Captain Foster, our company commander, was also our intelligence officer. He was someone I had only met on parades but we all knew that he was well respected by all the officers and non-coms. I walked quickly to the tent they used. Sergeant Greely was waiting at the entrance. He waved me in impatiently. Captain Foster and Lieutenant Ashcroft were looking at the map. "Ah Harsker, I understand you did well today." I did not know if that required a reply and so I just inclined my head to one side. Sergeant Greely rolled his eyes. The Captain just smiled, "You used your head today. I hear you speak German and French. Any other skills in your repertoire?"

"Skills sir?"

"Well, I know you are a good shot and have mechanical skills. What else can you do? Play any sports?"

I was confused. What had this to do with the patrol or the war or anything? "No sir, but I enjoy running." He encouraged me with a smile and the wave of his hand. "And I can drive. I have flown a single-seater. I can sail a little and I like canoeing. Oh, and I am not a bad swimmer. That's about it."

He laughed, "An impressive list. Well, I have asked the Lieutenant to keep you for such patrols as we had today. You have shown an ability to think and to move quietly. Well done. Dismissed."

Sergeant Greely walked me out. "You shouldn't be so modest, you know." He looked at me, "Fly an aeroplane?"

I shrugged, "I grew up on airfields and my Dad is a pilot. It isn't that hard you know. Driving a car is harder in my view." I pointed to the skies. "They are a lot emptier." It is strange but I pointed to an empty blue sky and, as I looked up, I saw an aeroplane flying from the east.

Sergeant Greely snapped, "That's a Hun!" He turned and ran back to the intelligence tent. Willy and the others came out of the tents to stare at the buzzing black cross high in the sky. The Germans were scouting. The solitary aeroplane allied to the four Germans we had spotted in the woods put us on high alert.

We were set to improving the defences of the camp. We already had slit trenches and sandbags. Lieutenant Ashcroft had us conceal the Bren gun and Vickers' emplacements. Sergeant Jennings took our squad to dig some hidden pits beyond our perimeter. The next day we were issued more ammunition and another four Mills Bombs. Our patrol had changed the war. To us, it no longer felt phoney.

For a day nothing happened, nothing that is except that Captain Foster disappeared. That sounds dramatic but one day he was there and the next day Lieutenant Ashcroft was beaming like a cat that had the cream. He was acting company commander until the return of the Captain. The following morning we were awoken in the early hours by the drone of bombers passing over towards the west. The numbers were hard to estimate but I guessed that there were at least two squadrons. Stand to was sounded and we hurried to our rifle pits.

A few hours later we heard their drone as they headed east. This time we saw that they were twin-engine bombers. Corporal Higgins took Willy and they fetched us a dixie of tea from the mess tent. "Keep your eyes peeled, lads, the colonel is out and about. It seems Jerry has started something over in Holland."

Jack Jones spat and said, "That's miles away Corp. We are safe enough here."

I was not so certain. I thought I heard something and I cocked my head to one side. I hated these helmets. Sergeant Jennings asked, "You hear something?"

"I thought I heard an engine. I could be wrong."

Sergeant Greely appeared from nowhere. "Let's trust your ears eh? Stand to. Eyes front."

The engines not only became louder they were augmented by the noise of aeroplane engines. I looked up and saw single-seaters. They were gull-winged. I pointed and Sergeant Greely shouted, "Stukas!

Take cover!" We were all in our trenches anyway but we tried to get as deep in them as possible. I suddenly wished that we had dug them another foot or so deeper.

The noise of the dive bomber's engines became a high pitched scream as they dived. Sergeant Major Campbell roared, "Open fire!"

I raised my Lee Enfield. I had hunted birds before and knew that you aimed ahead of them. The ducks I had shot, however, had not been diving at me. I squeezed five rounds off. In the time it took to fire the Stukas had begun to open fire with their machine guns. Before I could fire again Sergeant Greely shouted, "Bombs! Take cover!"

I buried my head into the trench. Willy's back was in front of me and Nev's helmet rammed into my back. I felt the concussion from the explosion before the wall of heat rushed over us. I heard the clang of shrapnel on metal and then the screams and shouts of those wounded began. I don't know how long we had to endure the bombs but I do know that something clanged off my helmet and made my already deafened ears ring. In the maelstrom of flying metal, branches and soil which fell like rain, I heard, "Medical Orderly!" I did not envy the poor sods who would have to leave the safety of a trench to brave the bombs and tend the wounded.

And then the bombing stopped. It was bizarre. Our deafness made it seem like a silent world. As if from far away I heard a voice shout, "Stand to!"

I raised my head. The sky was lighter because most of the trees had gone. I looked to our right and saw a crater where there had been a trench with four men before the Stukas had struck. Medical orderlies were carrying bloodied bodies back to the medical tent. I reloaded as quickly as I could. Nev snarled, "Bastard Stukas! I had enough of them in Spain!"

I found my hearing returning and I caught the sound of engines coming from the east. "Tanks!"

My shout grabbed everyone's attention. Sergeant Jennings, in the next trench, shouted, "Get some Mills bombs ready!"

I felt the ground vibrate as the tracks of the tanks drew closer to us. We could see nothing. Then a spout of flame erupted from the woods ahead as the first of the tanks fired. It was not a big gun but it sounded big to us. The crack followed and I felt the force of the explosion as the shell exploded some way behind us. Then I saw the flickering flames of the machine gun as it chattered out. Our own Vickers fired in reply but I knew it would be a waste of ammunition. The bullets pinged off the shell of the tank as it drew ever closer. There was one slit trench ahead of us. As the next five tanks emerged two of the lads in the trench tried to clamber out and flee. Reg Johnson and Welsh Paul stood no chance. The bullets of three machine guns tore into their bodies making then dance as though they were puppets. Their shredded corpses fell feet in front of us.

Corporal Higgins shouted, "Stay in your trenches!"

That was easier said than done as the German tanks drew ever closer. By the standards of later in the war, these were not particularly big tanks and their guns were not enormous but they were big enough. There were only six of them but they cut a swath through our defences. All of our traps and fallen trees were no obstacle and they climbed them easily. I saw the leading tank as it rose above the trench ahead. The survivors screamed as the weight of the tank came crashing down and crushed them.

"Grenades!"

Sergeant Jennings' voice gave us something to do. We could fight back although I knew that our death was inevitable. We could not stop tanks with grenades and rifles. I pulled the pin and released the handle then I threw. Some of my comrades threw as soon as they had pulled the pin. The result was that the grenades went off in succession. Miraculously they tore the left-hand track from the tank and it slewed to the right. It was just forty yards ahead of us and its angle stopped the other tanks from being able to fire at us. I ran from the trench as fast as I could. I had another grenade in my hand. I saw behind the tanks the grey uniforms of the German infantry. I saw the turret as it traversed. I was in a race now. Could I reach the tank before the machine gun fired?

I pulled the pin as I ran. I reached the side of the Panzer as the barrel of the cannon appeared above me. I put my rifle against the tank and hauled myself up. The hatch began to open just as the German infantry began to fire at me. Had the hatch not opened I would have been dead as bullets struck the metal. A head appeared and I punched it with my right hand. As it disappeared I dropped the grenade and slithered from the tank as a hail of bullets smacked into the hatch cover. I grabbed my rifle and ran. I suspect they were seeking the bomb and that saved me for they did not fire the MG 42. I had just dived into the trench, head first, when there was a crump from behind me and I heard a cheer as the tank was disabled.

I looked up and saw Nev and Willy grinning at me. "You mad bugger!"

I scrambled to my feet. My sudden charge appeared to have invigorated the rest of the company and hand grenades were thrown towards the German tanks. The others were further away but two lucky blows disabled two machine guns. We were learning that the machine guns were more deadly than the cannon they carried. One of the tanks with a disabled machine gun ran afoul of a broken branch. The hatch opened and a head appeared. We all fired our rifles and the German slumped halfway out of his turret. Suddenly, Sean McGuire, one of those who had joined up with me stood and pulled the pin on a Mills Bomb. Sean had been a gifted cricketer and he pulled his arm back and lobbed the grenade. It struck the dead German and trickled down into the turret. Poor Sean just had time to cheer before the other tanks' machine guns scythed him in two.

The tank spewed metal and smoke as the bomb exploded inside. There were two tanks which were disabled but, more importantly, they were almost together. Sergeant Jennings shouted, "Right lads, shelter behind the tanks." We sprinted to the shelter of the tanks. They formed a V, there was a small gap between them and Smith and Jones set up the Bren. I leaned against the back of the tank I had destroyed. We could now see, less than thirty yards away, the advancing German soldiers.

"Fire!"

The smoke from the second tank was blowing towards the Germans and they had no idea that we had advanced. The first line was cut down as the Bren and our Lee Enfields shredded them. Away to our left the company Vickers still barked away and I realised that we had halted them. Only two of the Panzers had escaped damage and they began to back towards the shelter of the trees as more grenades were hurled at them. We had shown that we could blow their tracks off.

Sergeant Greely pointed, "Look, Tom, there is a German officer trying to rally his men, can you hit him?"

I looked. He was well over two hundred yards away and partly hidden. "I can give it a go Sarge."

"Even if you don't hit him you can worry him! Do your best, son."

I licked my finger and thumb and moistened my sight. I breathed slowly and took a bead on him. I aimed at his chest, even though it was partly hidden by the undergrowth and I squeezed off four shots. The second one struck him and he spun around. I switched to the man on his left and hit him with my fifth shot. The whole line halted.

More of the battalion raced to join us and more Bren guns added their firepower. It became too hot for the Germans who pulled back. "Cease fire!"

Chapter 6

We all stood in silence, wreathed in smoke and surrounded by the sour smell of spent cordite. We had held them. I turned and saw Sergeant Jennings. He was looking at the crater where half of his men, the rest of our section, had died. Our squad was all that remained of his section. Sergeant Major Campbell shouted, "Reload and await orders."

Sergeant Jennings and Sergeant Greely went around our dead and took their dog tags and any papers they might have had. Corporal Higgins said to the rest of us, "Collect any spare ammo and use the knapsacks from the lads to carry them."

Mike Carr said, "That's like robbing the dead, Corp!"

Jack Jones snorted, "If you were dead, Sonny Jim, would you give a bugger if your mates had your spare ammo?"

Once we had done that we were ordered to collect the dead, our dead, and lay them out. While we were doing that Lieutenant Foster came over to us. "Sergeant Jennings, take your squad and see if the Germans have gone or if they are regrouping. If you find any German maps or papers then grab them eh?"

"Sir. Right lads leave the bodies where they are. Harsker," he pointed and I trotted off to head the line of nine men. Just then we heard the drone of aeroplanes and we looked up to see another two squadrons of twin-engine aeroplanes heading west. I recognised them this time. They were the Heinkel 111. I heard Jack Jones say, "Some poor bugger is going to cop it!"

"Shut it, Jones, you should know better."

I found the first German body. He looked to be the same age as me and had been hit by a number of bullets. I bent down to check his tunic when the sergeant snapped, "You keep looking ahead, Harsker, you are our eyes and ears!"

I waved to show I had heard and I moved a little quicker. I did not move in a straight line. The Germans might be regrouping and waiting for me. After the first ten or twelve bodies, I found fewer until I came to the German officer I had killed. I saw that I had hit him twice. The other soldier was not there. They must have carried off their wounded. I impulsively grabbed his Luger and jammed it in my battle dress. A handgun always came in handy, at least that was what my Dad had said.

The ground rose and I heard the noise of diesel engines. I dropped to all fours and clambered up the small rise. I found the German tanks. Already they were refitting and repairing the damaged machine guns.

Some of the assault troops were drinking from their canteens while others were having their wounds dressed. I had seen enough and I slithered down the bank. The rest of the squad had almost reached my dead German and I waved them back. Sergeant Jennings halted them, "What is it?"

"The Germans are over that rise and they are refitting the tanks. I reckon they will be coming back soon."

"Right. Back lads."

We returned much quicker than we had left. The rest of the battalion had worked quickly and we saw the line of graves each draped with a helmet. We had buried our dead and there were thirty men who would never walk the streets of Manchester again. Lieutenant Foster approached us, "Well?"

"Harsker spotted them regrouping. They are coming again. Do we dig in?"

He shook his head, "Apparently we are the only ones who held. We are surrounded. We have been ordered to pull back. The battalion is the rearguard. Keep your squad at the back. I'll send Sarn't Greely and the remains of his squad to help you." He looked at me. "If we get out of this Harsker, I'll see that you and McGuire get medals for what you did. Between the two of you, you saved our bacon. Well done."

"Thanks, sir." I took my helmet off to scratch my head. I saw a hole and a large dent in the tin lin. As I scratched my head I found a tiny piece of shrapnel caught in my hair. I had been lucky. I put the grisly souvenir in my battle dress pocket.

When Sergeant Greely reached me he slapped me on the back of the head, "What's that for Sarge?"

"For being a dozy bugger and almost getting yourself killed."

"But the Lieutenant said he is putting me in for a medal."

He shook his head, "Forget being a hero and keep your head down!"

Corporal Higgins and Willy arrived with a dixie of tea and a tray of sandwiches. "Cooks had this all ready but they are pulling out. Seemed a shame for it to go to waste."

Mike Carr asked, "What kind are they?"

"Are you choosy or what? They are corned dog now eat them while you can. I reckon we will be scavenging from now on."

We ate the curling sandwiches and drank the lukewarm, sweet tea. It was a feast. By the time we had finished were almost the only soldiers left. We heard the sound of a tank but they were in the distance. "Right lads let's go."

"Sarge, how about leaving a few booby traps. It will slow them down." We all looked at the veteran of the Spanish Civil War, Nev Wilkinson. "It takes two shakes and if the lads watch me then they will be able to do it too. I reckon we will need tricks like this if we are the rearguard."

"Righto. Show us but make it quick. Holden, keep a good lookout."

We watched as Nev took a Mills bomb and threaded a piece of cord through the pin. He jammed the grenade in the tracks of one of the tanks. He ran the cord between the tanks and tied it to the broken wheel. "That's it."

"Right lads, each of you leave a present for Jerry. Holden?"

"Nowt yet Sarge."

Nev said, "Let's go and find some German potato mashers." We ran to the first of the German dead. He took the stick grenade and unscrewed the porcelain cap. There was a cord. "When you pull this there is a five-second fuse. Lift the body." I raised the body and he carefully put the cord around the button of the tunic. "Now lower it. When Jerry comes to check his kamerad the fuse starts and Jerry dies for the Fatherland."

We had rigged four bodies when Willy shouted, "Krauts at twelve o'clock."

We picked up our rifles and we ran. We were both exposed and bullets zinged around us. We had almost reached the two brewed up tanks when Nev fell to the ground. I turned and sprayed five random shots at the advancing Germans. He had taken a bullet in the leg. I picked him up and pulled him into the shelter of the tanks. Harry Mac was the medical orderly from Sergeant Greely's squad and he tore open the trousers as we fired at the advancing Germans.

"You are lucky. It passed through." He quickly applied a dressing.

Sergeant Jennings said, "Get a move on, I don't fancy spending the war in a prison camp!"

"Done!"

"Right get Wilkinson back we will buy you five minutes." He turned to the rest of us. "Pair up. One man fires and one falls back." He paused, "We are the rearguard if you fall no one comes for you!"

Willy appeared at my side, "I reckon your German will come in handy, Professor!"

I nodded, "Ready?"

"I was born ready, old son."

"Run!" As he ran I aimed at a Feldwebel urging his men on. I clipped his shoulder and he fell. I fired a second shot at the man who was aiming at me. I missed and so did he.

"Run, Tom!"
I turned and ran. I saw Willy firing as I passed him. I stopped twenty yards beyond him and was aiming when I heard the crump of a grenade beyond the tanks. It was followed by two others. They had found our body booby traps. It halted the pursuit. We jogged after the others and were gratified to hear more explosions as more of our booby traps were triggered.
We heard but didn't see the German bombers as they returned east. Once we cleared the trees and found the road we saw the devastation caused by the Stukas. The road was littered with damaged vehicles and bodies. They were not the 1st Loyal Lancashires. It was getting on towards six o'clock when we heard the high pitched engines of the Stukas again.
"Take cover!
Willy and I threw ourselves into a ditch. I saw, to my horror, that there was the headless corpse of an engineer there. I forced myself to concentrate on the dive bombers. I aimed my rifle at the engine. This time we could see their flight. The whole of our rearguard squad opened fire. I heard the two Bren guns as they added their chatter to the crack of the rifles. I saw smoke appear from the first Stuka. It billowed against the cockpit and I knew that the pilot would be struggling to pull up the nose. It was a vain hope. It zipped over our heads to explode in a fireball just fifty yards down the road. The shock wave made my head buzz. The column of debris threw off the aim of the other Stukas whose machine-gun bullets and bombs hit the adjacent fields. As the remaining five aeroplanes climbed for another attack, Sergeant Greely shouted, "Fall back!"
We clambered from the ditch and sprinted down the road. We had to take a detour into the field around the burning aeroplane. The two charred corpses were still in their seats. I glanced over my shoulder and saw that the Stukas had turned. Their bombs had been dropped but they could still strafe us.
"Cover!"
Willy and I took shelter in the ditch. This time it was mercifully free of the dead. The machine guns and the rifles all threw up a wall of lead but we did not bring any more of the dive bombers down. They turned and headed east when their ammunition was depleted.
"Right lads, let's find the battalion."
We were dead on our feet when we found the commandeered farmhouse. Nev Wilkinson was waiting for us smoking a cigarette, the bloody bandage on his leg clearly visible as we approached him. "I

wondered where you lads were." He gestured behind him with his thumb, "The Lieutenant said to wait for you here."

I grinned at him, "Your booby bombs worked Nev!"

"A little trick I picked up in Spain. Another one we can try is filling a bottle with petrol. Put a rag in it and then light it. It stops tanks better than grenades."

"How's the leg, Wilkinson?"

"I've had worse. It'll ache like buggery tomorrow Sarge but Harry Mac cleaned it up nicely."

"Where is he?"

He shook his head, "He bought it along with Major Marston and some of the Headquarters squad. Stukas did for them!"

The Lieutenant reached us. "Well done lads. Tomorrow I will be with you. We have the remains of the company to help us." He looked at the two sergeants. "You two are the last of my sergeants."

Sergeant Greely nodded, "Any grub sir? We have had nowt since the butties and that was hours ago."

He shook his head. "We left most of the food at the camp. It is just the rations you have with you."

I saw the farmhouse. "Sir, has anyone searched the farmhouse yet?"

"I am afraid so Harsker. There is nothing in the kitchen left."

"Do you mind if I have a look, sir?"

"Be my guest!"

"Willy."

We left our rifles stacked with the others and headed across to the farmhouse. I could see where the roof had been blown off. It was a shambles. The only item of furniture which remained undamaged was a huge ancient oak table in the middle of the room. The Lieutenant was right the kitchen had been picked clean but I was not looking for food in the kitchen. "Willy, grab this table and shift it." We moved the huge table to the side and I reached down and pulled the handle of the trap door to the cellar.

"Well, I'll be. How did you know about this?"

"I didn't but I spent enough holidays in France to know that the local farmers use their cellars to store food." I spied a broken candle. "Grab that candle and light it." I opened the door of the cellar and felt the rush of cold air.

I turned around and began to back down the step ladder which led down. I reached the bottom and my head was still above the floor level. Willy handed me the candle. I ducked my head and peered around. It was an Aladdin's cave. I reached in and took the huge ham I spied. I hoisted it proudly like a football trophy. "Best get the rest of the lads, Willy, there is too much here for two of us."

By the time he had returned I had two hams, two cheeses, a dozen bottles of wine and a small sack of beans. Sergeant Jennings actually smiled at me. "You know Harsker, the Lieutenant was going to give you a medal for blowing up the tank. I want to give you one for this."

Sergeant Greely nodded. "And we might as well eat in here. We'll have a bit of shelter too."

Sergeant Jennings held up the sack of dried beans. "These aren't much use. Pity."

"That's all you know Sarge." The rest of the squad were busy carving the ham with their bayonets and dividing the cheese. "Willy, find me a dixie. Nev, can you get a fire going in the stove?"

He had changed since we had brewed up the tank. He seemed more approachable. "Your wish is my command."

There was a water butt and I used a small pan to ladle the water into the dixie. Nev used the broken furniture in the kitchen and the farmhouse to get a fire going in the stove. I put half of the beans in the dixie. Turning I saw that they had carved the meat from one of the hams. I took the bone and dropped it into the dixie. "If we keep this going all night we will have bean and ham soup for breakfast. It will keep us going."

Sergeant Greely handed me a hunk of ham and a wedge of cheese, "You are a constant surprise to me, Professor. Where did you learn this trick?"

"Mum learned it from a French woman. They live off this sort of stuff." I chewed happily on the ham. Willy passed me the bottle of rough red wine and I washed the ham down. After we had eaten the cheese I felt a little better.

Nev disappeared and when he returned, limping, he had a handful of greenery. "And I learned a few tricks in Spain. Herbs and spinach. They will give us a little more flavour too." He put them and the second ham bone in the pot. We emptied almost all of the bottles of wine. We had dined like kings.

The two sergeants had saved some food for the Lieutenant who arrived when we had just finished all but a quarter of a bottle of wine. He cocked an eye and Willy said, cheerfully, "Saved you some wine, sir. It goes well with the cheese!"

Laughing the Lieutenant ate his share. The company looked after their own. We had left many comrades on the battlefield but the ones who remained still had spirit. We were split into three groups to keep watch.

Our team had the middle shift. When I was woken I had the lovely aroma of herbs and ham soup to greet me. Before I went to relieve the other team I stirred it. There was a reassuring *'gloop'* as I did so.

When I reached the road it was pitch black. I looked west and saw a glow in the sky and I heard the sound of gunfire. Sergeant Greely came over to me. "It looks like we have been caught with our trousers down again. I thought we had learned our lesson in the Great War. Belgium is too close to Germany to defend."

"What about the French, Sarge?"

"Not good I am afraid. I was talking with the Sarn't Major. Jerry has isolated us from the French. They have attacked Brussels and Antwerp. They are trying to stop us from getting home. We are heading for the sea."

"Dad told me about that. He was in the cavalry and they barely made it to the coast. Will it be trenches again do you think?"

He pointed to the sky. "With the German bombers and dive bombers I don't think that is possible and they have tanks."

I chuckled, "Do you know the irony, Sarge? We invented tanks and now the Germans are using them against us."

"It's always the same." I saw his face from the glow of his cigarette. "I am glad you joined up young un. The University's loss is our gain. You and McGuire did save our bacon today."

"You have changed your tune, Sarge, this morning I was an idiot."

"Oh you are still an idiot but I am glad you are here with us."

We did not have to finish our watch that night. We heard the sound of tanks. They were coming down the road.

"Stand to! Tanks."

The Lieutenant was woken and he sent a runner to the colonel.

Sergeant Jennings said, "Right lads, let's make some of Wilkinson's booby traps."

Nev said, "I filled up the twelve bottles from last night with some paraffin I found. We have some bombs."

Sergeant Jennings said, "Well done but you are wounded. You sort the soup out for the lads. I'll be buggered if we are going to let Jerry have any of it."

Nev nodded and scurried off. The Lieutenant handed one of the bombs to each of us. "The rest of the company will make some booby traps. You twelve go and hide along the ditches. When the tanks come light the tops and throw them at the tanks. Four to a tank. We make sure they burn. The road is narrow. If we can block the road then we have a chance."

Mike Carr asked, "A chance for what, sir?"
"To escape this trap and fight again."
We could not see the tanks but we could see the trees moving above them and feel the ground vibrating. We ran, in pairs, to hide in the ditch some fifty or so yards from the farmhouse. The rest of the company was busy setting up Bren guns and improvising barricades. I hoped that the Colonel would be sending back fresh troops to help us. There were just two men ahead of us in our ditch and they were both from Sergeant Greely's. None of us had rifles. They would be too cumbersome but I still had, tucked in my knapsack, my Luger. I had managed to clean and load it during my sentry duty. It was reassuring. I also had my last two Mills bombs. Our booby traps had taken their toll.

Now I saw the dark shapes of the tanks as they came past us. We had to wait until the first tank had come by before we launched our attack. The lads ahead of us had to endure two tanks. We lay flat in the ditch. The muddy water covered my face effectively camouflaging me. I risked a look up and saw that the tanks had pairs of German infantry clinging to the back. As the second tank approached I tapped Willy on the shoulder. He had a petrol lighter. He flicked it and lit his fuse. As soon as the light flared I heard a shout in German. I lit mine from his and then we both hurled them at the tank. It was just six feet away. As they shattered the flames lit the fumes and I saw two of the German soldiers erupt into flames like huge Roman candles. As we turned to run I heard the chatter of a machine gun. Then there were two more walls of flame, one ahead of us and one behind us.

I heard a shout and as I turned I saw The two men from Sergeant Greely's squad pitched forward as the machine guns of the other tanks riddled them. The tank we had struck suddenly exploded as the flames and the petrol found the ammunition. We were both thrown through the air. When I landed the wind had been knocked from me and my ears were ringing. That probably saved my life as the first tank in the column exploded just twelve feet away. The fact that we were in the ditch meant that the force of the explosion went over us but I found I was deaf. I just lay there with my face buried as deep as I could get it. I had cursed my helmet but it had saved me again.

After what seemed an age the flames died a little and I forced myself to my feet. I could hear the muffled sounds of firing but my hearing had gone. As I stood I saw the crisply charred corpses of the Germans who had been on the back of the first tank. I pulled Willy up. I saw his mouth moving but I heard nothing. I pointed to my ears and shook my head. He grinned and nodded.

We stepped over the body of Bert Williams. He was the first of our squad to die. He would not be the last. We ran towards the Bren guns which were covering us. We ran past them, picked up our rifles and then turned to face the enemy. The flames showed the position of the enemy column. There were eight tanks behind the three we had destroyed. I raised my rifle to fire but there were no targets. Suddenly there were eight sharp cracks as the 20 mm tank guns began to fire.

A runner ran up to the Lieutenant. "Colonel's compliments sir and you can withdraw your men!"

"Right lads, you heard. Let's go. At the double."

Willy and I stood with our rifles at the ready. Nev Wilkinson hobbled over with two mugs in his hand. "You made it Prof, you best drink it." He hobbled off using his rifle as a makeshift stick.

I swallowed a mouthful. Sergeant Jennings's hand clapped me on the shoulder. "Right lads. You are the last. Let's go and be sharpish."

We turned and jogged down the road. I swallowed every last bean and flake of meat. It is funny but close encounters with death made me hungry. When I had finished I put the mug in my respirator case. The respirator had long gone. I would rinse the mug later. Some of the soup would have clung to the sides. Who knew when we might eat again?

Chapter 7

Soon we found the road filled with refugees fleeing west. Our progress became a crawl. Sadly the Germans were no respecters of civilians and the Stukas returned. This time we stood our ground. We formed up in blocks of men and fired at the diving Stukas. They screamed down at us; their cleverly placed sirens made them even louder. They were a weapon of terror; at least they were to the civilians. Our battalion brought down four of them but the roads were littered with dead and dying civilians. Our doctors patched up those that they could but the trucks and tanks in the distance meant we had to scurry away again ourselves.

There was chuntering and complaints from many of the men. It did not sit well to retreat.

"But we have held our own every time we have faced them, Sarge. We can stop them!"

"Jenkins, you dozy sod! We have been lucky so far and we have destroyed a couple of tanks. Every time we have we have lost men and the Germans are to the north, south and east of us."

"I know, Sarge, but ..."

"But nothing. How many grenades have you got left?"

"None."

"And I bet you have less than thirty rounds of .303."

"Yes, Sarge."

"Then focus on walking. The brass will tell us when we hold them."

We did stop. Just beyond Ravin, we halted at the river. The engineers were there rigging the bridge to blow when we crossed. We were exhausted. Since the soup, we had eaten nothing and our canteens were empty. We looked more like brigands than British soldiers. The Colonel, when we saw him, looked to have aged by thirty years as he waited on the other side of the bridge to greet us. The last four of us who crossed were Willy, Corporal Higgins, Sergeant Jennings and me. The Colonel shook each of us by the hand. "Your squad, Sergeant Jennings, has done the battalion proud. I intend to name a number of your men in despatches. Your sacrifice has been worthwhile." We all saluted.

"Stand clear! We are blowing the bridge!"

We hurried to the shelter of some nearby houses as the engineers exploded the frail-looking pillars on the old bridge. I had no doubt that it would not delay the Germans for long but any delay was necessary.

We had no tents and we just collapsed close to the river. Once again it was the sergeants and corporals who organised us. Our company which had begun the war with three platoons now had a mere one and a half. Some wounded had been evacuated. The Lieutenant wanted Nev Wilkinson to go but he refused. "The leg is healing nicely, sir. All I need is some new trousers and I will be right as rain."

I could not get over the change in Nev. Since we had begun to kill Germans he was a different man. A lorry arrived to take away the wounded and to bring much-needed food, grenades and ammunition. We even managed to boil some water so that we could shave. I just shaved my beard. This seemed a good opportunity to grow a moustache. I also took the opportunity to strip down and clean my rifle. I saw the nods of approval from the two sergeants. I suspect Sergeant Jennings had seen a studious young recruit when he had first met me. I hoped that I had shown him a different side to me since then.

We had lost all of our tents. Some had been destroyed when the Stukas had attacked the lorries while many had been left when we had to leave so quickly from our camp. We had only our blankets. I prayed it would not rain. Our greatcoats also acted as a groundsheet for us. It was the food which made all the difference. The cooks made an improvised field kitchen while we dug slit trenches and prepared our Bren positions. The Vickers machine guns had been abandoned. We helped Jack and Pete to load the Bren magazines. They were our only automatic weapons.

As we had had the longest duty the night before our team had the first duty. We could hear, to the north and south of us, gunfire. German bombers droned overhead as they continued to bomb the Dutch and Belgian cities. At midnight we woke our reliefs and headed, almost like men in a trance, to our bivouacs. I slept like a baby. There is nothing like curling up and sleeping especially when you are exhausted.

When we awoke I was surprised that we were not under fire. I had expected the Germans to be hot on our trail. There was gossip aplenty which I ignored. Dad had told me that gossip was bad for morale and I was beginning to see that he was right. All we had to do was our duty. The enemy were to the east of us and our salvation was in the west. We were the rear guard. It was as simple as that. For some reason, our squad all seemed more relaxed about the whole thing than some of the other companies. Perhaps because we had only lost one man and we had bloodied the Germans on a number of occasions we were all more confident.

The reconnaissance aeroplane flew over us at about noon. We knew that would not be the end of things. We had all eaten and so we dug our trenches just a little bit deeper and found whatever we could to make barriers before us. I used the holes in my helmet as repositories for twigs and leaves. It helped to camouflage me a little more. Others who had similarly damaged helmets did the same. To while away the time I sharpened my bayonet. When I had the time I would get myself a proper knife. The bayonet was too long.

The rest spent their time smoking. One or two had pipes but the rest all had cigarettes. The lorries which brought the supplies had also brought more cigarettes. I gave mine to Willy. I didn't smoke but I knew I would get myself a lighter. That would come in handy. Of that I was sure. I patted my knapsack. It now had six grenades. We had made sure that we had more than we were allocated. The rear guard needed them.

The Stukas found us at three o'clock. They had a harder target this time. The battalion had had time to dig in and we threw up a barrage of Biblical proportions. We had grown teeth and we had grown more creative. We used the strength of the Stuka against them. They employed a steep dive for accuracy. It meant you could throw a cone of fire through which they would have to fly. We only shot one down but six were smoking as they left and they merely succeeded in destroying the last of the pillars of the bridge.

The tanks arrived an hour later. They lined up on the other side of the river and they blasted away with machine guns and cannon. We burrowed down into our trenches. The damage they did merely added to the strength of the trenches by depositing more debris before us. The tanks withdrew. We could not hurt them but they could do nothing until they crossed the river and for that, they needed to winkle us out.

It was getting on for dusk when we heard the sound of German trucks. We were ready and there was a ripple of bolts being pulled back. We were prepared for an attack across the water. Nothing happened until it was completely dark and then I saw a shadow move across the river.
"Sarge, movement!"

"Thanks, son."

Sergeant Jennings fired the Very pistol and the flare flew high into the sky. As it came down we saw German soldiers trying to manhandle rubber boats down to the river.

"Fire!"

The flare descended slowly and we used every second we had to kill as many as we could. We heard the splashes as their bodies fell into the water. Then there was silence broken only by the moans of those who had been wounded. The night was shattered when the German heavy machine guns began to shred the river bank. I dived to the bottom of my trench but some were too slow and, perhaps, a little unlucky. I heard their shouts as they died. We did not get much sleep that night. I heard the noise of diesel engines in the hours before dawn and I wondered if that meant tanks again. When dawn broke it was worse than tanks. They had brought artillery and mortars. The dawn chorus was the crump of mortars and the crack of artillery pieces.

"Fall back! Retreat!"

We could not stand against such a barrage at such close range and we grabbed our belongings and we ran. Once again we were the last but we would gun without fear of being caught. There was no one behind us to delay. The German troops would have to throw a bridge over the river if they were going to catch us. They had driven us out and it would just be a matter of time. We stopped running when we outran the shells that their artillery continued to lob at us. We gathered around Sergeant Jennings and caught our breath. Corporal Higgins said, "Well we held them up for a day."

"Aye we did but we ran away again and that is a bad habit to get into. Best do a roll call."

Pete Smith did not answer the roll call. He had fallen or been hit after we had left the river. Old Jack Jones was the last of the original squad. We were being slowly pared down. We marched west. The Meuse was ahead and that wasn't far from the coast. We were running out of land. The Germans were doing a good job of driving us into the net. We began to run into German patrols and advance units from the north and the south. We heard the fire from the flanks. We had delayed them at the river but the other forces, French, Belgian and British had not. We were in danger of being caught.

Nev Wilkinson had recovered quickly from his wound. He was tough and hardened by his time in Spain. He now marched with a pronounced limp. He had a sixth sense and he suddenly hissed, as we marched down a leafy hedgerow. "I smell German tobacco!"

There were just our squad and we were the last men. We dropped to the ground and peered into the fields to our left. We had no sooner done that than a fusillade ripped through the bushes. I saw, through the thinner lower branches grey legs. I fired five shots rapidly at the legs. I saw blood gushing and Germans fell to the ground. I fired into their bodies. Willy took a grenade and hurled it, from a prone position over the hedgerow. I heard a German shout, "Grenade" and a few seconds later it exploded. They fired again and this time it was lower. I took out a grenade, took out the pin and released the handle. I counted to three and threw it. I covered my face for I knew it would explode in the air. Shrapnel whizzed back on our side of the hedge as my grenade exploded. I heard screams. I jumped to my feet, my ears were still ringing and ran back up the lane until I found a gap in the hedge. I ran into the field and saw the carnage I had caused. Three men were still standing and I knelt and began to fire at them. The first fell without realising that they had been flanked. The second two turned. I fired my second shot and the German was thrown backwards. The last German was taking a bead on me. I forced myself to aim and I squeezed my trigger. I saw his muzzle flash as he fired a millisecond before me and I waited for the bullet which would end my life prematurely. It zipped across my battle dress and tore a hole in the epaulette. My bullet smacked into him between the eyes.

I stood and walked over to them. One or two were not dead but from the blood pumping from their bodies, it would not take long. Sergeant Jennings and Willy appeared behind me. "That was a risky thing to do with a grenade, son. It could have killed us all."

"It worked though, Sarge."

Willy reached down and took the Luger and holster from the dead officer. Sergeant Jennings said, "See if they have grenades and food. Nev, get down the road and tell the Lieutenant what has happened. Be sharpish." He limped off down the road.

We gathered what they had and used a German rucksack to carry them. When we reached the other side we saw the others gathered around a body. Jack Jones had been hit in the initial attack. He had been too slow to heed Nev's warning. Corporal Higgins took his dog tags and papers. "Hogan, Carr, you take the Bren."

Nodding, Sergeant Jennings said, "Let's get back to the war. Double time."

We all took one last look at old Jack Jones and then we ran down the lane. We had travelled no more than two miles before we heard firing from our right. We heard .303s in return. That had to be our lads, the rearguard. Sergeant Jennings halted and waved us into the field on our right. Two hundred yards ahead of us we saw a line of Germans; they were setting up mortars and a machine gun.

Corporal Higgins said, "What do we do Sarge? If we fire on them they will turn on us."

"We are the rear guard lad. We'll do our duty." He turned. There was cover from a ditch and overhanging bushes. "Set up the Bren here.

Harsker, Holden, do you think you can make your way down the hedge on the left and get a bit closer. Try to pick off the officers."

"Right, Sarge."

He smiled, "If owt happens to us then you make your way back to the others right? You are smart lads. You'll be all right."

We crawled to the ditch and began to make our way down. The first of the German heavy machines began to chatter and then I heard the crump as the first of the mortars fired. We reached to within forty yards of them before the Bren fired. They cut a line through the machine crew and two mortar crews. Pandemonium ensued as the Germans turned to face the new enemy. I placed my last hand grenades before me and then took a bead on the officer who was giving orders. I squeezed one bullet off. More would have been a waste as I was just fifty yards from him. Willy fired too but he fired a number of shots. I switched to a Feldwebel and hit him. Then I saw the Germans trying to crew the machine gun again. Three bullets took care of them. I saw grey uniforms rushing towards us and I took out the pin from a grenade, released the handle and then threw it. "Down Willy!"

I pushed my face into the ground. I felt shrapnel whizz over my head. When I looked over I saw that the charging Germans had fallen. The troops who had been attacking our rearguard began to run towards the sergeant and the Bren. I saw them switching the mortars around and I fired as fast as I could at their crews. They were too far away for a grenade. We were now the target of the Germans and it was only the ditch and the camouflaged helmets which saved us. I watched in horror as the first mortar exploded to the right of the Bren and took Mike and George out. Corporal Higgins and Sergeant Jennings crouched and emptied their magazines at the Germans.

"Let's buy them some time, Willy!" I took out the pins from two grenades and half stood to hurl them at the Germans. Willy managed to throw one before a furious fusillade rattled out. We both managed to dive to the ground but I felt the impact as a bullet hit my tin lid. As soon as I heard the explosions I stood with my last hand grenade in my hand and threw it as I had seen Sean McGuire. It arched high and, as I hit the ground, it exploded in the air.

Willy grabbed my arm, "That's it, Tom. Time we were going too!"

He half dragged me through the gap at the bottom of the hedge. The thorns tore at my clothes but we made it. Bullets shredded the leaves above our head and, once we were through, we crawled. I heard boots on the road and turned to see Corporal Higgins helping a wounded Sergeant Jennings.

"Help them Willy and give me your last two grenades."
The three of them hobbled down the road. I pulled the pin and hurled one high above the hedge and then I ran after my comrades. I slung my rifle and took out my Luger. I could fire that one handed and it had nine bullets. More bullets came my way and I heard the Germans ordering the mortars to switch targets. I had an idea and I shouted, "Don't shoot this way the English have fled!"
I know my accent was poor but I just needed them to doubt that we were English. I ran as fast as I could. Ahead of me, I saw another entrance to the field and grey uniforms emerged. I fired four shots from the Luger and they dived for cover. I pulled the pin from my last grenade and as I approached the gateway I released the handle. I rolled it into the gap. I fired one blind shot and then ran just as fast as I could.
There were two shots in reply before the grenade went off. I reached my three comrades as we passed the dead men of our battalion who had been killed by the German ambush. There were six of them. We could do nothing for them and we kept on running. Night was falling and we still had to reach the rest of our company. There were just four of us left now and we had had ten just a few days ago. I suddenly felt lonely. Every few yards I stopped and turned but my last grenades must have slowed their attack. I was not certain that I had killed that many Germans but my grenades had caused wounds. They would be cautious. We had to stop once to apply a field dressing to Sergeant Jennings' leg. The bullet had broken his tibia from the look of it.
It was almost two o'clock in the morning when we found Lieutenant Ashcroft and the rest of the rear guard. I saw Nev Wilkinson. He was leaning against a wall and smoking a cigarette. He looked all in.
"Thank God you made it. Where are the others?"
Sergeant Jennings had passed out and Corporal Higgins said. "This is it, sir."
Sergeant Greely said, "Was it you lot who hit the German ambush?" Corporal Higgins nodded, "Then you saved us again." He turned to his men. "Take the sergeant to the doctor."
The Lieutenant nodded to Corporal Higgins. "You had better take charge of the squad until the Sergeant is recovered."
He nodded, "Any idea where we are headed, sir?"
"The Colonel has been told to head for Arras. The wounded are being taken to Boulogne, Calais and Dunkirk." He shook his head, "I have a feeling that this disaster is almost over. All we have managed to do is to slow down their advance."

"Don't worry sir, we have hurt them more than they expected. What we need is a couple of Matildas and that would stop their Panzers."

"You might as well wish for a squadron of Spitfires to take out their Stukas, Sergeant Greely."

I smiled, "Well on the bright side, sir, we haven't seen them all day have we?"

They all began to laugh, "Well if that isn't optimism I don't know what is. Get some rest. There's little enough food but others can do the watching tonight."

Chapter 8

Sergeant Greely was now in command of our company. We had lost Lieutenant Green from the HQ squad when he had been wounded and our Lieutenant had taken his place. The village we had reached was tiny. We were off the road and behind a row of small houses. The inhabitants had fled but the interiors were being used by the Colonel and his headquarters staff. We could hear, from our new bivouac, the crackle of the radio, our only link with the rest of the British Expeditionary Force.

"Jeffers, go and fetch a jug of tea." The Sergeant lit a cigarette and gave an apologetic shrug. It is little enough lads, but it's better than nowt."

"Things look bad Sarge."

"They do, Holden. Don't worry, that's when Tommy Atkins is at his best. Look at you lads. Most of the officers had given you up for dead except the Lieutenant of course. He knows you. You came through. Look at Wilkinson here. I thought he would have been carted back to Blighty with his wound but he dug in and even told us about your ambush." He nodded towards Nev. "That gave us a little warning about our own attack so don't you lads let this get you down. We are doing fine."

The mugs of hot sweet tea arrived. Jimmy Jeffers said, "Make the most of this lads, we have run out of sugar and there are only a few cans of milk left."

As I drank the tea I realised what we took for granted. I had been ill-prepared for this campaign. I had thought that I had brought enough of everything but I hadn't. The tea was welcome. I was so hungry now that I was beyond eating. Whatever food had been left was now gone. The rest of the battalion, thinking us dead had not left any for us. I curled up in my greatcoat and fell asleep behind the tiny Belgian village whose name I did not even know.

We were up before dawn. We used the village tap to wash and to rinse out our mouths. After filling our canteens we watched as the rest of the battalion marched off. No one had suggested replacing us as rearguard and we would have been offended if they had. It was a place of honour. We had endured it for six days now and another two or three would not hurt. At least we knew where we were going; Arras. As we began to trudge down the cobbled Belgian road I remembered the name. Dad and his squadron had been involved up there. I couldn't help glancing, involuntarily, up into the air. He would have seen a brown column snaking its way east. I prayed for the roundels of a Hurricane. Air cover would have been a luxury.

Willy lit the stub of an old cigarette as we marched. "Well Tom, there's not many of us left from the training platoon is there?"

"No Willy but at least some of them were evacuated out. They aren't all dead."

"I know but I thought we might last more than a couple of months. How can we fight these German tanks? Hand grenades and petrol bombs aren't enough."

"We have good tanks it's just they weren't here. Unless I miss my guess there are boffins in England making new weapons. My Dad began flying in a pusher aeroplane called the Gunbus. It flew at just eighty miles an hour. The Germans flew rings around them but, by the end of the war, they had the Sopwith Camel which flew at over a hundred and thirty miles an hour and they ruled the skies. The Sarge is right, we British might be slow starters but we are dogged and we don't give up."

The refugees appeared to have fled this particular road but the corpses in the ditches and discarded belongings by the side were a sad testament to the enemy's tactics. Terror. That terror was brought home to us when we heard the noise of Stukas in the distance. "Stukas!"

There were officers' whistles and then shouts of, "Take cover!"

Willy and I were already in the ditch. There was an old tin bath lying at an angle and we sheltered behind that. Our eyes now automatically chose the best and most efficient cover. We both leaned our rifles on the bath and waited until the first Stuka closed with us. Perhaps we had hurt them in the previous days for they all released their bombs early. Their machine guns rattled first and then they pulled up their noses. The bombs struck the roads, creating new potholes but they did little damage to us. Two of the twelve were smoking as they headed east.

As we resumed our retreat I reflected that the terror of the Stuka was aimed at civilians. Resolute soldiers could fight them off. We had done so and there was a spring in our step. We saw, to the north and the south, flights of Heinkels as they continued to bomb the towns and supply lines.

"How come the Royal Air Force aren't up there doing something about them? Where are the Brylcreem boys?"

Dad hated that nickname and I felt honour bound to defend them. "Those who wanted peace and disarmament decided that we didn't need as many fighter aircraft. We haven't got enough. You can train a man quickly but a fighter takes a long time to manufacture. The pilots will be as frustrated as us. It was the politicians and those who didn't see the danger in the Nazis." I saw him nod and consider my words. Willy was not well educated but he was not stupid and he began to process my words and to think on them.

I had no idea how far we marched each day but those cadets at the OTC would not have managed half of what we did. When we saw the rest of the battalion halt at the crossroads then we knew we had marched enough for that day.

Lieutenant Ashcroft greeted us. "Sergeant Greely, take the company down the road to the south. This is an important crossroads and we have been ordered to hold it for a few days to allow the rest of the army to get to Arras."

"Yes sir, is there any food? The lads have just had a can of corned dog each and there is nowt left now."

"Sorry Sergeant. If you send a couple of lads to the mess area, they can get a jug of tea as of food…" he shrugged, "you will need to forage."

Wearily the sergeant saluted and said, "Right, sir." He turned to us. "Harsker, you seem to have an eye for this sort of thing. Take Wilkinson and Holden and see what you can find."

"Right, Sarge." We took off our greatcoats and slung our rifles over our shoulders. The two of them looked expectantly at me. The village would have been pillaged by the rest of the battalion. I spied a farm about a mile away across the fields. "Let's try over there."

We clambered over the hedge and walked across the field. The cereal in it was growing but there was nothing there for us. "Is this Belgium or France now, Tom?"

"Not sure, Willy. We are on the border so I am not certain." As we neared the farm, I thought I saw a movement. "Best have our guns ready. I think I saw movement there." We swung our rifles from our shoulders and, spreading out, crouched as we hurried towards the wall. I saw that the movement was an arm, an arm in a brown uniform and it was waving us forward. I began to run. When I was just twenty yards from the wall behind which I could see the arm I slowed. I approached more cautiously. This could be a trap. As I stepped closer I could see that the arm belonged to a dead Tommy and it was moving because it was caught on a washing line and as the wind blew the washing it moved his arm back and forth.

Stepping over the stone wall I saw that there had been British soldiers here but, from the crater I could see, they had been attacked by Stukas.

It was a squad of the 1st Battalion Lancashire Fusiliers. Nev knelt next to one of the dead soldiers, "I know this one. It's Bert Grimshaw. He lived in the next street to us."

"Best get their dog tags. You do that Nev. Willy let's see if there are any inside the building." We had our guns ready as we entered. The blast from the bomb had covered everything in shards of glass but there had been no fire. There was some food too. There were tins of beef, obviously from the Fusiliers but there was also a cheese and a ham. We stuffed them in our bags. We moved the table but found that the cellar was totally empty. We went out of the front door and found another crater and the dead sergeant and corporal from the Fusiliers. Both had machine-gunned bullets across their chests. I took their identity discs and papers. "Best take their ammo. I can't see us getting any more soon."

Just then I heard the clucking of a chicken. It was followed a few moments later by another. There was a barn. I waved Willy towards the barn. There were a dozen hens. They had escaped some time ago and they were high in the rafters. They were beyond our reach. "Here Tom, there are some eggs!"

Fresh eggs were like gold and we carefully gathered the two dozen we found. We took off our helmets to make improvised carriers. Reluctantly we left the chickens and made our way back to Nev. He looked shaken. "Poor sods. It looks like the bomb fell in the middle and killed them all."

I gestured with my head. "We found two more on the other side. They were machine-gunned."

As we trudged back across the field carrying our treasure and grisly mementoes from the dead Nev said, "You know what this means don't you?"

Willy asked, "No, what?"

"The Germans are ahead of us. They are between us and the coast. We are trapped."

Sergeant Greely was delighted with the food but, like Nev, he was disturbed by the implications of our discovery. He took the discs and the papers. "I'll take these to the Lieutenant. Distribute that food. Make sure we all get a fair share."

"Right, Sarge."

Willy chuckled, "Like feeding the five thousand eh? Instead of loaves and fishes, we have bully beef and eggs!"

The Lieutenant and Sergeant Greely joined us. "Well done lads. The Lieutenant here wants you back in that farmhouse. You can guard the road to the south. If Jerry comes up that road you can give us warning. Corporal Higgins, you take the rest of your squad and these six orphans we have found. We have been feeding them for the last three days. They might as well sing for their supper."

The Corporal nodded. The six trudged towards us and none looked happy. Sergeant Greely shook his head at their attitude. Corporal Higgins was a good sort. He tried to get on with everybody. "Right then, let's get to know you all. I am Corporal Higgins, this is Nev Wilkinson, Willy Holden and Tom Harsker. Who are you blokes?"

"I'm Reg Brown and this is Harry Smith, Royal Engineers."

"Eddie Cartwright, 99th Bucks Yeomanry."

"Bert Entwhistle 1st Battalion Royal Berks."

Two had said nothing. "And you two? Are you a pair of Harpos?"

They both looked sullen, "We're Royal Artillery and we shouldn't have to do sentry duty."

We had reached the farmhouse and Corporal Higgins turned to them, "Listen, pal, you are in for the duration and if the Lieutenant says you do duty then that is what you do. Names!"

"Private Brian Peters, Royal Artillery."

"Private Phillip Harris, Royal Artillery."

"That's better. Find yourself a bunk. I'll work out a rota and you new lads better have a clean rifle which is ready to fire!"

The six reluctant heroes went upstairs to check out the bedrooms. Nev shook his head, "What a shower we have."

"Corp, why do you reckon we got lumbered with them?"

"Dunno, Willy. Perhaps the Lieutenant thought we could make soldiers of them."

Nev lit a cigarette. "This is no bloody schoolroom."

"And that's no word of a lie. Tom and Willy, you take first stag. I'll get two of the charmers to relieve you in a couple of hours or so."

"Righto Corp."

We dumped our greatcoats and our bags. We had had spare knapsacks with the German grenades we had captured. We headed along the track to the main road. We could hear the noise of battle but it appeared to be more south and west than south. The road looked empty. Willy threw away the tiniest vestige of his cigarette. How he did not burn his lip I would never know. "Well, Tom, we are almost veterans eh? There are just the three of us left now."

"You are right."

"What do you make of Nev? He's a dark horse and that's no error."

"I think he suffered in the Spanish Civil War. I know my Dad is reluctant to talk about the actual fighting in the Great War. He'll talk for days about the fine fellows he flew with. It may be that Nev has had to exorcise his demons."

"You what?"

I forgot that I was not talking to my Dad. "Sorry, getting rid of the problems he had inside. Since he laid those booby traps he has been a different fellow."

"He'd make a good sergeant. I know that."

The two Royal Engineers tramped up the lane. "Seen owt?"

"Bugger all." Willy pointed to the south and west. "There was some shooting over there a while back."

"That is only thirty miles from Boulogne. They are getting close to our way out."

When we went back into the farmhouse we saw that Nev and the Corporal had organised it. It looked almost homely. "We have sorted the food out." Nev gestured upstairs with his thumb, "Mind with the extra mouths to feed we will still be on short rations."

Willy said, "I have an idea. Come with me, Tom."

We went into the back place. It looked as though it had been a repository for anything they couldn't find a home for. Willy rummaged around in what looked like a pile of junk to me.

"What are you looking for?"

"When I see it I will know." His hand suddenly emerged holding a thin piece of leather triumphantly. "There you are, this will do."

I was intrigued and I followed him outside where he kicked the gravel from the farmyard and then reached down to select about eight or ten round pebbles. "Now we hunt!" We returned to the barn. The chickens were all in the same place, they were out of reach. Even as we watched two of them laid an egg but both struck not the rotting hay but the wood of the cow byre and smashed. I remembered this happening close to our cottage. When hens did this the farmer had no recourse but to shoot them and begin again. We could not waste bullets on chickens. We had perilously few as it was.

"Right, Tom. I am going to hit one with this slingshot. It will probably only stun him but when he falls take your bayonet and chop off his head. I'll try and get a couple."

I took out my bayonet glad that I had recently sharpened it. "Ready when you are William Tell!"

"He had a crossbow. It's David and Goliath you are thinking of."

He whirled the improvised sling around his head and then released the pebble. It smacked against the side of one hen's head and the bird tumbled to the ground. I pounced upon it amidst a cacophony of squawks and squeals. It was as though a fox had entered this particular hen house. I hacked down on the side of the chicken's head. Amazingly the body still thrashed for some time after its head had been removed. It was not until there was a puddle of blood that it stopped.

Looking pleased with himself he said, "Ready?"

"Whenever you are."

He repeated the trick but it would be the last one. The remaining birds fluttered up to hide in the rafters of the barn. They were dumb animals but even they recognised a predator. We carried the two chickens into the kitchen. Willy gave a dramatic, 'Ta-Da!' as we flourished them.

"Well done lads! Let's get them plucked." Nev pointed to the two artillerymen, "Right Muff and Chuff go and relieve your oppos."

One of them stood up, "You aren't a corporal. You're the same as we are."

Nev laughed, "Don't make me laugh, that's like saying a poodle is the same as a hunting dog. One is bloody useless and the other works for a living now get on stag before I kick your arse!"

Willy and I had to cover our faces as the two of them made a hasty retreat. Willy was right. Nev would make a good sergeant.

We had a fine meal. The only thing lacking was some bread and some wine but we ate every scrap. I collected the bones, after the meal, and put them in a pan of water with some of the herbs and green vegetables we had gathered. Corporal Higgins asked as he lit a cigarette. "What's that for Tom? More soup?"

"We have no idea how long we are going to be here do we? I'm fed up with being hungry."

"Can't hurt. Well, lads, it is you two again. Me and Nev will relieve you at midnight."

"Righto, Corp."

We took our greatcoats. It might be summer but the nights could still get nippy.

"That chicken was lovely Tom. Where did you learn to cook? Were you planning on being a chef or summat?"

I shook my head, "No I was supposed to be at University when I joined up. Mum believed that everyone should know how to cook. I enjoy it."

Willy shook his head, "You really are a daft bugger. You have the chance of a cushy time in Blighty and you volunteer."

"So did you."

"Aye because there was nowt else for me. I can barely read and write and there were precious few jobs in Fallowfield."

I shrugged, "It seemed the right thing to do."

"Do you regret it?"

"Not for one second."

We had a quiet watch and we had the luxury of a roof over our head and the cushions from the chairs as a bed. It was like a four-star hotel. We were all rudely awakened at about four o'clock in the morning by the sound of machine gunfire. We were up, dressed and armed in an instant. Corporal Higgins went to the door and opened it. We joined him. To the north, the dawn was lit up by machine gunfire and explosions. The battalion was being attacked. I looked to the road, There was a column of tanks heading up it. There was no sign of the sentries. "Corp who was on duty?"

"The two artillerymen."

"Well, they aren't there now."

We looked at the other four. One of the engineers said, "They said they were fed up of this and were heading to the coast. They asked us to join them."

Nev shook his head, "I will gut the bastards if I get my hands on them."

"We have no time for that. Get everything you can. We'll head west and try to rejoin the battalion. Tom and Nev use the German grenades and booby trap the front. We will have some warning of their arrival."

"They are tanks! We have no chance. We should surrender!"

The Corporal looked at the Engineer. "Over my dead body."

The two infantrymen said, "How about heading back across the field and rejoining your regiment."

Corporal Higgins shook his head, "You'll never make it."

"We could try. We could let the officers know that there are tanks from the south too."

"Go on then but keep low. They haven't seen us yet."

Nev and I were busy with the booby traps while the Corporal and Willy were stuffing our bags with the last of the food. None of us saw the Engineers run towards the road. We had just finished the last booby trap when we heard rifles from close to the farmhouse. "Willy, go and have a butcher's from upstairs!" There was another flurry of fire from the front. Willy hurtled down the stairs. The lads heading to the battalion have been shot and those two Engineers are prisoners. The Krauts are heading this way."

"Right lads out the back and be quick!"
We shut the door and Nev put one last booby trap with a Mills bomb this time at the back door. As we ran we saw that the German tanks had advanced to the west. We were cut off from the battalion. We were alone!

Chapter 9

We heard shouts and a rattle of bullets struck the farmhouse. We heard them clatter off the stones. The sky was becoming much lighter and soon, once they had cleared the farmhouse they would be able to see us. I was the fittest of the four of us and I found myself in the lead. I saw that the fields seemed to go on forever but there was cover to our left. The only problem was it was away from the battalion. "Corp there is a wood on our left. We might lose them there."

The Corporal was not a man to dither, "Lead on Macduff! It's as good a way as any."

Just then there was an explosion behind us as the first of the booby traps exploded. They would be more cautious and we had a minute or two. I hoped we could make the shelter of the woods by then. There were two more explosions and then a rattle of gunfire. The wood was just twenty yards from us when the back door exploded when they tried to open it. We saw the explosion and we dived to the ground. We would crawl the last few yards.

Once in the safety of the eaves of the forest we turned and looked at the farmhouse. The explosions had set it on fire and it was now an inferno. We saw the Germans silhouetted against it. I saw an officer with binoculars scanning the fields. "Jerry has binoculars and is looking for us."

"Then we keep still until they have gone."

I kept looking from the farmhouse to the north. The tanks had rolled over the position our battalion had held. They were now between us and safety. "Have you got a map, Corp?"

"Aye, Tom, why?"

"We will need to find another way to Boulogne. Jerry has shut that door."

The Germans searched for an hour or so and then gave up. We slipped into the woods and then stood up. From the map, we had about fifty or sixty miles to go to reach the coast. To reach Calais we would have to cover more than forty and Dunkirk would be over a hundred. We knew that we were supposed to halt at Arras. That was just a few miles away. Between Arras and the Belgian border was my parents' holiday home. I knew that it was on the way to Boulogne. We could kill two birds with one stone.

I could see that the Corporal was perplexed about the decision he had to make. "Look, Corp, if we head to the north of Arras we might get ahead of the tanks. That was a big column coming from the south. If not then the road takes us to Boulogne anyway." I pointed to the map. "The fields will give us cover. We just keep parallel to the road. We can see Jerry. When we can't see him then we head north and catch up with our lads."

He looked at the other two. Nev nodded, "I can't see any flaws. It is better than sitting here and doing nothing. The battalion is getting further away by the minute."

"Right! Out in front Professor. You take the map and lead us home."

I slung my rifle and begin to move through the woods. According to the map once we were through the woods and some open fields we would cross the main road the battalion had used and was now being used by the Germans. That would eventually reach Arras but the Germans were using that one for their tanks. We would have to sneak across the road unseen. It would not be easy. I suddenly remembered the broth I had made. No one would enjoy it now. At least we had all the supplies in our bags. We would eat, for at least two days anyway. Every time an aeroplane was heard we dived for cover. We no longer had the protection of the battalion. We were four soldiers with four rifles amidst a sea of grey-clad Germans.

We crossed the first road with such ease that I began to think that it would be a picnic. The next fourteen miles were equally easy. Perhaps we had exaggerated the problems. There was one more road to cross and then we would be within a dozen or so miles of the cottage. We were cautious at the road we had to cross for it was the main road to Arras.

We reached the last obstacle and froze when we heard engines. We cowered in the undergrowth. We could not go forward until they had passed and to go back would be to take us deeper into enemy territory. We had no idea where the front line was. The engines turned out to be half a dozen German trucks. A small German car, a Kübelwagen, with a machine gun at the back led them and they trundled past us heading towards the north. We waited until their motors disappeared in the distance. When it became silent I waved the others across the road. Willy led and then the Corporal. Nev was just moving across the road when I heard the high pitched roar of a motorcycle. A German motorcycle and sidecar came around the bend. I had not started across and I swung my rifle around. Nev ran as fast as his leg would allow him. The machine gun on the sidecar rattled. I squeezed two rounds and struck the driver. He clutched his arm and the whole contraption slewed around and rolled along the road.

I glanced up, as I moved across the cobbles, Nev was lying in the ditch. Willy and the Corporal were close by him. I ran to the motorcycle. They were both dead. I grabbed the hand grenades and the ammunition. Who knew when they might come in handy.

"Quick Corp, get him undercover. Those Jerries in the trucks might come back."

As they dragged him to safety I tried to clear any sign that we had been here. Even if the Germans did not return others would be using the road and they would find the dead Germans. I followed the trail of blood and found a white-faced Nev lying on the ground. Willy was tying a tourniquet around his thigh. He grinned weakly, "Same bloody leg."

The Corporal looked up at me and shook his head. "The kneecap is shattered."

"So I guess my dancing career is over with?" He tried to laugh but ended wincing with the pain.

Willy looked up, "What do we do then? Surrender and get him to a doctor?"

Nev grabbed Willy's battledress, "Listen, sonny, you can shoot me if you have a mind but we are not surrendering. Leave me with a gun and I'll take a few of the bastards with me."

"No-one is surrendering and if you have nowt intelligent to say, Holden, then keep your gob shut! We need to get Wilkinson to some shelter. But where?"

"There is somewhere. It is a few miles south of here."

Willy scoffed, "A few miles? It might as well be a few hundred with his leg in the state it is."

"Willy, I will punch you myself if you don't shut up. Go and find a path to the north will you? Do something useful."

He nodded, "Right Tom. Sorry, Nev."

"We carry him, Corp. We keep one on point and the other two carry. We keep swapping over. We can cover the few miles in two or three hours."

Nev looked like he would say something. "Wilkinson, you shut up now. We are carrying you and that is an end to it. We will use two rifles to make a chair. This place how do you know it?"

"My Dad and two of his mates built it. My family own it. Dad and his gunner used the original farm when they were shot down in 1915. They hid there for a couple of days. It is remote and it is secluded. We haven't visited since 1938 so I guess it will be overgrown."

"It's worth a shot."

Willy arrived back. "There is a farm track leading through the woods. We have to cross a little stream."

"Good." I pointed to the path we had just used. There were drops of blood all along it. "They are like a beacon. We need to throw them off the scent. You two carry him while I rig a booby trap here."

The Corporal nodded and they used their rifles and a pack to make a kind of sedan chair. Nev put his arms around their shoulders and they headed south. I walked back along the trail. I put myself in the German's position. They would follow the trail of blood and their heads would be down. I took out a can of bully beef. I opened it and put the meat back in my pack. I put some soil in the tin to give it some weight. I put the filled can to the side. They would spot it and examine it. I took a grenade and removed the pin. Very carefully I covered the grenade with tufts of grass and weeds I pulled up and then I put the can on the handle. As soon as they lifted the can the handle would be released and they would have eight seconds to live. As I followed the others I decided that I would make the fuses just five seconds from now on. Uncle Lumpy had shown me how to do it. He had used them as aerial bombs in the Great War.

I soon caught up with them and took the lead. We crossed the first stream and headed down the trail. I intended to change direction soon. I recognised where we were. This wood was quite extensive. Dad and I had hunted here because it was so remote. We had little chance of accidentally shooting an innocent walker. There were plenty of streams and we used those to replenish our supply of water as we made our way south. At the second stream, I swapped with the Corporal and we changed to a north-westerly direction. It took us away from the coast and I hoped that it would throw any pursuit off. After an hour the Corporal replaced Willy. It was as we were changing over that we heard a dull crump. They all looked at me. "They have found where we bound Nev's wound. I left them a present. We are nearly there. Willy, take over from me in half an hour. Keep on this trail until then."

I was now worrying about pursuit. The Germans could move much faster than we could. I hoped that the booby trap would have hidden our trail. I knew we had another turn to come and that would, I prayed, be enough to hide us from the Germans. I whistled, "Time, Willy."

He came back and we swapped. I point to the right. "We are going through that scrubby bit of land. You go ahead and I will tidy up our tracks. Wait just over there."

Corporal Higgins said, "You are giving a lot of orders, Harsker."

"Sorry Corp. I didn't think we had time to be a debating club."

"Just so as you remember who is in charge, eh son?"

"Right Corp." They headed through the bushes and I lifted the branches and leaves through which they had trodden. It would fool a German briefly. I went down to the left and found a stubby tree. I hauled myself up to the lower branches and then swung myself to land on a few stones which lay there. I hoped from stone to stone until I caught up with my bemused comrades.

Nev laughed, "Tarzan the bloody ape-man."

"Just trying to put off the pursuit."

I ran ahead and led them through a twisting path which was almost overgrown now. When we had lived there this had been much easier to use. It gave me hope that the cottage was still hidden. I approached it from the rear. There was a hedge fence and a wicker gate. The gate only opened reluctantly. The cottage looked to be deserted but I took the safety from my rifle as I went towards the door. We never kept it locked and I turned the handle. The hinges creaked as I pushed it open. The musty smell told me that no one had been here since October 1938.

"It's safe. Bring him in. There is a bed here in the backroom or he can use the seat in the front room." I took off my helmet, packs and greatcoat.

I went into each room just to confirm that it was empty. I knew we needed hot water but I was reluctant to use the fire. I decided to risk it. I took some kindling and lit the stove. The dry wood would not give off smoke and we had to see to Nev. I grabbed a pan and slipped out of the front door and went to the well. I dropped the bucket and heard the reassuring splash. The well had never let us down. Dad and Uncle Ted had dug it and lined it with bricks when I was still a toddler. I filled the pan with water and went back inside.

The Corporal had cut the trousers off Nev. "How is he Corp?"

"I have no idea. I did a first aid course but this needs surgery. The bullet has gone through."

"Then we just clean it up and apply a field dressing. I have some water boiling on the stove. I reckon he needs splints."

Willy said, "I thought the water was for a cup of tea!"

For some reason that made us all laugh. "I am sure there will be enough left for tea." I turned to the Corporal. "Do you want me to give you a hand or shall I get things sorted out here, Corporal Higgins?"

"It is your house. You know where things are."

"Righto."

I had not opened the curtains when we had gone in. They were heavy-duty black curtains which kept out all light. In hot, bright summers they kept the cottage cool while we were walking or out for the day. I took an oil lamp from the cupboard and lit it. "Here, Corp, it helps if you can see what you are doing."

I checked all the cupboards. I only vaguely remembered what was here. I found the tea, a little old now but still usable and a teapot. There was sugar but, obviously, no milk. I took them back into the kitchen which doubled as a sitting room. Dad had told me that was how Albert had had it and he liked the idea. It was comfortable. There were two bedrooms on one side and two on the other. Mum liked the idea that we could have guests. The rooms were cosy but they suited us. I went to the wardrobe and rummaged around. I found a pair of Dad's trousers and a few pairs of spare socks. A soldier could march all day on a clean pair of socks!

When I walked in I could see that they had bandaged the leg. I threw the trousers to Nev. "Here you are. You can at least have a little dignity. I found spare socks for you all too."

"This is damned civilised, Tom." Nev's words came through gritted teeth.

"You are welcome, Nev."

"I have cleaned it up as best I can but I don't think he can move for a few days."

I nodded, "We have the supplies we were given by the sergeant and we have these." I went to a cupboard and opened it. There was an array of tins. To my delight, I saw some condensed milk. We could have milk with our tea. "We won't starve."

"Tom, you are a wonder. Willy, get that tea poured."

In the distance, we heard the sound of an engine. Everyone started. "Don't worry. The road is a mile from here. Cars and lorries, even buses, pass up and down all the time. I will walk to the end of the lane and have a look-see if it will make you all feel happier."

The Corporal nodded and I left. I suppose the Corporal was right to worry; if there were Germans on the road then we were, effectively trapped. I was gratified that the overhanging trees had not been damaged by traffic and that the track was overgrown. No one had been here for some time and we were, effectively, hidden. I did not go to the end of the track, instead, I forced my way through the undergrowth and peered through the leaves. If I remained still then no one would see me. I had always been the last one to be found when we had played games of hide and seek near to the airfields when I had been growing up. I heard the steady grind of a struggling engine. An old lorry came past driven by, what I assumed, was a local farmer. I did not recognise him.

After another ten minutes of watching, I saw no military vehicles of any description. We were safe, for a while.

I turned to look at the cottage as I walked back up the greenway. I was gratified to see that there was barely any smoke visible from the chimney. We were so far from anyone else that the wind would dissipate the smell and the smoke. When I got back to the cottage there were just Willy and the Corporal. They were smoking and drinking tea. Willy handed me a cup. "Where's Nev?"

The Corporal gestured with his cigarette, "We put him in one of the beds. He was all in. I'm afraid the sheets will be a mess. There was a little blood seeping from the wound."

"Don't worry; Mum was a nurse although I am not certain she will be back here for some time eh?"

He laughed, "Still this is a little lifesaver; literally. You know that even when we do move he is going to slow us down."

"I know."

"By that time our lads might have held them and started pushing them back."

We both looked at Willy who was looking cheerful. "Holden, we have barely stopped running since the Germans started their attack. What makes you think we are going to change that now?"

"The Lieutenant said that we were going to hold them at Arras."

The Corporal nodded and took out the map. He jabbed his finger at Arras. "Do you see where Arras is?"Willy nodded. "And do you see how close the coast is?"

"Yes Corp but the trenches were here in the Great War and we held them then!"

"Aye, and they didn't have Stukas, heavy bombers and tanks then. No, my son, we are going to be pushed back to Blighty. As soon as Nev can move then we are going to make for Boulogne. That was one of the three places the Lieutenant mentioned. If they manage to hold them at Arras we might even make it there before them." He stubbed his cigarette out and folded up the map. "Of course we have to work out a way how to get a one-legged man more than seventy miles to Boulogne."

"Through German troops."

"Aye, you are right."

I went to the cupboard and brought out a walking stick. "There is a stick here but we will need to re-splint his leg so that he can put weight on it.

"I was going to do that but we'll leave it until just before we actually leave. We need to build up his strength."

"Then we make sure that he eats for England."

Willy threw his empty cigarette packet into the stove. "Any cigarettes in this Aladdin's cave?"

I shook my head, "Sorry, Willy, Dad smokes a pipe. If you find one of his old pouches here you will find some dried up tobacco inside but that's all."

He sank back into his seat, "Well that is a bugger!"

I smiled. That was the British soldier all over. He could endure almost anything so long as he had a cup of tea, an occasional meal and his cigarettes. I went to a wall cupboard and brought out a bottle of local brandy. It was rough and Mum used it for cooking but it was drinkable. "Here, lads, we can all have a drink and it will help ease Nev's pain!"

"Harsker you are like Merlin the bloody magician! You'll do for me old son."

The Corporal emptied his dregs into the sink and poured himself a measure. We slept well that first night. We were so tired and full that we even forgot to set a sentry. When we woke undisturbed we risked it every night. We recovered far quicker that way.

We enjoyed three days in the cottage. Nev spent most of the time in the bedroom with his leg raised. That had been my suggestion. I had learned as much from Mum about nursing as I had from Dad about flying. We might have stayed longer had we not heard the distant sounds of battle coming from the south about the twenty-first of May. The Corporal had more experience of these sorts of things and he estimated it to be about twenty to thirty miles south of us. We looked at the map. Arras. The Lieutenant had been right; we were trying to hold them. The morning after we were woken by the sound of heavy vehicles moving down the road. Without waiting for an order I ran down the greenway. I did not even get to the end for I saw the German trucks moving west. I ducked into the trees as I saw German infantry with them. Our holiday was over. We were going back to war.

Chapter 10

"The Germans are here!"

We had been ready for such an eventuality. Willy and I began to pack the bags with as much food as we could carry. We were leaving bare cupboards. The Corporal went to splint Nev's leg with sturdier wood we had taken from the forest. Nev would not be able to carry anything and so we split his belongings between us. We had cut two sturdy branches from the trees around the cottage and we took them with us in case we had to make a stretcher. Two greatcoats and the branches would suffice. Nev insisted that he would walk. I was not certain. That would slow us down but he was a determined man.

When he was ready I led us out of the back. There was a track which led to the village of Dadizele. We would then head to Ypres. I hoped that the Belgians still held that most symbolic of places. We intended to avoid roads. This time we were in no position to fight and run. If trouble came then we would fight and die.

The first two miles were the worst for Nev. His leg had been rested but the shock of using it brought waves of agony. After a mile, we stopped and added another branch to splint both sides of his leg and that made it easier. We reached the outskirts of Ypres just after noon on that first day and we approached no further. The German flags fluttered from the buildings we could see and the road was thronged with Germans soldiers. We heard, to the north, firing.

Safe in the woods and hedges some mile or so from the road we debated our next course of action. "It looks like Ypres is out of the question. That rules out Dunkirk and Calais. It will have to be Boulogne which is closer."

"That's further to travel, Corp."

Nev shot an angry look at Willy. "We are going to get home, Willy, so button it!"

I knew it was the pain talking. I took out the compass I had picked up in the cottage. "Then we need to head a little south of west. We head for the sun."

We made slow progress across country. Corporal Higgins looked at the pain on Nev's face. "We need to use the road. We'll make quicker time."

"I'll be fine."

"I am still in charge, Wilkinson. We will wait up in those woods by the road. We will risk the road tonight."

The three of us took turns to watch while the others slept. I know in my case it was a cat nap but it was better than nothing. I watched columns of Germans marching west and, more alarmingly, columns of British soldiers being marched east. They were prisoners. It was not constant traffic; sometimes there was no movement for twenty or thirty minutes. I was woken after the sun had set. I ate a handful of food and washed it down with a mouthful of water. We headed down to the road. The click of Nev's stick seemed to echo and reverberate in the dark. I stopped, "Look, Corp, if Nev drapes his arms around our shoulders he can swing himself forward on his good leg. We will travel faster and make less noise."

We tried it and found that we could go at normal marching speed. There was little extra weight and it was pain-free for Nev. We had to keep stopping when a vehicle came down the road but we used that as an opportunity to change our carriers. We covered almost twenty miles in the dark. We found another place to hide, this time a semi-destroyed barn and we waited for nightfall.

The lines of British, Belgian and French soldiers continued to trudge disconsolately east. It confirmed that things were not going well. We made excellent progress again that night and dawn found us close to Eperlecques. The French signs told us that we were within twenty miles of the port of Boulogne. During the night we had taken a smaller side road which was north of the main road to Boulogne. There had been more nocturnal traffic and we knew we would have to cross their lines sometime. We hoped it would be easier on the smaller side road than the main one. As we ate our frugal meal and listened to the sporadic firing, which seemed to always be in the distance, the Corporal said, "What worries me is that we haven't heard heavy guns and machine guns. At least we haven't heard any to the west. We have heard them to the north and the south but not the west."

"You think that Boulogne might have fallen?"

"It looks that way, Nev."

I angled the map to catch the little light which remained, "We could head north now then. Make for Calais."

The others nodded their agreement. Willy shook his head, "More marching."

"Have you got something else planned, my son?"

"No, Corp, just saying."

I was woken by a sudden burst of gunfire during the late morning. I grabbed my rifle but Corporal Higgins shook his head and mimed for me to be silent. I bellied up next to him. Willy and Nev were already there. There were two dead Tommies lying in the road just forty yards away. There were two Germans and they had a soldier on his knees. One had a Maschinenpistole 42; a deadly little machine gun while the other held a standard German rifle fitted with a bayonet. I heard one of them say, "Another English coward who thinks to surrender!"

"He is not worth a bullet. Use your bayonet."

I pulled up my rifle and shouted, "They are going to kill him!"

I fired as the bayonet entered the soldier's belly. The killer flew off to the side of the Tommy. The machine gunner tried to turn and fire at the sudden sound. He was thrown from his feet by three bullets. We ran to the soldier who lay in a pool of blood. I saw, from his badge that he was from the Lancashire Fusiliers. He opened his eyes as I tore open his battle dress. "I hope yer got the bastard."

He was a Scouser, he was from Liverpool.

"Aye, he's dead. Lie still."

"Ave yer got a ciggy there lah?"

"Sorry, we are all out."

Corporal Higgins said, "Willy, search the Krauts." He cradled the soldier's head. "What happened, son?"

"We were in Boulogne when it fell. That was two, three days ago." He winced. Willy had found some German cigarettes and he lit two and gave one to the Scouser. "Thanks, pal, you're a lifesaver." He took a long drag and coughed, "Jesus Christ if they smoke this shit then they are bound to lose the war."

"Then Boulogne has fallen?"

He nodded, "Aye and Calais. We were trying to get to Dunkirk we heard a rumour that the army was going there. We had been hiding up when these Krauts found us. Bastard SS!" He closed his eyes and I thought he was dead. He opened them and said, "Joey there," he gestured to one of his dead comrades, "coughed when they were near and they opened fire. I put my hands up to surrender. I'm not stupid and…"

I looked at the wound. The bayonet had torn his stomach open when the German had fallen to the side and I could see intestines and guts. I shook my head.

"I know pal. I ain't going back to Liverpool. Could you do us a favour? There's a letter for me mam in my pocket. See she gets it and me watch. Th…" He rolled back and he died.

The Corporal said, "We have to get a move on. Those shots might bring someone else and we know now there's no point in surrendering.

Not with the SS around. Nev, get the dog tags and any other papers from the lads."

I took the blood-stained letter and the watch and put them in my own pockets. Corporal Higgins took the machine gun and the spare ammunition. I saw that one of the SS had a black-handled dagger. It was smaller than the bayonet I used as a knife and I grabbed it. It was not a souvenir. I knew it would come in handy.

We hurried back to our cover and then headed west. As we were going cross country Nev had to use his stick. We were not able to move as fast as on the road. When we were a mile away from the massacre we stopped. It was mainly to give Nev a breather. We slumped to the ground. "Well, we are up shit creek without a paddle. What do we do, Corp?"

With the pain, Nev's short temper returned, "Well, Sonny Jim, surrender is no longer an option is it now?"

"Hey Wilkinson, it will get us nowhere if we argue with each other. Get the map out Harsker."

I spread it out. "Calais is in the same direction as Dunkirk. We could head there."

"Were you not listening? The Scouser said Calais had fallen! Any other suggestions?" The other two were silent. "The problem we are now going to have is that they will be looking for lads like us." He gestured back in the direction we had just come. "So we have to move even slower than we did before. How much food have we?"

I opened my pack. "I reckon another day." The other two nodded.

"Then we tighten our belts. I am sorry Nev but we will have to keep moving and get as far west and north as we can."

"We can stay in these woods until we get close to Calais. We just have to avoid the roads during the day." I looked at the map again. "I reckon at least twelve hours before we reach Calais."

Nev stood, "Then the sooner we push on the better eh?"

He was a tough customer. I had the map and the compass and I led. We knew that Nev was in pain and we stopped every hour. I saw that the wound was leaking blood. When he had been hopping there had been no pressure on the wound. Now his weight was reopening partially healed wounds. We had travelled eight miles or so and we were taking advantage of a stream we had found when disaster struck. Willy was lighting one of the cigarettes whilst keeping watch on the high ground and the Corporal and I were filling our canteens. Nev was further upstream and pouring water on to his leg. The cool water seemed to ease the pain slightly. I wished now that we had not drunk all the brandy. That would have numbed the pain.

Five German soldiers appeared from nowhere. I reacted first. I dived for my rifle, ignoring the fact that it meant I was lying in the stream. Even as I swung it around they began firing. Nev was between us and them. Their bullets all struck him. His body danced like a marionette. I fired five shots in quick succession. The Corporal began firing too. I wondered why Willy had not fired. I saw two Germans fall and a third held his arm. I fired again and then I heard the chatter of the machine gun and the last of the Germans fell.

I jumped from the stream and ran to Nev. He had been hit by all five and he was stone dead. He had been a unique character and I was sad that he was dead. The Corporal took charge. "We are in bother now lads. These five will be missed." He grabbed Nev's dog tags and his papers. We both looked at the body. "We have no time to bury him."

"I know Corp." I took the last two grenades from his bag and ran to the Germans. The machine gun had made a mess of them. I found the one who was the least damaged and booby-trapped his body with a grenade. I did not do it to be vindictive. I wanted to know when they found their bodies.

Willy said, "Bloody gun jammed on me!"

Corporal Higgins snapped, "And that is why Harsker and I clean ours every time we fire them!"

With just three of us and no Nev to slow us down, we were able to race through the woods. We kept running until I smelled the sea. I stopped and held up my hand. "The sea!" I took out the compass. We had not cared if we were heading west or north; we had just been trying to escape. I pointed to the left. "How about it Corp?"

He nodded, "Let's head over there. The woods look to be thinning anyway."

It was coming on to dark when we saw the sea. I saw lights to our left and I waved the other two to the right and the sand dunes. We found a hollow and I consulted the map. "I reckon that is Wissant down there, Corp."

"What's that, a port?"

"I doubt it. A village I think. Why what are you thinking?"

"That if it was a port there might be a ship or something there."

Nev's death had shaken the Corporal. He was not thinking straight. "That's no good, Corp. They would guard ships."

"There might be something there." He sighed. "I know it's asking a lot of a young lad like you but you are resourceful. I have seen that. Could you get close to the place tonight and see what you can find out. You speak the lingo. If you don't want to..."

"That's no problem but I will strip down a bit. If I take my battle dress off and just use my comforter then I might look like a fisherman or something."

Willy asked, "Fisherman?"

"Yeah, I have been thinking. This isn't a holiday place, not that I know. Boulogne is a port and I have heard of Wissant mussels. There may be fishing boats."

"Good lad. What about a weapon?"

I took out the Luger and the knife. "I can hide these and they are easier to use than the rifle." I nodded to the east. "We haven't heard my booby trap going off so they can't have found the bodies yet."

"Perhaps."

As soon as I was ready I turned. "It will only take me a couple of hours. If I am not back by dawn, say four o'clock then assume I have been captured." I pointed north. "Dunkirk is that way."

They both nodded. There was a dull crump in the distance. "Looks like they found Nev!"

Chapter 11

I felt naked without my battledress but I hurried over the dunes towards the lights. Darkness had fallen and I knew that I would be hard to spot in the dark. I took a chance and headed for the beach and the shoreline. I reached the sea and the tide was on its way in. I strolled as though I was a fisherman who had finished work for the day. I put my hands in my trouser pockets. I just tried to look as though I didn't care if I was seen. I worked out that the worst thing I could do was to look furtive.

When I neared the town I climbed the dunes to get a better view. It was a smaller place than I had thought. I had been wrong about what was here. There were what looked like holiday homes but I breathed a sigh of relief when I saw the half a dozen fishing boats drawn up on the sand. There were a couple of larger ones tied up to the jetty. I wandered to the road which led into the village to afford a better view.

I was so excited at my discovery that I failed to hear the approach of two German guards. They spoke to me in German and I nearly made the mistake of answering them in the same. I shrugged my shoulders and said, in French, that I did not understand them. One of them tried French. It was execrable! "What you do here?"

"I dropped my pipe on the beach and I was looking for it?" I spoke slowly as though to an idiot.

"Pipe?" He did not understand the word. I mimed smoking a pipe and he nodded. "Go home!" He struggled for a word and then said, in German, "Curfew!"

I pointed to the boats. "I sleep on my boat."

"Then go!"

They watched me descend to the beach. I knew I was taking a chance but if I had walked into the village then they might have seen my trousers in the light. They would have marked me, along with my boots, as British. It was why I had mimed. I wanted their attention on my face and my hands. My moustache and rough growth of beard had also helped with my disguise.

I wandered down to the boats. There was no one near them. I walked to the smallest of them. It looked like it would hold no more than four crew. There was a tarpaulin across it and I lifted it. I risked a furtive look up at the road. The two Germans were heading back down the road. This was obviously their duty. They would walk to the end of the jetty and then back into the village. I saw that the boat had a coil of rope and a couple of buckets. I quickly fashioned them into a pile which might resemble a body and then I pulled the tarpaulin back over it. When the sentries came back they would see the bump and assume it was me. I did not want them investigating it. Of course, the fishermen would be confused when they came the next morning.

I did not climb the slope to the road. Instead, I headed back down the beach. I wondered if I would remember where the others were. I saw my footsteps where I had descended to the beach and after another hundred yards or so I headed into the dunes. After a few moments, I heard a hiss, "Here Tom!" I turned in the direction of the voice. Willy's grinning face greeted me. "Well?"

"Where's the Corp?"

"I'm here." He appeared behind me. "I was just keeping an eye out in case you were followed."

"There are fishing boats but the Germans have a curfew. There are guards watching the boats."

"That's that then."

"No, Corp, it isn't. This is better than we could have hoped. The tide was on its way in when I walked down there. In a couple of hours, it will turn. We can slip back and steal a boat."

"A boat? We need someone to sail it. We have to get some French fishermen to take us."

"That wouldn't work, Corporal. Firstly we would have to risk being in the village amongst people secondly if the French took us they would risk being arrested when they returned. I can sail."

"I know you have many talents, Harsker but don't start making them up now."

"I'm not Corp. I swear to you I can sail the little fishing boat I saw. It has a simple sail and we have a compass. We head north-west and we are bound to bump into England. It's either that or we fight our way to Dunkirk."

I saw him chew his fingernail. I put on my battle dress and my greatcoat. I had already decided. I was going to sail home with or without him. He nodded, "Right then! But I hope to God you know what you are doing because I am no sailor."

"Right, we go down the beach." I took a deep breath. We will need to get rid of the two sentries." I saw the Corporal nod. I took out my new knife, "Silently!"

I led them back down the beach. It would be light in less than four hours and I was taking a chance but the sentries would be getting towards the end of their duty and they would be tired. Now was our best chance to escape. I waved them both to their knees when we came close to the end of the dunes. I took off my packs and my greatcoat. I suddenly realised I had left my helmet behind. It was too late to go back for it now. The other two copied me. I took out my newly acquired knife. I led the other two up the slope of the dune. It was hard going for my feet kept sinking into the sand.

Once near the top I stopped and peered over. They were just twenty feet away and they were talking and smoking. I heard them say how the British army was trapped at Dunkirk and that soon they would be invading England. The other two joined me and I mimed slitting throats. They both nodded and we rose and moved towards them. Willy was not watching where he was going and his foot disturbed a pebble. It clattered onto other stones. I leapt the six feet which separated us and my left hand went towards the German sentry's mouth. We crashed to the floor. His teeth fastened on to me like a dog but I heard the gasp as the wind was driven from him. I rammed my dagger up into his throat. I pushed so hard it went up into his skull.

I rolled on to my back and saw that the other two had disposed of the other sentry but the Corporal was clutching a bleeding arm. There was no time for first aid now. We ran down the dune and grabbed our gear. I led them along the beach towards the boats. I tore the tarpaulin from the boat and cut through the rope securing the anchor. We had no time to haul it aboard. I pointed to the boat and they clambered awkwardly into it. The tide had not quite turned. This was as good a time as any to leave. I threw my greatcoat and pack into the boat and pushed it out into the water. When the water was up to my chest I tried to pull myself up. My trousers were too sodden. Willy reached down and hauled me up. We nearly flipped over as I landed in the bottom of the small boat.

I went to the sail and, grabbing the sheet, began to hoist the sail up. I had not had the time to check the wind. If it was a headwind then we were dead men. We still dared not speak. I gave the rope to Willy and mimed holding it tight. The Corporal would have to tend to his own wound. I went to the tiller and pushed it to port. Looking up at the masthead I saw that the wind was coming from the south-east. Willy was not looking at me and I kicked him. He looked around, affronted, I mimed loosening the rope a little. He did so and was nearly thrown overboard as the wind caught us. I pointed to the port side of the boat and he moved. As soon as he did we levelled out. We were just a hundred yards from the beach and we still had to keep silent. I realised I should have briefed them in the dunes. I would have to give sailing lessons while we sailed.

As soon as the lights of Wissant disappeared I risked speaking. "Sorry about that Willy."

"It's all right Tom. I thought I was going over for a minute."

"I'll just tell you when to change sides, is that all right?"

"Aye no bother. Piece of cake this sailing lark."

"Wait till we see the white cliffs of Dover before you get cocky." I looked ahead, "You all right Corp?"

There was silence. "Willy, there is a cleat next to you."

"A what?"

"A piece of metal. Wrap that sheet around it a couple of times and then drag the Corporal back here." He looked at me blankly, "Sorry we call ropes sheets."

"Righto!"

I looked up at the masthead. The pennant had not moved. It was too dark to see my compass and I was sailing where the wind took us. The boat began to pitch as Willy dragged the unconscious Corporal towards me. "Keep it steady, this is not the Queen Mary! Take off his greatcoat and battle dress." I watched in trepidation. There was a great deal of blood. I saw, from the battle dress, that the German had bayoneted Corporal Higgins. The blade had entered his lower arm. I breathed a sigh of relief. It was a loss of blood that had made him pass out. There was nothing more serious.

"Willy put a tourniquet on his upper arm." When he had done that the blood stopped flowing so freely. I reached over with the bailer and cupped some seawater. "Pour this over the wound to wash it. The salt will help disinfect it. Then stick a dressing on it."

I glanced up and saw that wind had veered a point or two and the sail was not taut. I turned the tiller slightly and our motion became smoother.

"Cover him with the three greatcoats and then open the last tin of sweetened condensed milk. Get some into his mouth."

"How?"

"Lift his head, hold his nose and then when he opens his mouth pour it in."

"Why?"

"He needs the sugar. The body will make up the lost blood but the sugar will speed things up." I mentally thanked my Mum for telling me such things.

Once he was covered and Willy had forced some of the milk down his throat I could concentrate on sailing. "Right Willy, untie your rope again. We are going to have to come about."

"What?"

"You are going to have to change seats."

"Oh right."

"Ready? Go!"

Once on the other tack, we sped through the water. Willy was a quick learner and we began to operate as a team. It was when the wind began to get up that I worried. Willy could not shorten sail and if I left the tiller then we risked capsizing. At least we were free from the Germans; for the present.

When dawn broke we were not a pretty sight. Willy and the Corporal were covered in blood and their faces were rimed with salt. As soon as I could I took out the compass. We were heading too far to the north. The currents had carried us off what I had thought was the correct course.

"Willy we are going to have to come about again."

I saw the Corporal stir.

"Willy, give the Corporal the rest of the condensed milk."

The Corporal turned his head, "Where are we?"

"Admiral Nelson here is sailing us back to Blighty. Here you are, Corp, get this condensed milk down you. You need the sugar apparently."

"I'm all right! I don't need milk."

"Now don't argue with the ship's doctor, Corp, or the admiral here will have you keelhauled."

I smiled. Willy's sense of humour had returned. The Corporal obeyed.

"Corporal could you get into the front end of the boat. It will make it easier for Willy."

"Aye aye captain!"

Once he had moved I risked a turn. For a moment we were beam on to the rollers and the boat tipped alarmingly. If we had not moved the Corporal we would have capsized. Willy shouted, "Whoa, you bugger!"

"Come about!"

I put the tiller over and Willy moved. We became more stable and, once again we flew. After twenty minutes of smooth sailing, the Corporal shouted, "How long until we get home?"

"I haven't got the first clue, Corp. It could be a day or two. I just don't know. We are only twenty odd miles from Dover but we have to keep tacking. The visibility isn't great but if you want to get to the bow and have a shufti you might see the coast before we do."

Willy groaned. "That's all we need." He pointed into the sky. "A Jerry!"

"Take off your battle dress." I did the same. "When he passes over just wave. He might think we are friendlies."
I saw that it was a Messerschmitt 109. They were extremely fast and powerfully armed. If he chose to fire at us then we would all end up at the bottom of the Channel. He flew low over us and we waved. He was only fifty feet or so from the sea. I saw him climb and head east. Willy said, "That fooled him he's... oh, bloody hell. He is coming back!"
We had one chance and one chance only. Dad had told me that at a hundred and odd miles an hour you only had a stationary target in view for a few seconds. The 109 was much faster than that. I saw him wave hopping. "Willy, get the machine pistol. When I give the word then give him a burst. He won't be expecting that and brace yourself. I am going to try something."
The Corporal said, "Give me the machine gun. You made a right cock-up of it the last time."
Willy handed him the machine gun. I knew the German would not waste bullets. He would wait until the last moment to fire. He was closing so fast that I thought I had misjudged it. "Fire!" As the Corporal fired I turned the boat into the wind so that we just stopped dead. The German's machine guns tore into the water just twenty feet from us.
"Come about." I had played my only ace. We had to get moving and hope that he had no more ammunition. It was a vain hope for we saw him bank and turn east. He was coming again.
The Corporal suddenly shouted, "I see the coast!"
Willy murmured, "I hope they find our bodies then because this bugger is going to get us for sure this time."
"Ready with the gun, Corp?"
He shook his head, "Out of ammo!"
I turned to look on my death. The yellow propeller grew ever closer. I braced myself for the impact of the bullets. When I heard the eight Brownings I could not believe it. The Spitfire's bullets tore into the 109. He had been so keen to finish us off he had not noticed the Spitfire diving to attack. As the 109 crashed the pilot gave a victory roll. I shook my head, Dad would not have approved of such a manoeuvre.
An hour later we saw a destroyer heading from the east. She changed course to intercept us. Once alongside a young lieutenant came to the scrambling nets and said, "One of the Brylcreem boys said there were three unlikely sailors who needed a lift. Care to join us?"
We clambered aboard an already packed destroyer bringing back the BEF. We had made it. We would get home.

Part 3

Commando

Chapter 12

Corporal Higgins was the only one of us afforded any space on the grossly overcrowded warship's deck. The doctor cleared space and we joined the upright brown herd; the survivors of the disaster of France. We saw many regiments on the decks but not our own. Willy cadged a cigarette from a matelot and, once the familiar tobacco was in his lungs he smiled and began to ask questions. "How's it been going then?"

A soldier from the West Yorkshires asked, "Where have you lads been then? The far side of the moon?"

I shook my head. "We were with the rear guard. We were cut off on the 16th. We had a long journey to get here."

The soldier nodded. He pointed to the fishing boat now being riddled with machine guns to make it sink. "I can see you have had an interesting time. One of the crew said the captain was diverted to pick you up. Something about a Spitfire?"

"Aye, a 109 tried to sink us and the Spit sorted him out. So is it bad then?"

"Bad? It's a cock-up. Every gun we had has been left. We held them for about an hour when the tanks slowed them down but there were less than twenty and the Germans just pounded them into scrap when they brought their 88s into action." He gestured with his thumb. "We left hundreds of thousands of lads on the beaches. I hope the Navy and the flyboys are up to it because there will be bugger all of us left if they don't get the rest off soon. It was a shambles. There were blokes wandering all over looking for someone to take charge. There was no one."

I watched the white cliffs draw closer and Corporal Higgins joined us. He gave five cigarettes to Willy. "Here the orderly gave me these."

"Cheers Corp."

He turned to me, "A disaster eh?"

"Aye, the lads were just telling me that the army is finished."

The Corporal threw an angry look at the Yorkshireman, "Some people need to keep their gobs shut! Listen, lads, we have taken a licking. This is round one. You don't throw the towel in when you get knocked out at the start of a fight. You get up and work out how to come out and beat the bloke who smacked you one. I was a boxer when I was younger and I fought plenty of blokes who punched heavier than me. You just use your strengths."

The Yorkshireman snorted, "What strengths?"

"The fact that we are English and the best soldiers in the world." He seemed to notice that the man came from Yorkshire, "And in Lancashire, we have a backbone as well as a pair of balls!"

The Yorkshireman was big and he balled his fists. Willy and I stepped between him and the Corporal. I said quietly, "He's just been given medication so back off."

The Yorkshireman said, "When he takes back what he said then…"

I put my face in his. I was as tall as he was though not as wide. "Then how about this, back off or I'll throw you over the side."

I wondered if this would start a fight but he must have seen something in my eyes for he stepped back a little. "You're not worth the effort."

The three of us remained huddled together. We had been to hell and back. We were now comrades. I understood, for the first time, the bond between my Dad and my 'uncles'. This was something closer than family. The three of us had been in each other's hands for so long that we had become one.

Disembarkation gave me hope. Volunteers stood at the quayside with blankets, mugs of tea and cigarettes. I took some even though I didn't smoke. I would give them to Willy and the Corporal. The Yorkshireman had said there was no organisation on the other side of the Channel. Here there was. It looked chaotic but it was not. The Corporal was whisked away by a couple of orderlies with the other wounded. He shouted over his shoulder as he was put in the ambulance. "Harsker, you are in charge now!"

We waved to him. I never saw him again after that day. I have no idea what happened to him but he would always be part of me. As would Nev and all the other lads we had left behind. A sergeant with a clipboard snapped, "What unit?"

"1st Loyal Lancashire, sergeant."

He looked up. "You are the first of your lot." He pointed to a row of tables lined up along the quayside. "Go to the end table and the bloke doing bugger all. Tell him your story. He will issue you travel warrants."

We walked past long lines of men who were lined up at the tables. I deduced that each line represented a regiment or unit. The private at the end looked up, "New lads eh? I am guessing that you are the first of your regiment to land." We nodded, "Name and rank." We spent fifteen minutes giving him all the information we had. He wrote it all down. At one point he looked up and said, apologetically, "Sorry about this but the first ones always get this. When the rest of your lot get in they won't have as long."

"We were the rear guard."

He looked genuinely sorry, "I am sorry about that."

Willy said, "They'll get back, don't you worry!"

"Of course they will." He handed us a travel warrant each. "The odds and sods are all being sent to Shoreditch. I am sorry but that area might be a bit crowded. Most battalions are being sent to their own barracks. When your lot arrive you'll be heading north again."

We boarded a crowded train and headed for London. For Willy, this would be a novel experience. He had never seen the capital. He was full of questions. "Do you reckon we'll see the King?"

I laughed, "I doubt it, Willy. Shoreditch is miles away from Buckingham Palace."

I knew that there had been a barracks at Shoreditch. I guessed that they would be hard-pressed to accommodate all those who had been rescued. It was late afternoon when we reached the barracks. For the first time since we had been rescued, we had space. There were the remnants of a dozen battalions. This time we were interviewed by an officer from Intelligence who asked us much more searching questions. When he had finished he said, "You were lucky. Those tanks you talk about at the crossroads were Guderian's Panzers. They nearly cut off the whole of your battalion."

"What happens now, sir?"

He smiled, "To you?" I nodded as did Willy. "You wait here for the rest of your battalions. The rescue from the beaches can't last much longer. The Germans have them hemmed in pretty badly. When they get here you'll be sent back to your home depot and begin training. Both of you have a great deal of experience now. We have conscription. The lads who join from now on won't have the training that you were given. Anything I can do for you?"

"Well sir, is there a telephone I can use?"

He looked surprised. "A telephone?"

I smiled. The other men I had trained with had been most impressed that we had a telephone in our home, "My father is a Wing Commander, sir and we need a telephone for his job."

"And you signed up as a squaddie? You were keen." I nodded. "You can use this one. I have finished here anyway. Come on Private Holden I will show you where the mess is."

The office was a bare affair. Apart from the table and chairs, there was just the telephone. After asking the operator for a line I carefully dialled and realised that my hand was shaking. I heard my Mum's voice on the other end. I said, quietly, "Mum, it's Tom."

There was what sounded like a sob and a silence.

"Mum, it's Tom."

"You are safe! Thank God!" Mum had been a nurse and she was the most organized person I knew. Once my voice had sunk in she began to organize. "Where are you?"

"Shoreditch at the barracks there."

"Your Dad will want to know. Thank God you are alive. Were you over there? Dunkirk? We heard about the evacuation on the wireless. Are you..."

"I am fine, Mum. I came through without a scratch unlike some of the other lads."

"I can imagine what you have been through and I am just pleased that you are alive."

Just then the call was interrupted by the operator, one of the clerks in the office, "I'm sorry son. We need this line now for an important call." I was cut off. At least Mum knew I was alive. I left the office and headed towards the smell of food. I joined the short queue. Willy was seated already and he waved to me indicating that he had saved me a seat.

He had lit up his first cigarette when I joined him. "I was ready for that. Did you get through then?"

"I did."

"It's a rum do, isn't it? I mean our squad was the back end of the battalion and we are the first back."

"I know."

I ate in silence. Willy couldn't keep quiet. "That officer reckoned the likes of us will all get promotions out of this. You know because there will be a bunch of new battalions and they will need experienced soldiers like us."

I had finished and I pushed my plate away and drank some of my tea. "Probably." I suddenly remembered the Scouser who had died close to

Boulogne. I took the bloodstained letter out of my battledress. "I won't be a minute. I might as well write this letter now while I remember. His mum will be worried."

"Mam."

"What?"

"He called her his mam."

I nodded, "See you in the barracks."

"Aye. I'll have another fag and another cuppa. It's nice having tea with proper milk in it."

The letter took an age to write. How do you tell someone that their son died? It was far harder than I had imagined. It made me think what would the others have written about me if I had fallen.

We both slept well but forgot that we were back in camp. Reveille sounded ridiculously early and we found ourselves back on parade. Until our officers returned we were in the charge of the camp. The Sergeant Major might have served in the Great War and was ready to be put out to pasture but he knew how to bark. After being told to ***'shave off that fuzz'*** and ***'get your kit cleaned up***! ' We were sent to breakfast.

We went to the Quarter Master's stores and discovered that we could have new uniforms. I guessed the generosity would not last and we gratefully received a new issue of everything, including boots. We spent the morning with the back of a spoon and a tin of polish making the boots gleam. After lunch, we were heading to the barracks when I was summoned to the guard room.

"What's up Corporal?"

"Dunno son but a bloody big staff car has pulled up and I was told to get you." He glanced down at me and nodded, "Well you look presentable anyway."

He knocked on the door and the duty officer shouted, "Come!"

We both marched in and snapped to attention. I looked up and saw my Dad. The duty officer said, "Group Captain Harsker has asked permission to take you off camp for twenty-four hours. In the absence of your officers, I have seen no reason to deny the request. You are given a twenty-hour leave beginning as of now."

I hid my smile. It would be a brave second lieutenant who would challenge a Group Captain. I would ask Dad about his promotion as soon as we got in the car. "Thank you, sir." I turned to the Corporal, "Could you let Private Holden know that I haven't gone AWOL, Corporal."

He grinned, "Righto Private!"

I saluted and followed Dad out to his car. His driver opened the door. It was a little awkward for both Dad and myself. There was a stranger in the car and we had to watch what we said. Dad began. "You look very smart, son. You have turned out well."

"Thanks to John and his lessons, Dad. And you. When did you get the promotion?"

"The day war broke out. I would have told you sooner but…."

"But your idiot son went and left University and joined up."

He laughed and I saw, in the mirror, the driver smile. "That's about it. Any regrets?"

"Not a one. They are a fine bunch of lads."

"It was tough though?"

"It was but I have to thank the RAF for being here."

"How's that?"

I told him the story of the escape in the boat and then the rest of the journey to Central London telling him the tale of the ill-fated campaign. He nodded, "I knew it was tough. I am just pleased that you have emerged alive." We were approaching Westminster Bridge. "Now, listen, old chap. I have a meeting at the Ministry." He looked at his watch. "It is nearly eleven now. It should be over by three. I thought you might like Jenkins here to take you around London."

"No thanks. I thought I would pop along and see John. His hotel is just off Piccadilly. I shall get out when Jenkins here drops you off and meet you later."

"Are you sure?"

"Certain," I smiled, "there is a war on you know. Can't have petrol being wasted eh, Dad?"

"Good lad. We'll have dinner at my club. I have rooms nearby."

We reached the Air Ministry and I got out. He waved cheerily as he went in and I saluted. I noticed that all the people I saw now carried a khaki bag with their gas mask. We seemed a little more prepared for war and what the Germans might do this time. I knew that John's hotel was just along from the fabulous Mayfair Hotel. He had persuaded Lady Mary to invest some of the little money she had left after death duties, in the hotel. Over the years it had grown in popularity and was now a large part of the income for Lady Mary. It was all down to John and his skills. I hoped that the war would not cause too many problems for either of them.

There was a liveried doorman at the steps. He looked to be a veteran of the Great War for he had only one arm. He saw my uniform and saluted with his good one as I approached. He opened the door for me and I felt immediately guilty. When I walked in I could see John's influence. It was most tastefully decorated. There were none of the garish colours you saw in some hotels which were trying to be fashionable. John's hotel would never be fashionable, it would be timeless. I saw him, behind the desk as I entered. He was speaking to a young lady who looked to be the receptionist. He had a flower in his lapel and was impeccably turned out; I would have expected nothing less.

He glanced up and saw me. His face lit up into a huge smile and he came scurrying around to greet me. Unlike the formality of my father, he gave me a hug; much to the surprise of the receptionist. "Dear Tom, how good to see you and how fine you look! What brings you here? Not that you need an excuse to visit with your Uncle John."

"Dad has a meeting at the Ministry and, well, I wanted to see you."

"And I am delighted. Come we will go to the lounge." Over his shoulder, he said, "Miss Devine turn your attention to today's bookings and stop admiring this young man."

I glanced over my shoulder and saw her blushing. The lounge had a bar. It was not yet opening time but there was a barman on duty. "David, a pot of coffee and ask the cook for some biscuits. I am certain my guest will be hungry." We sat in two leather lounge chairs. "Well, you look well. Your mother wrote to say you had joined up."

"Aren't you disappointed that I am only a private?"

"What nonsense. No wonder your parents were annoyed with you. They did not disagree with your decision but were cross that you acted so hastily without talking to them. That was not the way you were brought up."

I brightened at that. I had thought they were both disappointed in me. I explained my reasons to John who nodded. "Perfectly understandable reasons but had you delayed by a day or two would the outcome have been any different?"

"No."

"There you are then, the impetuosity of youth. Your father was the same. Acted first and thought about it later. Ah here is our coffee."

The barman put the tray down and took the silver coffee pot, cream jug, sugar bowl, china cups and biscuits from it and arranged them on the table. I could see he was aware that John was watching him and he would get it right. He stood upright waiting for instructions. John said, "Thank you, David, but your tie., that will never do. It should be square. We have standards you know."

"Sorry, sir."

"Well don't let it happen again." As he went off John sighed, "He is a good fellow but I fear I shall lose him. All the decent chaps are being conscripted, or like you, volunteering." He shook his head and poured the coffee. "Now you will enjoy this. Javan beans although with the war I am not certain how much longer we will be able to get them."

"This will be the first coffee I have had in a long time. I am looking forward to it." I sipped the rich black brew. It was, as I had expected, perfect.

"Now what have you been up to? Your mother told me you were training up in Manchester."

"I was with the BEF. I just landed back home yesterday."

He looked genuinely upset. "Oh, dear. That must have been a terrible ordeal. I read about the evacuation, the little ships I think they called it. Don't worry. Britain has had dark times before. Mr Churchill will make a difference." We chatted about life in the army and he gave me some sage advice. As noon came and went the bar filled up with drinkers. "Come along. I shall give you a tour." As we reached the door he asked, "Would you like lunch? I am sure I can squeeze you in?"

"No Dad is taking me to his club."

"Do you need a room for the night? I should have asked earlier. How rude of me."

"No, that is fine. Dad has a flat here."

"Your mother and Mary are not here are they?"

"No, they are still in the Midlands in our home in the country."

"Good. I would hate to think of your mother being in danger. The Germans will bomb us you know. They did so in the Great War. I know their Kaiser was related to Queen Victoria but they, as a people, do not understand the idea of rules of war. Do you know they sank the Athenia? A passenger ship! It was the Lusitania all over again. We seem determined to make the same mistakes we made a quarter of a century ago. The war to end all wars failed eh?"

I had a lovely two hours being shown around a hotel which showed John's touch all the way through from the tasteful decorations to the obvious affection in which he was held. I left him, at two o'clock feeling more positive about life than I had in some time. With stoics like John, it would take a worthier adversary than Hitler to defeat us.

Chapter 13

I posted the letter to Mrs Gillespie in Liverpool at the post box close to John's hotel. That was a weight off my shoulders; a promise to a dying man was something which had to be honoured. Wandering the streets of London was depressing. The whole place was prepared for war. I arrived at the Air Ministry early. I saw the sentries, the sandbags outside and the tape over the windows. They were preparing for the worst. John had been correct. The Zeppelin raids in the Great War had given us an inkling of what was to come. Jenkins saw me approach and leapt out to open the door for me. Dad was a little late and it was almost three-thirty before he emerged. He looked a little flustered but smiled when he saw me. "Bloody red tape! My club, Jenkins, and then I have finished with you until the morrow."

"Thank you, Group Captain."

I could tell he was distracted for he did not speak all the way to his club. Once he left the car he looked over Green Park towards Buckingham Palace. "You know the King and Queen have refused to leave the capital? They want to share in the hardships of the people. That is another reason we shall win. That and Mr Churchill."

"What about the soldiers, sailors and airmen?"

"Thank you for putting me in my place. You are quite right." The door opened and an ancient retainer greeted us. "Ah Group Captain will you be staying for dinner later? We are going to be busy. I will need to reserve you a table."

"Yes, Smyth. A table but we shall go and have cocktails first. This is my son."

"Pleased to meet you, Private Harsker."

I had expected some snobbery, especially from the servants; this was the reserve of officers and normally high ranking ones. I did not know if this was because of my father's name or just customary. One cocktail turned into four or five. I found myself becoming a little light-headed. I had not had much to eat. Dad seemed exactly the same. When we went in to an early dinner at seven Dad said, "You will enjoy the food here. Especially having eaten so frugally for the past weeks."

I grinned, "And you will need to restock the cottage. We ate everything."

He burst out laughing, "Well I think that deserves a medal; depriving the enemy of comfort! I hope you polished off the brandy too?"

"We did indeed."

He was right about the dinner. Surprisingly there were some serving captains and majors at the club although most of them appeared to be staff officers based in London. "We'll have a quick brandy and then get off back to the flat. I am afraid I have an early meeting in the morning."

We had just sat down in the lounge when I heard a voice from behind us, "Private Harsker! Is that you?"

I turned and stood to attention as I saw Captain Foster. "Yes, sir!"

He looked at my father and snapped to attention. "I was your son's company commander in the Low Countries. I left before the retreat. Damned glad you made it."

"Please join us, Captain Foster. A drink for the Captain please."

He sat down and I noticed that he had on a new uniform. I was about to comment on it when he said, "Did you get the medal then?"

Dad looked at me, "What medal?"

"It was nothing."

"Nothing my…" The Captain then told the whole story of my attacking and destroying the tank.

I saw the pride in my father's eyes as he heard the story. He nodded, "I think we will moderate that story when we tell it to your mother. I am not sure she would understand although I most certainly do."

"And you, young Harsker, what happened during the retreat after I left?"

I told him and finished with the attack by the 109. He waved over for another round of drinks. "The stuff of adventure stories." When the drinks came and he had signed for them he said, "Cheers!"

"Cheers!"

"You know I think I was meant to come here tonight." Both of us were intrigued at the comment. He smiled and tapped his shoulder, "I have joined the Commandos. Actually, that isn't quite true. The reason I left the battalion was that I was asked for by Colonel Dudley Clarke. I had served under him and he knew of my particular skills. I am on my way to Shropshire to begin training my men."

I nodded and Dad said, "I was talking to Admiral Keyes about you chaps last week. Churchill's brainchild eh?"

"That's right, sir, and we train and fight in a totally different way to the rest of the army." He then went on to describe the training and their methodology. "And we get to choose the men who fight with us."

I began to get excited. Dad said, "I think I can see where this is going, Captain."

He smiled, "I think your son has all the qualities we need in the Commandos or Special Service Brigade as we are officially known. I don't think that will stick, not with SS in it! He was the best scout we had. He has shown his skills at sailing. He is a whizz at booby traps and he can handle himself. Finally, his two languages are impressive qualifications. What do you say? Do you fancy joining a brand new unit?" He gestured towards my father, "Your father did something similar with the Flying Corps and it didn't turn out too badly for him, did it?"

I hesitated and Dad burst out laughing so loudly that heads turned. He shook his head, "Sorry Captain it is just that my son here has been reprimanded by a number of his family for making impetuous decisions and once he has one he should take he is debating with himself."

"You think I should do it?"

"Look me in the eyes and tell me you don't want to do it!"

He was right. It sounded perfect for me and I turned, "Yes Captain. Where do we go from here?"

"You said you were based at Shoreditch at the moment?"

"Yes, sir."

"I am here for the next week interviewing prospective candidates. What say I pop down next week and get the paperwork sorted out and a couple of travel warrants? We can get a train from Paddington and be in Oswestry by the evening eh?"

"That sounds grand, sir!"

He stood and shook my Dad's hand. "It has been an honour and a pleasure to meet you. I can see that you and your son are made from the same mould."

When we got to the flat we sat down and talked. For the first time in my life, and not the last, Dad spoke to me soldier to soldier, man to man. He gave me advice in the same way that John had. He told me things he had experienced in the Great War, including the times he had had to kill close up and personal. I learned more about my Dad that night than in the previous nineteen years. He smiled as he handed me the blankets. "I'll tell Mum about this. I have a little more experience explaining things to women than you do." He paused at the door. "I am inordinately proud of you son. I always was but now that you are a man I can see that your Mum and I didn't do a bad job."

He left the next morning before I was even awake. There was nothing to keep me in London and so I caught the first train back that I could. I surprised the Lieutenant who was on duty. "You are back three hours early!"

I grinned, "I am keen, sir."

"Some more of your lot arrived yesterday so you have your own officer now."

I hurried to the barracks. It had been almost empty when I had left and now it was full. Willy was regaling them with our story when I arrived. I was touched by the welcome. I began to feel guilty. I would soon be leaving them.

"Who is the officer who has returned?"

"Lieutenant Wilson."

"Any idea where he is?"

Willy shook his head. "He went back to Dover to meet the next batch of lads who were arriving. He said he would be back this afternoon." He took me to one side, "He is a pal of Ashcroft's and he said he knew that we would get through. Lieutenant Ashcroft wants to promote us both to Corporal. Apparently, after we left he asked the Colonel to promote us and Lieutenant Wilson was the first one back. He was made up to see me."

I said nothing then. I didn't want to upset Willy by telling him I was transferring. He went back to his stories and I heard laughter as he made some of the things which had been serious, funny. He had that natural humour which was irrepressible.

I spent the next week pussyfooting around telling Willy of my decision. It was when I saw Lieutenant Ashcroft heading through the gates with some more of our chaps that I decided to speak with him. "Willy, can I have a word?"

"Aye mate, is there a problem?"

Once outside I said, "It's not a problem but I am transferring. I met Captain Foster last week and he has asked me to join the Commandos."

"But if you stay here you'll be a Corporal!"

"I know but I want to join the Commandos. Sorry."

He held out his hand, "Don't worry mate, you'll be a success no matter where you serve. I'll miss you. You might talk posh but you are a good lad. "

"And the same to you. I think you will soon be Company Sergeant."

"I don't know about that."

He looked over my shoulder. "Looks like Lieutenant Ashcroft is back."

The Lieutenant grinned when he saw us. He put his hands on his hips, "Like a pair of bad pennies eh? Where are the others?"

"Only Corporal Higgins made it and he was wounded. We only made it by the skin of our teeth, Lieutenant."

He nodded, "Captain now, I got promoted."

"Can I have a word then Captain?"

"Sounds serious but of course, Harsker."

Willy went with the rest to show them the barracks. "It's like this sir, I met Captain Foster last week and he wants me to join the Commandos."

"The Commandos?"

"I think they are raiders who will go behind enemy lines and cause trouble."

He laughed, "It sounds like it was made for you. I'll be sorry to lose you, The Colonel and I want to promote the two of you to Corporal."

"I know sir."

"And you still want to join the Commandos."

"Sir."

"Then I won't stand in your way. Besides if captain Foster is involved it will be well planned. I'll try to get the paperwork done as quickly as I can."

"The Captain said he would be down here by the end of the week. That's tomorrow, sir so don't put yourself out on my account."

"Make sure you have all the equipment you need. I expect you lost a lot in France like the rest of us did."

"Yes, sir."

As well as the new uniforms I managed to acquire a new kitbag I went to the Quarter Master's store to see what else I could get. I needed a mess kit. When I had it all I went into the barracks and packed my bag. Captain Foster arrived first thing the next day as he had promised. He and Captain Ashcroft spent half an hour talking and I took the opportunity to say goodbye to the lads and get my gear.

By the time I was ready the two captains appeared. "Well, Harsker I guess I am losing you. I have to say that I am disappointed and if it were anyone else but the Captain here I would refuse the request but I know you will be a first-rate Commando. We still haven't heard about the medal but you were mentioned in despatches so it is on your record now."

"Thank you, sir and it was an honour to serve with the 1st Loyal Lancashires. Er sir, what happened to Sergeant Greely?"

His face darkened, "Like you, he became separated from the battalion. I hoped he might be with you lads but Holden told me you hadn't seen him since the crossroads."

"No sir, but he is a tough character; if a couple of green recruits like us could survive then Sergeant Greely will have as well."

"I hope so. This country will need soldiers like Sergeant Greely."

"Well, we had better run, Harsker. We have a long journey ahead of us."

He shook Captain Ashcroft's hand, "Take care, Brian."

"And you Stephen."

I waved, "See you, Willy." I threw him the five packs of cigarettes I had bought in London. "These should last a wee while eh?"

"Tom, you are a gentleman!"

It took us some time to get to London and the captain had some last-minute details to sort out before we could get the train. The train for Oswestry left Paddington at ten past six. I noticed that the green liveried engine was the Powderham Castle. I wondered where that castle was. The chocolate and cream carriages looked totally different from the LNER ones I was used to. Luckily there was a restaurant car on this most modern of trains and the Captain and I shared a pleasant meal. Travelling with the Captain meant we were in First Class. It was a little bit of luxury for me. I was lost in my thoughts as we hurtled through the Midlands towards Gobowen where we would change trains. The train was relatively empty and the Captain and I had a carriage to ourselves. He lit his pipe. "You had the chance to be a corporal you know, Harsker."

"I know but I am not bothered about a rank."

"You should be. You are a natural leader. But you get more pay as a Commando anyway." I nodded, that was not important. "There are some things you need to know about being a Commando. We are different from other units. For one thing, you don't get to stay in barracks. It is up to you to arrange your own accommodation. You are responsible for getting to the base on time. There is no Sergeant Major to wake you up."

"That's fine sir. I can cope with that."

"We also have different equipment. You will find that out soon enough but I mention it because I know that you can handle a Lee Enfield and a Webley. We use the Thomson submachine gun and the Colt Automatic pistol. I hope you can adjust to them."

I smiled and reached into my kitbag. I took out the Luger and the dagger. "I am adaptable sir."

"Well done, Private! I take it these came from dead Germans."

"Yes sir, after I killed them." I held up the dagger. "The Waffen SS who had this had just bayoneted a prisoner. He deserved to die."

"Then that will stand you in good stead. We may well have to kill at close quarters. You are lucky, you will be in at the start of things. The training should take no more than six weeks. After all the men in the new unit have been handpicked."

"You have the others, sir?"

"I do. They were all volunteers. I whittled them down. We are B Troop. There are three officers and with you, there will be sixty enlisted men. As you can see we are different from other units. This is brand new. When I saw you yesterday it was after a meeting with our commanding officer, Lieutenant Colonel Dudley Clark. Churchill only gave his final go-ahead a couple of days ago."

"Then how were you able to choose your men sir?"

"Lieutenant Colonel Dudley Clark is a forceful man with interesting ideas. Mr Churchill had already asked him to look at raiding across the Channel even before Dunkirk. He likes to hit the ground running."

I took this in and became even more excited. There would be no precedent for whatever we did. No one would be able to talk about how they did it. We would be the first and that was exhilarating.

"And what do I do about digs then sir?"

"We are both in the same boat I am afraid. I think we will struggle to get anything tonight. I just hope that the pub has rooms."

I had already thought about that; I would sleep in the station waiting room and look for somewhere better the next morning. "When do I have to report for duty, sir?"

He smiled, "I'll tell you what Harsker, let's give you twenty-four hours from when you signed the papers of enlistment. Tomorrow, noon. How's that?"

"That will be fine sir. The other blokes will all be there will they?"

He shook his head. "No, Harsker. They are travelling from all over the country. I was surprised more weren't on this train. We won't be at full strength for a couple of days. We then have a couple of weeks of training and learning new skills like rock climbing, rope work and demolition. We will all have to get used to the new weapons too."

"So the camp is close to rocks and stuff."

"I am afraid not. Park Hall is a Royal Artillery and Plotting Officers training camp. We just share their facilities. Colonel Clark is up in Scotland getting us a more permanent training base but that will be for the ones who come after us. We are the first of the Commandos. The rules for us haven't been written yet."

I closed my eyes as darkness fell and the countryside became hidden. I knew ropes from sailing and I enjoyed scrambling over rocks. Thinking of demolition made me think about Nev. I now knew more than I had when the war had started and that was down to the veteran of the Spanish Civil War.

We reached Gobowen just after ten-thirty and we only had to wait five minutes for the ten-minute ride to Oswestry. As I watched the Castle Class engine pull the chocolate and cream carriages away I wondered what kind of train we would be on next. It was a tiny train with just two carriages. The train which looked like a toy train after the mainline train had a variety of passengers but many of them wore uniforms. We shared a compartment with four civilians, there was no corridor on this train, and conversation about the Commandos was not to be contemplated. I closed my eyes and thought of my future on the short train ride. The only ones who got off at our stop were dressed in khaki. The Captain shook my hand. "Well good luck Harsker. Your training starts here. You will have to find your own way to Park Hall."

"Right sir. Thanks for giving me this chance."

He slung his kitbag over his shoulder turned and headed out of the station and down the road. The other soldiers had already departed. I turned to go back into the waiting room. The Station Master was already locking it up. "Sorry son. There are no more trains until the milk train in the morning. The next passenger train is not due in until six."

"I was hoping to sleep in the waiting room."

"You'll be at Park Hall." I nodded, "It's just a couple of miles down the road. A young fit lad like you can be there in half an hour."

I decided upon honesty. "The thing is, sir, that we are a new unit and we don't sleep in barracks. We have to make our own arrangements." I remembered the benches on the platform. "Is it all right if I sleep on the platform?"

He laughed, "You'd sleep there?" I nodded. "You are mad." He was about to turn away and then he said, "Listen, son, I only have the one room in the station but I have a shed at the back where I keep the plant pots and the like for the station in the winter. I won't need it until October. You can use that if you have a mind. There's a toilet and washroom in the station during the day."

"That will do me, sir. How much rent do you want?"

He looked offended, "There is a war on and if a fellow can't help a soldier then it is a pretty poor show. I'll give you a hand to sweep it out."

"No that's all right. I am handy with a brush."

He supplied me with a brush and an oil lamp. The shed would be more than adequate. There was a hasp and I would buy a lock in the town. It would be cosy. In no time at all, it was swept out. I had my new blanket and greatcoat. I used those as a bed. The milk train woke me at four o'clock as it hissed to a halt and then chugged its way out. I tried to get back to sleep but I could not manage it. Before five I rose and went along to the toilets. Joe, the Station Master, had just opened them. He grinned at me, "Sleep all right then, Private?"

"Like a baby." He looked incredulous and went on unlocking the gates and the doors.

I had just finished when a small engine pulled in with three carriages. Joe said, "Here Tom, come and meet breakfast."

I was bemused. "Breakfast?"

He chuckled, "Aye." I followed him to the engine. He picked up a basket covered with a tea towel. The driver and his assistant were standing there with two shovels in their hands. As we approached they put them in the firebox. Joe handed the basket over, "Harry, Bert, this is my new lodger, Tom. He is staying in my shed yonder."

They nodded, "Won't take long and we'll have breakfast ready." I was curious. They lifted the tea towel off and underneath were sausages, bacon and half a dozen eggs.

Joe said, "I'll go and get the bread."

They put the sausages on one shovel and the bacon on the other. They thrust them back in the firebox where they spat and hissed as they cooked. The fireman brought his bacon out while the driver shook his sausages to move them around. The fireman took a homemade metal spatula out of his back pocket and he moved the bacon to one side. He nodded to me, "Joe normally does this. Could you crack the six eggs on the shovel here, young man?"

I climbed up on the footplate suddenly aware of the heat from the firebox. I cracked the eggs on the shovel which began to cook as they landed. They were in the firebox no more than seconds before they were cooked.

"Come on Joe!"

Joe hurried back out with a tray. "Coming!"

He had made a pot of tea and I saw that there was even a bottle of HP sauce. This was better than a hotel. The four of us sat on the platform bench and ate the best breakfast I had had in a long time. Once you learned to pick out the pieces of charcoal it was like eating in a fine hotel!

Joe explained, "The farmer who brings the milk drops the basket off. I get up early and load the milk for him. It saves him time, see. Harry and Bert here are the first train and it works out nicely."

I washed up for Joe while he checked the tickets for the passengers and, as the train pulled out, at six o'clock I headed towards Park Hall with my kitbag over my shoulder. Mindful of the Sergeant at Shoreditch I had shaved off my moustache. I did not want to start off on the wrong foot on my first day. As I marched through the deserted town I wondered which of the pubs the Captain had used. Joe had given me good directions. I had just left the town and was passing a park when I saw khaki uniforms emerge and begin to walk towards the road. I dropped my kitbag and waited. It was the Captain and the other men who had been on the train. They looked unkempt and unshaven.

He looked at me and smiled, "I see you landed on your feet. Found somewhere already?"

"At the station. I have my digs sorted. What about you, sir?"

He shook his head, "The two pubs were already full."

A sergeant said, "I felt like Baby Jesus, no room at the inn!" He sniffed, "I can smell HP sauce and bacon!" He looked around seeking the café.

"That would be me, sergeant. I had breakfast with the engine drivers."

The Captain laughed, "Well gentlemen we have had a fine lesson here on how to be a Commando. Tom Harsker is a natural!"

Chapter 14

Park Hall was a busy place. Now with three units using its facilities, I spent most of each day saluting officers. That first morning was spent in getting our new equipment. Some of it was familiar and some was not. The Bergen rucksack was definitely unfamiliar but I soon came to appreciate its clever design. It had a metal frame which enabled us to carry much greater weight. We were given a toggle rope. I had no idea of its purpose. We were also issued with a life belt. The Browning Colt and the Thomson machine gun I knew about, as well as the special pouch for the magazines. I was issued with a new comforter as well as a beret. The rubber-soled shoes we were given were another unknown quantity but when I received the Commando knife I knew that I was joining a unique unit. It looked like no knife I had seen before. Everything packed neatly into the Bergen.

Like the others who had just joined, we were all curious about each other. This was not like the University; here we knew we might depend on the men we now met for the first time. Suddenly we heard a whistle and a voice shouted. "Find the lecture hall. Last three men are all on jankers!"

None of us knew where the lecture hall was but I took a guess that it would a large building. I saw one just fifty yards away and I ran towards it. Others ran towards the main admin building while others just stood watching. Four or five men ran with me. A corporal threw a door open and we saw rows of seats and upon each seat was a notepad and a pencil.

"I am guessing this is it, boys." The man who had opened the door had a strong Scottish accent. He led us to the front row. I sat next to him. "Private Sean McKinley, formerly of the Gordon Highlanders."

I shook his hand, "Tom Harsker, formerly of the 1st Loyal Lancashire."

The others joined us. "Well," said Sean, "this is a rum do eh?" We both looked around as others came in to the hall. At first a trickle it soon became a flood. "Did you get some digs then?"

"Yes, I am staying in a hut at the station."

"That's clever. I found a farm with a barn. Cheap as chips!"

Captain Foster came to the front with two officers and the Sergeant who had shouted. He gave a smile when he saw me seated at the front. "Right lads, hurry up and settle down. Sergeant Johnson, have you the last three men yet?"

A voice at the back shouted, "Aye sir. They are just coming now."
When we heard the doors slam we knew that the three unfortunates who would be on punishment duty had reached us.
The Captain put his hands behind his back as he began to talk. "Well, that is just one of the ways we are different from other units. You have all discovered the joys of finding your own bed for the night. Some of you, like me, enjoyed life in the park last night." There was laughter all round. "Your officers all have the same rigours as you do. Every one of you was chosen by me. Many more than the men in this room wished to join but I was selective. I know that some of you were in the Rifles. Where are you?" Two men stood up. "Sit down, chaps. These two know more than most the value of what I am about to say. The Rifles have always fought in pairs. Each man watched his friend's back. We are going to use that esprit de corps here too. The difference is each ten-man squad will look after each other. We do not leave a man down or a man behind. We are brothers and each squad will be closer than family. When I dismiss you then you can go to the Admin Building and find who your new family is."
There was a murmur from some of the men. The loud sergeant snapped, "Silence in the ranks!"
"Just because we are a unique unit does not mean that we forget discipline and standards. If anything they will be higher here than in the units you came from and that includes the Guards! Lieutenant Reed here has transferred from the Coldstreams and he will confirm, if confirmation were needed, of our higher standards. I want men who can be self-reliant. I want men who can find a lecture hall instantly. We will be working behind enemy lines and we may not have accurate information about the terrain. You will all have to improvise and use your minds. All of you have shown me that you have that attribute. Each morning, whilst we are training, you will meet here at six-thirty. You will be briefed on the day's activities. You miss the briefing and you will be out of the Commandos. There are no second chances." He turned to the loud sergeant, "Sergeant Dean."
The Captain sat down and the sergeant stepped forward. "We have to cram six week's training into three weeks. We will work twice as hard as you have ever worked in your life." He glanced at the officers. "And that goes for everyone. Next week three PTIs will be coming to teach hand to hand combat and to put you through your paces. This week will be spent in getting used to our new equipment, our new role and our new brothers. I am the senior sergeant but each squad's sergeant will report to me at the end of each day. We will get rid of you before you

jeopardise the unit." He allowed that to sink in. "Now you have fifteen minutes to find out who your new family is. It is another initiative test. Then we will go on a little fifteen mile run to assess your fitness. Attention!"

We all stood.

"Dismiss!"

Fifteen minutes was not very long and we ran. Running had always been one of my strengths and I began to outstrip the others. Some of the ones at the back just ran out without thinking where they were running. I headed for the Admin Building. I was the second one there. I saw my name. There were eight privates in the list. It was the second on a list headed Number 2 squad. I went to the side to allow the others to see and then I shouted. Number Two Squad! Here!"

I almost laughed when the Gordon Highlander joined me. It seemed like Fate. We both roared, "Number Two Squad! Here!"

One or two others had decided to copy me but we had four members already. We all shouted a third time but our voices were drowned a little by the others. Even so, two more joined us. Finally, two men looked at the board and then asked. "Number Two Squad?"

Sean nodded, "And that makes us complete. Right lads let's move over there and get to know each other." The cacophony of noise made conversation impossible. We headed back to the lecture hall. I saw the officers, sergeants and corporals watching us with amusement. We stood in a circle. "I'm Sean McKinley and this is Tom Harsker."

He gestured with his left hand to the man on his left. "Percy Cunningham."

"Martin Murphy."

"Brian Davis."

"Dick Kirton."

"Harry Golightly."

"Dennis Grant."

The last man was the eldest of us. He had grey streaks in his hair. I wondered if he was too old to be in the Commandos. Before we could say anything else a sergeant and a corporal joined us. "Well done lads. That was smartly done. I have high hopes of you if you can keep that up. I am Sergeant Jack Johnson and this is Corporal Wally White. We are the other members of Number Two Squad. Right, let's get going."

He turned and began to run. We now knew to expect the unexpected and we all followed him. I found myself behind Sean and ahead of Dennis Grant. The Sergeant kept up a ground eating pace. It was not fast but it was steady. He led us out of the camp and along a lane. We turned and ran along the perimeter of the camp. I saw a second squad running too but others were still milling around.

I noticed that the lane was heading uphill. This was border country. Ahead were hills and mountains. I wished I had studied a map while on the train. It would have been handy to know where we were going. I did keep a close eye on the direction we took. The sergeant kept taking side lanes but always we went up. After two hours we stopped in the middle of a copse. We had left the last road half a mile back and had followed a trail until we came to the wood.

The Corporal and the Sergeant stood together. "Now my lovely lads. Your next task is to get back to camp. All of you! The last squad back is cooking the meal tonight." They sat down and lit up their cigarettes.

Brian Davis said, "Bloody hell anyone any idea of the way back?"

I stepped forward, "I think so. I was watching the turns as we came up."

Sean said, "Well old son, I guess you lead and we will play follow my leader!"

It was pressure but then Dad had told me to expect pressure. I had been brought up to make decisions and I took my first one. I began to jog through the woods. Martin Murphy said, "As soon as we see the other squads we will know which way to go."

Sean laughed, "I don't think they will make it that easy. They will all take different routes." He pointed and we could other sections snaking along the lanes.

Private Grant was behind me. "Still they all have to come from the camp, don't they? If young Tom here gets lost then we look for the ones climbing the hills."

That reassured me. There was a backup plan. Surprisingly I found the route down the hill easy. The fact that I had watched so closely on the way up meant I had a few waypoints in my head. As the ground began to flatten I grew hopeful. When we found the lane we had started on then I became excited. As soon as we saw the perimeter wall the whole squad began to cheer. We had made it. We could have slowed but I wanted to make a grand entrance. As we sprinted into the camp I saw Sergeant Johnson and Corporal White. They were leading their bicycles towards us with Lieutenant Reed behind. I heard Dennis say, "Crafty buggers." He clapped me on the back. "Well done, son. You did well then."

"So did you. I was surprised you were able to keep up."

He laughed, "Cheeky so and so. Don't let the grey hairs fool you. I was divisional cross country champion six years ago."

"Sorry. I meant no offence."

"And none taken."

The Lieutenant bounded up to us. "I say chaps, well done! The next squad is nowhere in sight!"

I saw that the two non-coms looked equally pleased. "Right lads. Your next lesson is about getting your body back to working order after a run like that. "Corporal White came along and gave each of us a half-pound bag of salt. "Go to the canteen and get a pint of water each. Put a tablespoon of salt in it and drink it."

I looked at Sean who shrugged. Dennis said, "It makes sense. When you run you sweat out salts and this replaces them. Come on son."

Sean laughed, "Right you are, Dad." We all laughed and in that instant, Dennis became Daddy Grant.

That was the moment when we became a team. A tiny thing in the scheme of things but it worked. It helped that we had arrived back more than fifteen minutes ahead of anyone else. In that short time, we became the ones everyone wanted to beat. While the team who came in last hurried to cook our meal the rest of us were allowed to go to the NAAFI where we could buy a beer or two. I was able to look at this in a detached manner. Dad would have done something similar to this to encourage the esprit de corps that Captain Foster wanted. Not surprisingly we sat in our squads. The officers of all ranks observed our privacy and let us get on with it. We found out what we had all done before joining the Commandos. We discovered that Daddy Grant was decorated. He had been awarded the Military Medal for gallantry in Norway. Although we had been driven from Norway Daddy Grant had fought with great courage.

I was the only veteran of the BEF retreat; even though I had not been to Dunkirk. It meant that the two of us were the only ones who had seen serious action.

"I think this is great," Percy had had more beers than the rest of us and was the most garrulous, "but how in the hell can we get to know each other if we all go our separate ways to our own digs. In a barracks, we would all be mucking in together."

Sean said, "You could be right but I dinna think we will be in our own little billets for too long. I have a feeling that we will have to be billeted together before we go into action. This is just for the training,"

Despite his brash manner, Sean was a thinker. He reminded me of a mature Willy. After we had eaten, and it was not the best food I had eaten, we all headed back to our own billets. We left together but, gradually the others all peeled off to go to pubs, farms and private houses. I reached the station and met Joe as he was heading back to his house. He smiled when he saw me. "How was your first day then?"

"It was good. I will buy a lock for the shed tomorrow." I held up my Bergen. "They keep giving us more and more gear."

He suddenly ran off and returned a moment or two later with the biggest padlock I had ever seen. "Here, you are, Tom. I've had this for some time. You might as well use it."

I spent the next hour examining my new weapons and tidying my new home. There was no lock on the inside and so I rigged my helmet on a cord. If anyone tried to come in the helmet would fall and clatter against the floor. As I snuggled down into my blanket I contemplated getting a camp bed but then decided against it. This would inure me against the privations to come.

The next week flew by. We learned how to rock climb. The rubber-soled shoes helped and my knowledge of knots was invaluable. My bowline was admired, even by Sergeant Dean who was the knot expert. I thoroughly enjoyed learning how to use the machine gun and the automatic. After the Lee Enfield and the Webley, they were a joy. When it came to booby traps the skills Nev had imparted proved to be superior even to some of those training us. I explained how to use a German hand grenade to make a booby trap and it made all of the officers sit up and take an interest. As we walked to the mess that evening Sergeant Dean said, "If we can get hold of a couple of potato mashers it would be good to try some of these booby traps out."

"No problem, Sergeant."

He nodded and then asked, "Was your father a British Ace in the Great War?"

My heart sank, I did not want to have to live up to his reputation. Equally, I could not lie to my new comrades, "Yes Sergeant."

He smiled, "My brother was a mechanic in his squadron. He spoke highly of your Dad. Said he was a good bloke. I can see you are a chip off the old block. Well done, son."

I breathed a sigh of relief. I was not being compared. It was the skills Nev had given me that made me stand out. My father was incidental.

We had lectures on blowing bridges. I could see that some of the lads struggled with that. My engineering background and knowledge of physics made it seem simple. We were told that we would, eventually, be able to practise blowing up bridges at Park Hall. The Royal Engineers based there would build them and we would destroy them. That sounded like fun.

At the end of the first week, on Sunday night, we were gathered in the lecture hall. There were three soldiers I did not recognise. Captain Foster stood. He had been ever-present during that first week as he had been observing and making notes on our performances. I knew from Sergeant Johnson that he was impressed with our squad.

"You have all done well this week. Only four of our number has had to be returned to their units. Believe me, that is a lower number than in many other troops. Next week we will be joined by Sergeant Geraghty, Corporal Horn and Corporal Lowe." He pointed to the three men. "They are Physical Training and hand to hand combat instructors. They will show you how to fight and how to kill with a knife." The three of them did not even nod an acknowledgement. They just stared ahead. "The last week we will be moving from here to Anglesey where we will be training with the Royal Navy and learn about boats." He grinned, pointedly at me, "I know that at least one of you has had experience of sailing and quite recently too!"

The rest of my squad knew about my exploits and I was patted on the back. It was ominous that Sergeant Geraghty's eyes narrowed as he stared at me. I had attracted his attention and that was not good.

I arrived early on Monday. I felt that I had some skills in this area. Nev had not only taught me about booby traps, when we had been in the cottage he had told me how to kill with a knife. He had been quite clear about hand to hand combat; *"You do anything to win! Forget fair play. If you can rip his balls off then do it! Kick, bite and gouge. It is dog eat dog so make sure you are the biggest dog! Just do the unexpected. You will win every time."*

The words still rang in my head.

We gathered on the rugby field and sat in a circle. The officers were with us. They were not exempt either. We were all in our battle dress. We were wearing our boots rather than our rubber-soled shoes for the captain wanted us to learn how to fight fully equipped.

Sergeant Geraghty stood with his two corporals behind him. He had muscle upon muscle. He obviously used weights. He had his hands on his hips. "Now you all want to be the best soldiers you can be. Our job is to do that. We have trained the Guards and we have trained the best. You will either become competent or you will be hurt! We will not go easy on you because Fritz certainly won't." He glared around our ranks. "Some of you think because you have a bit of fruit salad on your chest you know what it's all about! You don't'"

Our squad was seated together and collectively we bridled. He was having a go at Daddy who was the only one of us with a medal ribbon. His eyes fixed on Sean, "You got something to say, Sonny Jim?"

"I just think it is wrong to have a go at someone because he was brave and won a medal that's all."

"Ah, a Jock! I never yet knew a Jock who didn't think he was hard as nails and could piss whisky. I was looking for a volunteer and you'll do. Come here."

Sean got up and stood before the sergeant. He proffered a knife to Sean. "Here, Rob Roy, take this and gut me eh?"

Sean took the knife. From the way, he held it I could see he knew how to handle a knife. "I might hurt you, Sergeant."

Sergeant Geraghty laughed, "I don't think so. Come on you, Scottish Pansy! Use the knife!"

Sean widened his stance and then lunged. The sergeant grabbed the outstretched arm and in one swift movement threw Sean into the air. He crashed to the ground. At that moment it was a good demonstration of the skill of unarmed combat however the sergeant then brought back his boot and kicked Sean hard between the legs.

Captain Foster was on his feet in an instant, "There is no need for that, Sergeant."

"With respect Captain, you are here to learn just like your men and I say it is necessary. A Kraut will not hesitate to do what I did and more."

Sean crawled back to his place. I could see he was in agony. I knew that Dad had told me to keep my head down but Sean was one of our squad. I could not sit idly by but I knew a direct confrontation would only result in the sergeant winning. I knew I looked young and so I played the schoolboy. I held up my hand like a child in class.

The sergeant smirked, "Yes Sonny Jim? Do you need the toilet?" His two henchmen grinned.

"No Sergeant I just wondered, you are obviously so experienced where did you get that experience?" His eyes narrowed. "I mean where did you serve to kill Germans? Was it Norway? Were you in the BEF? I am certain we would all like to hear some of your stories. It would be illuminating and firsthand knowledge is always important isn't it, sergeant?"

He began to colour. I had guessed correctly. He had never been in combat. He regained his composure. "It looks like we have another volunteer." He turned, "Corporal Lowe, give the schoolboy your knife and we will see how he does."

"I think I saw what to do before, Sergeant. Why not let Corporal Lowe have the knife, I watched you in the last demonstration and I would like to try that too."

I saw the look of joy on their faces. "Your funeral son but we have a good doctor here. Off you go Corporal."

I was taking a chance but I was counting on overconfidence. Corporal Lowe held his knife behind him and then feinted with it. I pretended to be afraid and acted hesitantly. They were expecting me to go for the knife. Corporal Lowe was counting on that fact and when I did he would hurt me. I gave him his chance. I reached out with my left hand to grab his right wrist and he pulled his hand back as he prepared to stab towards me. I quickly pulled back and then spun on my left leg and brought my right fist into his ribs. He was not expecting that and he winced. I put my left leg in front of him and grabbed his hair to pull down his head down on to my left knee. There was a satisfying crack as his nose hit it. As he slumped to the ground I fell on his back and took the knife from his right hand. I looked up at the Sergeant, "You are a first-rate teacher, Sergeant." I threw the knife so that it landed between his legs as we used to do at school when we played the game called 'splits'.

I went back to my place and the other lads patted me on the back. I knew I had made three enemies but honour had demanded it.

The Sergeant glowered but he would save his revenge for another time. "Well done. There you are. That is how you do it. Now I will show you, with Corporal Horn here how to use an opponent's body weight against him." They showed us many moves. Most I already knew as I had done some work with experts who had been stationed with my Dad. I had been young and they had made it fun. But it was a good refresher course. After they had demonstrated we were divided up into pairs. I went with Sean.

"Are you all right, Sean?"

"I'll survive but I'll have that big bastard."

"That is what he wants; forget it. I'll come at you."

We spent an hour practising all that we had seen. The Sergeant and his corporals went around advising and coaching. They assiduously avoided the two of us. When they seemed satisfied they gathered us together again. This time Captain Foster stood.

"One of the skills you will need will be to disable sentries silently. That requires stealth. The first thing you need to do is to stalk them. Today you are wearing your boots; you have all been issued rubber-soled shoes. That will help us. There are two main methods we will use;

a knife and disabling them with your hands. We will come to the knife later; Sergeant, demonstrate the first of the hand methods."

Corporal Horn stood as though a sentry and the Sergeant crept up behind him. He spoke as he performed the actions. "Lower your body to help you to spring. When you are three or four feet from him spring forward and do two things at the same time. With the fingers and thumb of your left hand fully extended, strike him across the throat with the inner edge of your left forearm. At the same time punch him with your right hand in the small of his back. Then you clamp your right arm across his nose and mouth and drag him backwards. It should be easy because he will be unconscious if you have done it right. Now you try."

It wasn't as easy as they had made out because in some cases there was a disparity in height. We managed and then we were shown the second method, the Japanese stranglehold. This one proved to be an easier one for the smaller men as they could use it to pull back their taller opponent.

Finally, we were shown how to use our knives. The Sergeant demonstrated the best places to kill an enemy. Although we continued until lunchtime in the back of my mind was the thought that you none of us would really know if we could carry out the actions we had practised and actually kill an enemy until we were in the field. I realised that hesitation in a Commando could be disastrous.

As lunchtime approached the Sergeant said, "Any questions?" He pointedly looked at me.

"Just one Sergeant." It was Lieutenant Reed who asked the question.

"Yes, Lieutenant?"

"I have heard of a way of using your hands to strike an enemy's ears."

The Sergeant nodded, "You are right, sir. But this only works if your opponent isn't wearing a helmet. I'll demonstrate." He nodded to Corporal Lowe who came forward. "You cup your hands and strike your enemy over both ears at the same time. If you do it hard enough you can burst an eardrum or give him a mild concussion. Either way, he is disabled."

We heard the call for lunch. Sergeant Johnson said, "Dismiss!" We ran to the mess hall.

Chapter 15

Our squad sat together. They were all concerned about Sean who insisted he was fine. Daddy Grant smiled at me, "Thanks for the defence, Tom, but I have met the Sergeant's type before. All mouth and trousers as my old sergeant would have said. They are good at the theory but never have to put it into practice. It is much harder to kill a man close up."

I nodded, "Too right."

"You have done that already?"

"On the retreat to Boulogne. I had no time to think but it was messy."

That sobering thought silenced us.

The afternoon was spent with our new guns. We were shown how to strip them and reassemble them. We practised loading the magazines and all of this before we fired them. "You need to be able to do this in the dark so practise on your off duty moments as much as you can. Most of our work will be at night and guns can jam."

We were then taken to the range. We used the twenty round box magazine. "Now the last thing you want to do is to hold your finger on the trigger and blaze away. You will empty your magazine and then Jerry will have you for breakfast while you are reloading. Use it like a rifle. Two or three shots each time. It takes practice but that is why you are here."

The instructor was right it was hard to judge. There was a temptation just to hold down the trigger and keep firing. The Browning was a nice weapon. The seven-shot magazine was easy to change. It felt more like the Luger I had acquired. The difference was it used the same ammunition as the Thompson. I liked shooting and the time on the range was well spent.

After we had cleaned our weapons we returned to our digs. Sean said, "Let's go and have a pint in the local pub to celebrate and we can get some fish and chips from the chippy. It's Friday and they have fish." He pulled out his ration book. "And we have the rations too!"

Sean was a leader and we all followed him. We queued up with the locals who were also ready for their Friday night fish supper. It had been a long time since I had enjoyed them. The portions were slightly smaller than before the war but as Daddy said, "There is a war on and I reckon it won't be too long before we don't even get this."

It was a depressing thought. France and Norway had both fallen and we were alone. We heard stories of ships being torpedoed and there were daily rumours of invasion. As we sat in the pub Percy jerked a thumb at the newspaper being read by a local. "It looks like the RAF is doing well."

I saw the figures of downed aircraft. I shook my head, "Don't believe everything you read in the newspapers. The Germans have many more aeroplanes than us. And they have had practice in Spain. They know what they are doing."

Daddy nodded, "We had to endure Stuka attacks in Norway."

"They are a nasty machine even so you can bring them down." They asked me how I knew and I told them of the attacks during the retreat.

The door of the pub suddenly opened and we saw the two corporals, Horn and Lowe looming large. They saw us and they left. Sean shook his head, "They are like Frankenstein's monster and the Mummy that pair."

Daddy shook his head, "I'd steer clear of them two if I were you. They are not like us. They enjoy inflicting pain for the sake of it. Give them a black uniform and they could be Nazis. I am guessing that they want to pay back young Tom here. He showed them up good and proper today. "

"They are only here for another couple of days and then they go to show off to another Commando unit."

"That is a couple of days too many for me."

Daddy's words were a warning and I heeded them. When we all left, well before closing time, I kept to the middle of the road. The blackout restrictions meant that there were no street lights but it was midsummer and the sky was still light enough when we left to enable me to see if there was any danger. Joe was just sweeping out the waiting room when I arrived and I gave him a hand. I knew I had dropped lucky. He was a good landlord and if he wouldn't take my money he could take my help. I handed him the loaf I bought each day. It seemed a shame for him to have to use his own ration book for bread. After all, I was eating it too. I bought a loaf every day. I think the woman in the shop thought I lived on bread alone! As I went to my hut I noticed a bicycle in the corner of the station.

"What's that, Joe?"

"Some joker dumped it close to the line. The handlebars are twisted. I was going to give it to the rag and bone man when he comes around. With the war on they want all the scrap they can get."

"It looks like a good bike. It has gears and racing handlebars. An owner wouldn't have dumped it."

"It was probably stolen."

"Do you mind if I have a go at doing it up? I like to keep busy."
"Be my guest."
I worked for an hour or so and by the time I had finished, it could be ridden once more. I decided to see if I could work on the gears and the chain when time allowed.
After my normal breakfast with the engine driver and his fireman, I set off to the camp. One advantage of my early breakfast was that I was the first one in camp. I was surprised to see two policemen at the Admin building. I was curious. Oswestry was a quiet town and, despite the number of soldiers, there was no trouble. Even Joe had commented on the peaceful nature of our soldiery.
I went into the lecture hall for the usual briefing. Sean was there as was Percy. Their digs were close to the camp. "What are the police doing here?"
"Search me." Sean looked around guiltily, "Now if they were the polis from Glasgow then I would be feeling worried but I have been a good little laddie here… so far."
The hall filled up and Captain Foster came in. He had a serious expression on his face. "Settle down, chaps. I have some serious news this morning. We have suffered our first casualty. Private Grant was attacked last night and received a severe beating. The police will be asking you all questions." He looked at our squad, "When the rest are dismissed then I would like Sergeant Johnson's squad to remain behind. The police will question you first."
We were given a brief outline of the activities for the day. It would be more of the same; hand to hand and then gunnery. I barely took it in. There were only three people who would wish harm to come to Daddy and none of them were commandos. As we waited Sean said, "It canna be any of us! They should ask those bastard corporals."
Sergeant Johnson said, "Don't start a fight before you have to McKinley. They know that you lot were with him last night. They will want to know his movements."
The police did, indeed, just want to know what we had all done when we had left the camp. Sean and Percy were the last to see Daddy. "We left him close to the entrance to the camp. He went to his digs up yon lane."
"That is where we found him. Did you see anyone at the end of the lane?"
Percy shook his head, "No and he only had four hundred yards to go. We thought he would be home in no time."
"Had he had much to drink?"

"Two or three pints. Hardly a skinful. How is he?"
"He is still unconscious but he has broken ribs and a broken nose. He is lucky to be alive. If the farmer's dogs hadn't alerted the farmer then he might have died in the night. Well, thanks for your help lads and," the police sergeant leaned in, "from now on I would go around in pairs."
As we went to the rugby field I said, "It is those three, Sergeant, we all know that."
"No we don't and besides the three of them didn't leave the hall last night."
"How do you know, Sergeant?"
"No one left the Hall after we went back to our digs last night. I checked the duty log this morning."
I did not believe that. It would have been simplicity itself for them to slip out and wait for some of us to pass by. That was why they had attacked Daddy. He was the closest to the camp. This was a warning from the three of them for us to behave. It had all been my fault. They could not get at me and so they had attacked Daddy. I would be ready the next time they tried anything.
For the next four days, there was an air of tension in the camp. Due to their dubious alibis, the two corporals seemed to be above suspicion and there was bad feeling between the Commandos and the Royal Artillery. The Captain visited Daddy but our comrade could remember nothing, just that he was jumped from behind and he thought that there were two of them. I used it as an opportunity to hone my skills. Each day I went home by a different route. Sometimes I headed in the opposite direction. On the third night, I began by walking down the road. I had learned to trust my senses and I felt as though I was being followed. As soon as I could I ducked through a hedge and double backed on myself. I waited and sure enough, the two corporals were following me. They did not see me and I listened to their conversation. It was obvious, from what they said, that they were trying to get to me. I turned the tables on them and followed the two thugs. They went to the station. They knew where I was billeted. They hung around for a while but when Joe came around to empty the rubbish bins they disappeared back towards the town. As Sergeant Greely and my Dad had drummed into me no reconnaissance was ever wasted.
After our morning hand to hand session we were gathered in the lecture hall so that we could have our final lecture on demolitions. I enjoyed these more than almost anything. Precise amounts of explosives for different structures were explained to us. I made sure I kept copious notes. I knew that some of the others struggled with the

figures but that was the beauty of the Commandos. So long as a couple of us knew what to do then we would achieve our objective.

At the end of the session, Captain Foster stood. "Tomorrow is our last full day here. Our instructors will be leaving us in the afternoon to travel to Number Three Commando where they will repeat the training. I am sure we would all like to thank the three of them; we have learned much from them." The muted applause spoke volumes. "Tomorrow I want you all to bring your kitbags and equipment from your digs and place them at the back of the lecture hall."

I used my normal technique that night. I went down the lane and then went to the right rather than the left. No one was following me. That became obvious after a fifteen-minute wait. Had they given up? I was still suspicious and I took a really roundabout route back to the station. I was almost at the station when I smelled a cigarette. Joe smoked a pipe. I suddenly began to worry about Joe. These two were ruthless characters. They had shown me that when they had attacked Daddy and they had persistently tried to get me. This would be their last chance. Tomorrow they would be leaving and as the police were no closer to identifying them they had no reason to hold back. For Joe's sake, I had to act.

I reasoned that they were in the hedges behind the shed. They would be waiting for me to have my hands full with the padlock and then they would jump me. I went half a mile down the road and climbed the embankment down to the railway line. It was a risk but I knew that there was no train due until the ten forty-six from Gobowen. Joe had at least an hour and he would be in his office having a brew and catching up on his paperwork. I saw the two of them. Their attention was on the front of the station. I took in that they had iron bars with them. That explained the injuries Daddy had suffered. I had no weapon save my speed and Nev's sage advice.

I approached them silently. I would have been better with my rubber-soled shoes but I just made sure that I looked at where I was placing my feet before putting my weight on them. I needed them close before I alerted them. Nev had told me that surprise was a useful weapon. I intended to find that out. I was just five feet from them and I spoke, "Are you lads waiting for me?"

They both actually jumped as they turned and that tiny delay gave me my chance. I lifted my right leg and as Lowe tried to turn I rammed the heel of my boot at his knee. There was a crack and I saw the knee bend the wrong way. They called it pronation, my Mum had told me about it. Lowe collapsed in a heap but I was already dropping to my knees for I expected Horn to swing his iron bar at my head and he did. My move made him miss and he over swung. I hurled my shoulder into his midriff and his momentum carried him over my shoulder. He landed on the floor. I was on my feet and I stamped hard on the right hand which held the iron bar. There was a crack and he squealed with the pain. I used the thumb hold which, ironically, he had taught us and brought his left arm up behind his back.

Lowe was sobbing with the pain. I took out the German dagger I had taken. I placed it inside Horn's right ear. "Now I have a knife here. I could easily ram it into your ear and what passes for your brain. The express is due soon. I could drop your body on the line and then do the same with Lowe there. Nothing would remain of your bodies. Your deaths would be a mystery. Nod if you understand." He nodded, "Good. Now unlike you, I am an intelligent man and although I would not grieve over your loss I would prefer you to die in the service of the King. So I will let you both live. When I let you up you will take your friend here and go back to camp. If I were you I would tell a story of being jumped by the same men who jumped Daddy Grant. You would look very foolish if you admitted that a raw recruit took the two of you for I will have not a mark on me tomorrow."

I stood. "Get up slowly for I still have my knife."

His right hand was a mess. I must have broken every bone in it. Lowe was moaning. "The bastard broke my knee."

"I think you will find I merely cracked the patella. The pain you are feeling is the pain from the knee bending the wrong way. Help him up, Horn." I took the two iron bars. "You won't be needing these will you?" Lowe had to lean heavily on Horn. Even if they had wanted to there was no way that they could do harm to me now. I followed them out of the station. The road was still empty. I watched until they disappeared from view and then I went into the station. Joe was just pouring himself a cup of tea. "Cuppa Tom?"

"You must have read my mind, Joe!"

I thoroughly enjoyed my breakfast the next morning as I thought it might be my last. I had enjoyed the company of the three men who were both kind and funny. They reminded me of my Grandad.

When we reached the lecture hall Captain Foster had a strange expression on his face. He looked pointedly at me. Even Sean noticed, "The Captain is giving you a funny look. Have you been a bad boy?"

"Not that I know of." I hated lying to Sean but the less he knew the better. I could still be on charges for the fight. It could be construed as attacking a superior officer. If it came to that I would have to take my medicine.

"I am afraid that today only Sergeant Geraghty will be taking the last class. It seems that the two corporals were attacked by the same men who attacked Private Grant. Their injuries are not as serious but they will both be incapacitated for some time. We will have a shorter hand to hand session and I want you all back here." He pointed to the pile of kit bags at the back. "I will explain the reason for that when you return."

My squad was only interested in one thing. Even Sergeant Johnson was not immune from speculation. "It was you wasn't it? You were the one who gave them a good hiding."

I adopted my most innocent of looks. "Don't be stupid, Sergeant; how could I take on two hulking brutes like that." I pointed to my face. "Is there a mark on me? Do you think I could have inflicted injuries on those two and have nothing in return?"

"I suppose not. Still, I wonder who did it to them?" The fact that no one had seen the injuries meant that everyone had their own ideas.

Sean said, quietly, "I don't care what you say we both know it was you and I am not surprised you havna a mark on you. You are a tough sneaky bastard and I am bloody glad you are on our side."

The PTI Sergeant was in an even fouler mood than he had been when I had shown him up the first time. He set us off and, after a short exercise said, "Come here young man and I will show you how to throw someone much bigger than yourself, like me."

I went, I had no choice did I? I wondered if he would hurt me and pretend it was an accident. He told me and the others what he was going to do. He took out a Commando knife. I am going to sneak up on the Private. I will try to stab him in the ribs. Now Private what is your counter to that?"

"I will grab your hand holding the knife and I will pull you forward; at the same time I will thrust my buttocks backwards so that you fall over me."

"Good lad. Now we will not do this slow motion. We will do it in real time. This is our last exercise and we should make it as real as possible."

I smiled, "That suits me, Sergeant."

"Good now turn your back."

I had an idea about what he would try. He would hold his knife in his left hand rather than his right. I still don't know what told me that but I was ready. He was quick and, as the knife came up I grabbed his left arm and pulled but instead of using my buttocks, as he was expecting I stuck out my left leg. He tumbled over; as he had already said, he was a big man. As the wind was knocked from him I used the thumb grip and took the knife from him. I held it at his throat and allowed it to penetrate just enough to bloody the end. "You were right Sergeant, realism is the best form of training."

He hissed so that only I could hear, "You watch your back, Sonny Jim, because one day I am going to gut you like a fish."

I stood and held my hand out to help him up. As he came face to face with me I said, "Take your best shot but remember what happened to Muff and Chuff!"

Sergeant Dean raced up, "Well done, Private. You have done a grand job, Jack. You can be proud." I was not certain of the sincerity in Sergeant Dean's voice but his body was between us.

Sergeant Geraghty threw off my hand and stormed off without even acknowledging the officers. As he went Sergeant Dean said, "Son, you like living dangerously don't you?"

I smiled, "No one touches my mates and gets away with it."

He nodded, "Good."

My back was in danger of becoming black and blue as I took the plaudits of my comrades. I would be lying if I said I didn't enjoy it, I did. For the first time in my life, I was accepted because I was Tom Harsker, not because I was the son of a British hero. It felt good.

Chapter 16

Captain Foster had a wicked grin on his face as he stood before us. "You have all done well and we are now ready to begin our next phase of training. I am afraid it will not now be in Anglesey. Instead, it will be in Poole and we will be training with the Royal Navy. They, too, are part of the Special Service Brigade. That training will begin six days from now. However, we will not make it easy for you. You will have to make your own way there." I saw confident nods from many of the men. "But you will not be in uniform, nor will you have money. I want you all to strip down to your underwear. You may choose your own footwear but all else will go in your kitbags. They will await you in Poole."

We all looked at each other until Sergeant Dean began to strip and roared, "You heard the officer! Down to your skivvies unless you are shy!"

I actually smiled. I began to formulate my plan even as I undressed. I took off my boots and put on the rubber-soled shoes. Sean grumbled, "How the hell do we get to Poole from here? Where the hell is Poole?"

"It's on the south coast of Dorset about two hundred miles away."

"Bloody stupid if you ask me."

"It makes sense. If we can't operate in our own country without money then how will we do it in occupied France?"

"I suppose."

Captain Foster shouted for everyone was speaking, "There are some civilian clothes for you here. First come first served."

Everyone dived in and a battle royal ensued as everyone tried to get clothes which fitted. I was not bothered. When the frenzy had died down I took a pair of trousers, a shirt, a jumper and a jacket. The trousers were too short and the jacket too big but the shirt and jumper fitted. Lieutenant Reed laughed as he came towards us. We must have looked like circus clowns. "Lieutenant Reed has a simple map for you. It's the sort of map we might have if we were in Occupied France. For those of you who have not worked this out, this is a test for you. If you are picked up by the Military Police we will come and speak up for you but it means you will have failed and you may be returned to your own unit. Regard every uniform as an enemy." He paused. "Do you all have a map?" We chorused, "Sir, yes sir!"

"Then I will wait for you all by the Motor Torpedo Boat number twenty-three which will be waiting in Poole harbour. That is your objective. View it as an assignment in a hostile area and you will do well. Good luck gentlemen."

Everyone ran out of the mess hall. I walked. I had a plan. As I passed the Captain he said, "As cool as ever Harsker."

"We have six days and I estimate it will need about thirty miles a day. It should be possible but I have a feeling, sir, that you haven't told us everything and there will be a few surprises."

"And you would be right. Oh, by the way, Private Grant is too injured to be part of this exercise. He will be waiting for you all in Poole. I thought you should know."

"Thank you, sir." That made me feel much better.

When I reached the station I went to the shed and took out the bike. I had most of my plan worked out but not all. Joe had just checked the tickets from the Chester train. "Well Joe, I am leaving soon."

"I'll miss you and so will the lads. You have been a good chap to talk with."

"I have a favour to ask," I explained our task.

"That sounds difficult."

"It is. I am going to use my bike but I have a feeling that they will be looking for us close to here. Is there any chance you could get me a lift in the Guard's van of a train. Just to Wolverhampton or one of the stations further south."

He grinned, "It would be my pleasure." He looked at his watch. There is a Wolverhampton train due in about half an hour. Just enough time for you to have a bite to eat."

"No thanks, Joe, I have just eaten but I will make some sandwiches. I guess I will be hungrier tomorrow. I'll just go and check the bike and then make the sandwiches." I had a few things I had left at the shed. There was a pocket knife, my compass and a lighter. I put them in the small bag on the bike which had the tool kit inside. I took off the trousers and the jacket. I was wearing my PE shorts over my underwear. I intended to pretend to be a long-distance cyclist.

After I had made my sandwiches I put them in an old shopping bag I had found. By putting my arms through the handles it would be like a rucksack. Joe had a usable water skin which had been left in the lost property. I filled it with water and put that in the shopping bag. I was ready. When the train arrived Joe went to the Guard and had a word with him. I was waved over. "Right son, get your bike in yon Guard's van."

I shook old Joe's hand, "You are a pal!"

"And you have made me feel twenty years younger. Take care of yourself."

I seated myself on a wicker hamper amidst parcels and boxes. The train chugged out of the station and I was on my way.

It was mid-afternoon when I reached Wolverhampton. A busy town, it was the perfect place for me to disappear. I guessed that the Captain would have tried to catch people closer to Oswestry. Joe's friend got me through the ticket barrier; he said I was his nephew. Once outside the station I sat on the bike and pedalled. There were many other cyclists; admittedly few of them were wearing shorts but I did not attract any undue attention. I headed south. Hardly any of the roads had signs and I would have to rely on my compass and my own sense of direction. Even though I was already hungry I knew that I had to husband my meagre resources until I could replenish them.

I stopped after an hour. That was for two reasons: I was hot and needed to strip down to my vest and shorts, secondly, I was not used to the narrow saddle on the bike. I walked for half an hour and drank a little water. I had the salt we had been given and I added a little to the water to help with my dehydration. I knew that the train had saved me many miles. I rode through Kidderminster and Worcester. Night was falling and I did not want to risk being run down by a car or a lorry at night. I had no lights. I pulled over shortly after I had passed through a village called Bredon. I walked along a small lane and found a small lake or reservoir. I could not tell which. There were some trees where the ground rose a little to the south-east and I hid my bike there and then went down to the water. I stripped off and bathed. The cool waters helped my aching rear.

I towelled myself dry with the shirt and dressed. I was able to drink the contents of the water skin. I could refill it from the lake. I ate two of my precious sandwiches. I had six left. I could have four the next day and that would leave me two. After that… I had looked at the map while there was still light and, with the train and my cycling, I thought I had covered at least eighty miles. That was fifty more than I had estimated I might travel. It would leave me with about a hundred miles to ride. So long as the bike held up I would be able to make it in another two days. If I pushed it then I might be able to make it in one. However, as I had discovered during the retreat, one did not count chickens.

I had a good internal clock and I was awake by five. After filling my water skin and eating one of the sandwiches I set off. My rear was tender and it was agony to sit on the saddle. I found myself standing to ride, especially on the uphill sections. I made good time. I did see vehicles and meet people but the people just waved and the cars carried on their way. I did not see any uniforms. I knew that the Home Guard, the recently formed LDV would patrol at night but not during the day.

I was becoming confident and that is always a mistake. I was contemplating pushing on to Winchester which would leave me with a last day hopefully of just forty or so miles when I picked up a puncture. I was not far from Andover and the village of Penton Mewsey. I needed water to affect a repair. I saw the land, towards the village dip away. I took a chance that there would be a stream of some description there. I wheeled the bike across the rutted fields and found the stream. Luckily the puncture was on the front wheel and I soon had the inner tube out.

It did not take long to find the hole and, after I had repaired it I let the glue set. I knew from experience that if I pumped the tyre up too quickly I might undo my good work. I lay back on the grass and looked at the sky.

"Now then son, what are you doing on my land?"

I jumped up. My overconfidence had dulled my senses. I jumped to my feet. There was a farmer with a shotgun, broken, in the crook of his arm. "Sorry sir, I had a puncture and I was repairing it." I pointed to the inner tube."

"Ah. Is it done then?"

"It is. I will pump it up now and then be on my way."

"No hurry son but we are all a bit suspicious now what with Herr Hitler threatening to send paratroopers over." I replaced the inner tube and the tyre and began to pump. "How is it you aren't in the forces? You look like a fit young man."

I smiled. This was where I would have to pretend I was behind enemy lines and lie. "I am on my way to Dorset sir. I want to join up there."

I saw his face break into a smile. "And you are cycling all that way. Well done lad. Where have you come from?"

"I left Wolverhampton two days ago."

"You have done well. Where did you sleep last night?"

"Under some trees."

"And what did you eat?"

I had just fitted the wheel and tightened the bolts. I took out the last two sandwiches. "I had these."

He shook his head, "Come with me to the farmhouse. It would be a poor show if I let you spend another night in the open besides," he pointed to the sky, "it's going to rain cats and dogs tonight."

I was going to decline his offer and then I realised that I could not reach Poole any quicker even if I rode another twenty miles or so. I would be there tomorrow no matter what happened. "Thank you very much, sir."

Bert and his wife Edith turned out to be two lovely people. Their three sons had all joined up in 1939. One was in the navy, one was in the RAF and the last was in the army, based in Iceland. It explained his suspicions. I ate well. The farmer had been shooting and he had a brace of bunnies. Rationing did not affect them and we had their own potatoes and carrots in a stew with homemade bread. Bert's scrumpy had a kick to it and I slept that night, soundly, in a soft bed.

As I waved goodbye I felt more confident about winning this war. With solid folk like Bert and Edith, the backbone of England, Hitler stood no chance. He had underestimated the resilience of the British people. We might be alone but we were not cowed.

Gone were my cardboard sandwiches. I had freshly made ones with homemade cheese and cured ham. They gave added energy to my legs. My rear had hardened somewhat and I found cycling easier. As I hurtled along the back lanes of Hampshire and Dorset I was able to give thought to the traps the Captain would have set. He had told us to avoid the military. If I just turned up at the harbour I would find, I had no doubt, Military Police and soldiers. I worked out that I would arrive in the late afternoon. I would have more than enough time to scout out the MTB. Caution would be my watchword.

I was lucky in my approach. There was a roadblock on the main road, the A354. I saw it from the top of a small rise. I dismounted and pretended to check my tyres. It afforded me the opportunity of finding another way in. A small lane went to the east and looked to twist and turn away into the distance. I rode down it. I found a crossroads but the sign had been removed. I took the turn to the south. I found myself in the suburbs of Poole. I followed the road, which became a little wider until I reached the enormous harbour that was Poole. There were two old men fishing. They nodded at me. "Nice bike, son."

"Thanks." I laid it down and walked over to them. "This is a big harbour."

"Biggest and best harbour in the whole country. That's why the Navy uses it." He pointed to four ships: a destroyer a minesweeper and two frigates. "And out there, just t'other side of Brownsea Island are another few ships. Aye, we are safe from the Nazis here." He spat after he had said the word.

"Well, I'll be off. Good luck with the fishing." As I left I realised that this would not be as easy as I had thought. Captain Foster had been clever. The harbour had so many ships it would be like finding a needle in a haystack. There could be a flotilla of MTBs and I might not see them. I rode along the road which went around the harbour. I rode east first so that I could see beyond Brownsea Island. The fishermen had been correct. There were more warships there. They were all too big. It then struck me; the smaller boats could use some of the narrower and shallower parts of the harbour. They would not be in the deep water anchorages. I turned and rode west. I spied a channel just beyond where I had met the fishermen. I waved at them as I passed.

The roads were crowded as those who worked in the port were heading home. I joined those who were on their own bicycles and I became invisible. As we headed towards the A35 I saw, to my left in the shallow waters, four MTBs and two landing craft. They were moored fifty yards from the harbour. There was a small jetty and I saw Captain Foster standing there with half a dozen soldiers. I rode straight past him; he was no more than twenty feet from me but he just saw cyclists going home from work. I rode until we reached the main road and then I stopped.

I dismounted and wheeled my bike back along the road until I found a slipway. I walked my bike down to the water and I waited. I finished off my sandwiches and my water as I formulated my plan. I had a good view of the MTB I had to reach. I could also see the jetty. I smiled when I saw Sergeant Dean reach the Captain. I was close enough to see his smile turn to a frown when the Captain shook his head. As I had thought the captain was being devious. He wanted us to use our minds. He had told us to get aboard the MTB. Sergeant Dean had failed and would not be a happy man.

I made sure that I could identify the MTB before darkness fell. I slipped off my shoes and left them with the bike. I slipped into the chilly waters and swam out into the harbour. I wanted to approach the boat, MTB 23, from the seaward side. I saw the glow of the cigarettes from the ratings who were seated on the bridge. Although no lights showed from within the boat I could hear the other crew within her. She was anchored fore and aft. I used the stern as the best approach as I would be hidden by the 20 mm Oerlikon gun there. It was not as easy as I had expected to pull myself up the transom. I was helped by a passing guard boat a hundred yards into the harbour. The wake made the stern of the MTB rise and fall and I clambered aboard unseen. I crept along the port side. There was a sudden flash of light from below decks and I heard a voice say. "You lads keep a sharp look out!"

"Yes sir, quiet as a grave tonight."

I rose to my feet and said, "Private Harsker of A troop Number 4 Commando reporting for duty sir, as ordered!"

A torch lit up my dripping face and the officer began to laugh, "Well I'll be damned. And where have you come from, Private?"

I smiled, "I couldn't possible say, sir. But you can have my serial number if you like."

"Your Captain said that you were all a resourceful lot. Signal the shore and tell them that one of their birds has landed."

One of the ratings took an Aldis lamp and began to flash to the shore. The cold hit me and I began to shiver. "Able Seaman Leslie, go and get the private a blanket."

"Righto, sir. How about a cup of cocoa too eh?"

"Good idea, see if you can give him a tot of rum too."

"That's right sir, stoker's cocoa."

The Lieutenant held out a packet of cigarettes, "Smoke?"

"No sir, I don't."

The seaman called Leslie appeared with a blanket in one hand and three mugs in the other. "Here y'are. I brought us one each too sir."

"You are a good man, Leslie. Get back on watch now. I dare say they will send a boat."

The rating with the Aldis lamp moaned, "Well thanks a lot, Bill. You could have brought me one too."

"I'm not an octopus am I?"

"Really, Private, how did you get from Oswestry to here without being seen and so quickly?"

"I came by bike."

"You rode all the way?"

"Almost. It wasn't that hard sir."

"But your officer said you had neither money nor food."

"That's right."

He shook his head, "You are a new breed, Private. I look forward to working with you." He waved his arm at the boats. "We are in the same unit; Combined Operations."

I swallowed the hot rum-infused cocoa and felt it fill me with warmth. By the time the rubber dingy bumped into our side, I had finished it. Captain Foster's voice said, "Who is it then? Which one managed to reach the objective?"

I looked down and saw Sergeant Dean and Captain Foster, "Private Harsker sir."

"I might have known. Come on get into the dingy!"

I handed back the mug and the blanket. "Thank you for your hospitality, sir and I look forward to working with your men too. Especially if the cocoa is a regular feature of our association!"

Chapter 17

There was a small outboard motor on the rubber boat. The Sergeant steered. "Well come on then Harsker; tell me how you did it?"

"I cycled."

"Where did you get the bike from?"

"Someone had dumped it on the railway line and I repaired it."

"And how did you get out of Oswestry? I had men guarding all the main roads."

"But not the railway lines sir."

"Well, you have the right spirit. You are the only one so far who has made the boat."

"I thought so sir when I saw Sergeant Dean being captured."

I heard the Sergeant laugh in the dark, "Well sir it looks like the lectures worked. At least one of them listened to what we said."

When we landed I said, "Sir, could I go and get my bike and my shoes?"

"Of course." He pointed to the warehouse next to the harbour wall. "Your gear is in there and the ones who didn't make the boat."

I returned with the bike. I didn't know what I would do with it but I had grown attached to it. I wheeled it inside. Once through the blackout curtain, I heard a cheer as I stepped into the light. There were twenty of the lads there, including Daddy Grant. He laughed, "Look at him. Ten stone soaking wet and yet he manages to do the impossible and get to the boat. Here, Tom, get dressed. You are putting me off my supper!"

Sean and Percy were there too and they told me, as I dressed, how they had fared. They had gone together and hidden in various lorries. They had been overconfident too and were caught on the outskirts of Poole. Rather than resenting my success, they seemed to enjoy it. After supper, we sat at the trestle table and talked. Daddy had only just returned and Sean took great delight in telling him the story of the Corporals. "We reckon Tom here did for them but he is a secretive bugger."

"Well, they got what they deserved whoever did it to them. They were just thugs."

It took four more days for the rest of the men to arrive. Eight men were returned to their own units. They had been the ones who had either handed themselves in or had failed to get out of Shropshire. None were from our section. We then began training. We were working closely with the MTBs and LCAs. What we did not know was that on the day I had arrived in Poole Number 11 company had landed in Boulogne on a raid. It had been a fiasco. We discovered that in the middle of July when Admiral Keyes arrived to talk with the Captain. He watched us as we demonstrated landing on a beach from Landing Craft. He seemed impressed.

"Good, we have had a warning of what happens when men are rushed into action. You are doing the right thing here Foster. Training and discipline; they are key. Keep it up. By the way, do you have someone called Harsker?"

"Yes, Admiral. Harsker, front and centre."

"Sir!"

"You are Bill's son?"

"Yes, sir."

"He told me about you. He is very proud of you, you know."

"Yes sir and it is reciprocated. My father is a great man."

"He certainly is. How is he doing Captain Foster?"

"He managed to get from Oswestry to here and boarded an MTB without being seen, sir. I think that says it all."

The Admiral nodded and waved as he left us. Sean said, "Hobnobbing with Admirals eh?"

"I'll talk to anyone Sean, even Scotsmen!"

We began even more serious training in the last week of July. We went down to Lulworth Cove where we did a night landing and a night assault up the cliffs. That was where we had our first death. Private Bentine was startled by a roosting gull, lost his grip on the rope and fell to his death on the rocks below. It made us all more determined to do things right. We practised getting aboard the MTBs and landing craft as well as getting off. We even practised blindfold too.

In the middle of August, we were assembled by Captain Foster and Sergeant Dean. Lieutenant Commander Trimble who commanded the naval section was also there. "Right lads, I know you are all heartily sick of training and many of you have been itching for action. Well, it begins today." Although no one said a word, we had learned to remain silent, you could almost feel the buzz around the room.

We will go from here and board LCA 525, MTB 23 and MTB 18. We will be sailing to a location on the east coast. Sergeant Johnson your section will be aboard MTB 23 and Sergeant Pike yours will be on MTB 18. The rest will be aboard the LCA. Get your gear and move smartly and quietly."

We followed Sergeant Johnson outside. The boats were next to the dock. I saw Lieutenant Herd who commanded 23 and he smiled when he saw me.

"Aye, lads watch your wallets, the Army is here!"

I recognised the voice as Bill Leslie. I had seen him a few times on our exercises. Sean said, "Just what we needed, the Navy, rum, bum and baccy!"

"Stow it, McKinley! A bloke who wears a kilt should keep his gob shut!"

It was the normal good-natured banter between services. Dad had told me it existed in the Great War too. What we did not know was this would be the start of a very close relationship between the two services. By the end of the war, we were almost as one. The bosun stood with his hands on his hips. "Right lads stow your gear in the mess. It's a bit crowded down there. I should come back on deck when we get underway but for God's sake keep out of the way."

We ducked beneath the narrow entrance leading to the crew area. The mess was a table big enough for barely six yet I knew that the MTB had a crew of at least ten. The bosun was right. Once the kit bags and guns were stored there was little room for anything else. It was claustrophobic and I was glad to get back on deck. The LCA took longer to load but eventually, it was ready. We led the way followed by the LCA and then the other MTB.

The crew were all at their stations. The bosun steered the ship and Lieutenant Herd leaned against the side of the bridge. Able Seaman Leslie stood by the bosun. The three guns' crews were all closed up. The Oerlikon at the stern had a crew of two while the two Vickers also had a crew of two; that was not normal. I learned later that some of the crew doubled up and the Vickers usually had just one gunner while the others worked the torpedo tubes or the depth charges.

As soon as we reached deeper waters we noticed the motion of the boat. The Lieutenant smiled as Percy ran to the stern to throw up. "Sorry about this, lads. We have to go the speed of the LCA and that makes the motion more likely to induce nausea. Keep your eye on the horizon and you should be all right."

After an hour the Bosun said, "Righto Leslie, go and make a brew. Take one of these lads to give you a hand. They might as well earn their berth."

He nodded to me, "Come on Tom. I'll show you around."

The galley was tiny; it was barely big enough for one man let alone two. He handed me a huge teapot. "I hope your lads have mugs."

"We came prepared, Bill, we have our own mess tins."

"Good. There's a tea caddy in there. I reckon ten scoops should do it. I'll get the kettle on."

After I had put the tea in the pot he nodded to the cupboard to my left. "Open a tin of milk will you; just the one. We are a bit short of sugar too."

"Have you not tried condensed milk? It sweetens naturally."

"We'll try that. Mind you I have no idea when we will be near stores again. If we had known we were going out we would have stocked up."

"You didn't know then?"

"Not until five minutes before you lot arrived."

"Typical eh?" While we waited for the kettle to boil he filled his pipe. "I thought you smoked cigarettes?"

"I smoke owt but the baccy ration is better and I use a little bit of my rum ration to soak into it. It makes it last longer that way." He got it going and asked, "Did you join the Commandos directly or were you in the army before?"

"I was in the BEF. 1st Loyal Lancashires."

"Well, it's a small world. My cousin was in that lot. George Hogan, did you know him?"

"I did. He was in my section. I was there the day he bought it."

There was little to say other than that. He nodded, "He lived next door to me in St. Helens."

"I know St. Helens, my grandfather lived in Burscough."

"That's a nice part of the world. St. Helens is a bit grim by comparison. Anyroad up George was an only child. Poor Auntie Lizzie has no one. Now me, I am one of eight. If one of us goes there are replacements!" He put his pipe down, "Eh up, kettle's boiled." We poured the water on the tea and let it brew for a minute or two. "It won't be sergeant-major style but we have to watch the tea. Nowt worse than running out when you are sea!" We poured the milk into the teapot. "Grab the sugar and them mugs and I'll carry the pot. Watch your footing up there. If you lose any of the lads' cups they'll have your guts for garters."

He was right about the motion. The confined galley had protected us from the worst of the movement.

"Tea up lads! You Commandos better get your mugs out. Your oppo has the sugar."

I handed the mugs to the sailors and then waited for Bill to pour their tea. Finally, I took the sugar around. I notice that the sailors all took less than a spoonful. When I went around our lads I said, "They don't have much sugar lads so don't be greedy. We are their guests."

I was lucky I did not take sugar in my tea and what you never had you never miss. The Bosun said, "Right, Leslie, you take a turn at the wheel!"

Bill handed me the pot and juggled his tea so that he could steer. The pot was empty and I took it back into the galley.

The voyage was going well until the Lieutenant said, "Gun crews keep a close watch." Sergeant Johnson threw a quizzical look the officer's way. The Lieutenant pointed to the sky. "Aeroplanes. Normally they are bombing airfields or London but sometimes they have bombs left and we make an inviting target. At least we have the LCA this time. That normally draws fire like flies!"

Sergeant Johnson nodded. "Well we won't be much good; we just have Thompsons."

Half an hour later we saw a flight of German aeroplanes heading east. Having heard the Lieutenant's warning we were all a little nervous. We had our life jackets on but we were more than a mile from the coast. Fortunately, we were spared a strafing run. As we headed north through the Straits of Dover it became even tenser. We knew that less than twenty miles away was a huge army just waiting for their air force to clear the skies so that they could invade.

Sergeant Johnson asked, "Any idea where we are going, sir?"

The Lieutenant pointed north. "Harwich and you will find that much more dangerous than Poole. We'll be there in a couple of hours."

We did not have a couple of hours. The port gunner suddenly shouted, "E-Boats!"

The bosun came running back. "Right Leslie. I'll take over!"

The Lieutenant shouted, "Action stations! Sergeant, you might get your Thompsons. These E-Boats have a big crew and they are as fast as…"

"Right lads, get your guns and your tin lids!"

Even as we were arming ourselves the MTB was heeling to starboard as we steered for the E-Boats. There were six of them and they seemed to dwarf us. I cocked my gun. There was little point in firing until they were much closer. I had a thousand questions in my head for this was a first. I concentrated on the leading E-Boat. The two heavy guns on the E-Boat began to pound out. The Bosun was weaving our boat from side to side. We were a smaller target. Our Oerlikon could not be brought to bear for it was at the stern. I had no idea how the two Vickers were coping.

Suddenly the Bosun threw the boat to port. The Oerlikon gunner must have anticipated the move for he began to fire. I almost cheered when the shells stitched a line across the hull of the leading German. The captain of the Schnellboote took evasive action.
"Well done, bosun!"
We had turned our stern to the chasing E-Boats. The manoeuvre had been very clever. One E-boat had been taken out of the equation and we now had our biggest gun able to bear.
"If you Commandos want to fire now is your chance! This bugger will come like a bat out of hell!"
Sergeant Johnson shouted, "Let's show Jerry that we are Commandos. On my command..."
The E-Boats were so fast that they began to overhaul us. The fire from the Oerlikon gun made them swerve but, even so, they came closer and closer.
"Fire!" Ten Thompson submachine guns all fired at once. The range was less than a hundred feet and the cone of fire enveloped both the German boat's main gun and the bridge. I saw two of the gun crew fall and, as the boat veered to port, I saw some of those on the bridge duck. I had no idea what the LCA and the other MTB were doing. It took all my effort to cling on to the MTB. Then I heard the unmistakable sound of Brownings as a flight of Spitfires roared overhead and sprayed the E-boats. The one we had hit was hit repeatedly as the twenty-four machine guns tore into the hull. It began to sink into the sea and the crew hurled themselves overboard. The three Spitfires climbed and then dived to attack the fleeing E-Boats. They had briefly held the advantage but the Bosun's decision had given us the edge.
The Lieutenant shouted, "Any wounded?"
The lack of a reply meant that we had escaped and we all cheered. We turned west and headed for Harwich. Our bubble and euphoria burst when we reached the safety of the port. The E-boats had claimed casualties. Two Commandos and two sailors on the other MTB and LCA had been killed and another four Commandos wounded. We landed in a more sombre mood than in the moment of victory.
We marched ashore to the meeting hall which had been requisitioned for us. We trudged in with our kitbags aware that some of the men we had trained with were now dead. We had been lucky. "Right lads, find yourself a corner. We will get some food on the go and then there will be a briefing."
Sergeant Dean had been on the LCA and his battledress was still showered with the blood of dead Commandos. I began to strip and clean

my Thompson. This was the first time we had fired them in anger and they had worked well. I guessed that we would be in action soon and I wanted to be prepared.

After a basic meal of corned beef and bread, the Captain briefed us, "Tomorrow we strike our first blow on Mainland Europe. We will be landed on the Belgian coast and we will attack and destroy one of their newly built radar stations. They are called Freyas." A slide was shown with a picture of what looked like a Heath Robinson device. "We will leave tomorrow afternoon and reach Belgium after dark. We will land and Number One and Number Two sections will secure the beachhead. The rest of us will destroy the installation and try to capture a prisoner. The explosive expert in each company will draw the necessary explosives before we depart. All Sergeants will meet with me now and I will issue the maps. The Quartermaster will issue ammunition and explosive." He paused. "The raids in Norway and Guernsey have shown that the helmet does not help. We will not be using them. Just wear your beret. I want every Commando to have at least four Mills bombs. Get a goodnight's rest for tomorrow night we will be in action."

I was the explosives expert in our section and I went to collect my charges. I was issued with five pounds of TNT, two primers and four feet of safety fuse. It meant that we had four sets of explosives. If even two of us were killed then we could still complete the mission. It was a sobering thought that my death had been predicted and catered for.

Sean sat next to me. "Aren't you worried about carrying that TNT?"

"So long as there is no fuse it is as safe as houses."

"But if a bullet hits it then it might set it off."

I laughed, "And as you are the bloke going in with me you will know about it as soon as I do. Stop worrying. The Germans will not be expecting us. Besides if it is our time to die there is nothing we can do about it."

"You are a cheery sod."

I shrugged, "I am a realist."

We all had the luxury of a lie-in but I was awake and up by eight. I could not lie in bed. We began to prepare for the raid. And then, at twelve, the mission was postponed. "What's up, Sarge?"

"The Germans have just launched a massive air raid on Dover. The top brass reckon it is too risky to go tonight. We go tomorrow instead."

I did not like it. We were all ready to go. I could not see what difference a raid on Dover meant. Then I remembered Dad. He had told me that there was always a bigger picture. We were but a tiny cog in this huge machine. I lay back on my blanket and tried to relax. There was little point in getting upset. We would go when we would go. I had already said to Sean that if it was our time then we could not fight it. I idly wondered how Willy was getting on. Thinking about my death had made me think about Nev and the others who had fallen. Nev had come through so much and yet he had died. Willy had been unscathed and he was busy training. Anything could happen. Percy had told us of one of the men he had trained with who had lost a hand due to a faulty fuse on a Mills Bomb. We were soldiers and we knew the risks. With that happy thought, I fell asleep.

We boarded the MTBs and LCA in the late afternoon. We had no kitbags this time and I placed the demolition charges and their fuses under the table in the mess. We set off after six. It was still light but we expected to approach the French coast just after dark. We were going to land between Dunkirk and Calais. The photographs we had seen indicated that the Freya would just be a mile or so inland. When Sean had asked why the RAF could not destroy it he was told that it had been disguised. It meant we had an idea where it was but we would still have to find it. We were all acutely aware of the failures which the Commandos had experienced. Guernsey and Boulogne had been disasters. If it had not been for the Norwegian raid and Churchill's support then I suspect we would have been disbanded and sent back to our parent units. As darkness fell the three ships moved a little quicker towards the shore. It was a little choppy but the cloudy skies made the blackness complete.

We had covered up our faces and hands already. We wanted nothing white to show. Lieutenant Reed, who was with us aboard the MTB, said, "Get your gear."

I went below and put on the rucksack with the charges. I left my Thompson on board. I would need both hands for the demolition. If I had to use a gun I would rely on the Browning. The shadow of the coastline appeared. A month or two earlier and this had been thronged with the remains of the BEF. It was now, we hoped, empty. The LCA lowered its ramp and the others raced ashore. We had to jump into the surf and wade. I was lucky, it only came up to my waist. Some of the smaller men spluttered their way ashore. Everything was done with hand signals. Sean had been assigned as my guard and we followed Corporal White and Sergeant Johnson. Each section would make their own way to where we thought the target was. Behind us came Lieutenant Reed and the rest of the section.

We struggled to the top of a dune and halted while the Sergeant peered into the dark. The sand made everything look the same. We headed east and a large black shape appeared before us. It was a building and it was just a hundred yards away. It did not look like the photograph of Freya that we had seen. It appeared to be a small hotel.

Sergeant Johnson waved his arm and the rest of the section ran forward to cover the building. Once they had overtaken us we moved forward. I took out my Browning. The dunes had finished and I realised that we were running on sand which covered concrete. Had we been wearing our boots then it would have made a noise. The rubber-soled shoes were silent. The first of our section had reached the walls of the building. The other sections were moving around the side when there was a sudden flash, an explosion and screams. The night was then lit by the flashes of guns and the sound of shots. We had been spotted. This was not the time to panic. We had to keep going and complete our part of the mission.

Sean and I kept close to the wall. As we ran I slipped and steadied myself against the wall. It was hollow and it was wooden. Turning the corner I realised that it was a façade. Four men were down. We ignored them. Each section had its own medically trained Commandos. Two Germans loomed out of the dark, next to us. They were as surprised as we were. Having a handgun I was able to react faster than Sean. I fired six bullets at point-blank range and both men fell. Sean fired four rounds into each body to make sure they were dead and then we stepped through the door through which the Germans had come. There, ahead of us was the Freya. They had cleverly hidden the radar behind what looked like a hotel. It was now time for me to do my job. There might be other demolition Commandos but I was the first one there. I took out the TNT and placed it below the metal framework and on top of the metal box. I placed the fuse and looked for Lieutenant Reed. Our primers were simple timers and were set for five minutes. I had to wait for orders. The Lieutenant arrived, "Charges all ready?"

"Yes sir but it would be better if one of the other lads with charges put his under the metal box. It would do more damage."

He shook his head, "We haven't time." Just then we heard the sound of a heavy German machine gun. He shouted, "Everybody back to the beach! Blow it, Harsker!"

They all raced out leaving just Sean and myself. "Stand clear!" I primed the charge and I ran. As we emerged I saw a German half-track with a heavy machine gun and he was firing at the departing Commandos. I took out a grenade as Sean fired the rest of his clip at the gunner. The German ducked as the bullets came at him. He was swinging the gun around when the grenade went off. Although it exploded twenty yards from him shrapnel flew through the air. I heard the shouts as the grenade did its work. I thumped Sean on the back. "Just run, we have three minutes left!"

We turned the corner of the façade and we ran towards the beach. I could see Lieutenant Reed waving us on and then I felt myself thrown forward as the explosives were detonated. The concussion knocked me to the ground and then I was rained upon by sand and debris. I stood groggily and grabbed Sean's arm. He was lying face down in the sand. There was no point in shouting; he would have been as deafened as I was. We ran to the bow of the MTB which was already backing away from the beach. Hands reached out and hauled the two of us to land, unceremoniously, on the wooden deck. I looked up and saw the sergeant's face. He shook his head and began to laugh. He pulled me up and led me back to the safety of the bridge. The Germans had now set up machine guns on the beach. Thankfully the darkness soon hid us and the Germans fired blindly. We had completed our first mission. We did not know if it had been a success.

Chapter 18

As dawn broke behind us we saw the coast in the west. A flight of Hawker Hurricanes was overhead like an aerial umbrella. E-Boats would not surprise us this time. There had been desultory talk on the journey home. Lieutenant Reed had spent the trip speaking with Lieutenant Herd. I was lost in my thoughts. I had expected better things. We had trained well and I thought that we were a good team and yet there had been chaos. Only one set of charges had been laid rather than the four which should have been. And we had been surprised. Perhaps I had expected too much.

We trudged back to the meeting hall. I saw the bodies being carried from the LCA and I waited for them to pass us. The dead needed respect. There was a pot of steaming tea waiting for us and a pile of buttered toast. The local Woman's Institute, whose hall we used, had taken matters into their own hands. We were their guests whether we wished to be or not. Their smiling faces forced smiles on ours and stopped conversations about the raids.

I sat with the rest of the section and drank the tea. "You lads will need to get your digs sorted out today." Sergeant Johnson waved vaguely towards the town.

Percy waved a piece of toast around the hall. "Aren't we staying here?"

"We only used it temporary like. We will be here for at least a month, maybe more. The ladies will need to use it too."

It made sense to me. We were closer to enemy territory; it would be a good base to raid the French and Belgium coasts. However, that also put us close to them and their raids.

The officers were the last to enter and, after they had a mug in their hands the Captain said, "You did well last night chaps. If any of you have ordinance left in your bags take them to the Sergeant Dean and he will return them. You need to get your digs sorted out; get your heads down and we will meet back here at seven in the morning. We will have a proper debrief then when it is more private."

It seemed an anti-climax. I had used all of my explosives. I saw the other three as they handed their bags to Sergeant Dean. He glanced over at me and nodded. It was enough. Sean and Daddy tagged along behind me as we headed for the town. There were holes in rows of terraces and piles of rubble showing where German bombers had been. The billets here would be more dangerous than those in Oswestry.

"How did you two lads get digs in Shropshire?"

"We asked in the town if there was anyone who had a room to spare."

"There are three of us. Why don't we see if there is a house we can rent."

"Suits me."

We headed for the High Street. Although there were some boarded up buildings most seemed open for business. We were lucky; the second letting agent we tried had a property. "It's close to the docks I am afraid but I have a building with four rooms. It was the office of a German shipping line. They were interned and it has been empty ever since. There are no beds but it has a kitchen and even an inside toilet." I could see that impressed Sean. "The proximity of the docks makes it unpopular. I can do you, lads, a good price."

"We will take it for a month. We may need it longer but we will let you know." We paid him a deposit and then he took us down to it. It was perfectly placed. We could actually see our ships and the hall. After he left us we assessed what we would need. There were no curtains and no beds. The beds we could do without but not the curtains. We split up to forage and scavenge.

I headed for the part of town which still had smoke rising from the fires lit by the bombers who had made a nightly visit. It looked like they had hit a row of terraces. The ARP wardens and the fire brigade were still damping it down. I spied a couple of mattresses which had been blown from the buildings. They looked damp but serviceable. The chief warden saw my approach, "It's too dangerous to be here, Private. Some of these walls could fall at any time."

I pointed to the mattresses. "Are they going spare?"

He looked surprised, "They are wet and smoke damaged. We were going to dump them."

I smiled, "Then I will do you a favour and dump them for you."

"Be my guest."

I carried the first one back and laid it in the yard at the back of the offices. The yard faced south and the sun would dry it. I returned for the second. The kitchen was a smart one. The Germans had obviously liked their comfort. They had left in a hurry and there was a kettle, a couple of pans and even a coffee pot. It would double as a teapot. Their cups and plates were also undamaged. Sean and Daddy Grant arrived back with the curtains and they too had a mattress. This was not old and it was not wet. That meant we had three mattresses and curtains too. We soon had the blackout curtains in place. We used a hammer and nails to put them in position permanently. We would not win any home design competitions but it was functional.

"Well lads, we have a little home from home here. All we need is a couple of lamps for when the gas is out and we are well sorted."

I nodded, "I am going to get my head down now." I took my kit bag upstairs and laid my greatcoat on the floor. I piled my clothes neatly to the side. As soon as I lay down I was asleep.

We arrived at the meeting hall just after Sergeant Dean, "You lads were quick."

Sean proudly pointed to the office which was clearly visible. "We got handy digs."

"Good. You can help me sort out the room." We placed the chairs so that they all faced the small dais. "Harsker, see if you can find an easel or something." I went into the back rooms and found two of them. I brought them back out. "Stick them at the front. The Captain has aerial photographs of the damage we caused."

Soon the hall was full and we sat ready to be briefed. The Captain pinned up the photographs on the easels. "As you can see we did disable the Freya but I am afraid we did not destroy it. The antennae were destroyed but the metal box looks to be in one piece. Only one charge was laid. That is disappointing. However, I must take some responsibility for not securing our perimeter. We were surprised by the half-track and that will not happen again. We have learned lessons from this."

Lieutenant Reed stood, "We are going to practise today. We will be raiding again and soon. Obviously, we need to do it away from prying eyes. We are going on a ten-mile run. There is an old barracks building ten miles from town. It was damaged in the early days of the war and has yet to be repaired. It is perfect for what we require." He pinned up a piece of paper. "Here are the map coordinates." Grinning, he said, "We will see you there eh?"

We were on more familiar territory as each section humped bags and guns and began to trot out to the west. The good burghers looked up in surprise as fifty-odd men jogged through their town. I suppose to them it was as though we were running away. When we reached it I could see why they had not repaired the barracks. It had been almost totally destroyed. There were but three or four complete walls. The craters which proliferated would take bulldozers to fill them. However, it suited us. We were here to train and not to live.

We were the second section to arrive. We knew that the others all liked to beat us. We were known as the lucky section. We had not lost any of our men and we had had the greatest success thus far. Corporal White said, "Don't worry lads; we'll show them on the way back. Let them have their moment of glory. It will be brief!"

We spent the day using the damaged buildings to hone our techniques. It was a perfect place to practise; it was military and we were not under observation. We took it in turns to be the German guards and then the Commandos attacking. Both were good exercises. When I was a German guard it enabled me to see a raid through their eyes.

At the end of the sessions, the Captain gathered us together. "The Germans have begun to shell Dover from France. They are using heavy guns which can fire over twenty-five miles. The RAF is trying to find them. If possible they will bomb them and end the danger. However, if they cannot do so then we will be sent in to do the job. That means we might have to be in Occupied Europe for a day. We will spend tomorrow with the maps of the likely areas and become familiar with them." He pointed at me. "Private Harsker was in the area after the retreat. I, for one, will be picking his brains over this one."

Lieutenant Reed rubbed his hands, "Back to the meeting room. The Women's Institute has promised us tea and cakes!"

We were not as fit as we had been and some of the men were suffering on the way back. I saw an impatient Sergeant Dean noting those who straggled in some time after the rest of us. Daddy Grant, who had only recently recovered from the beating, was well ahead of some of them. Even in an elite force like the Commandos, there was a disparity in the ability of some of the men.

Once again we worked behind closed doors. We had many maps and photographs of the region. Captain Foster arrived an hour after we had started examining the maps. He had been briefed by senior officers. "It seems that the Germans have four guns and they are built-in new concrete emplacements. The RAF is sending Wellington Bombers in tomorrow to try to destroy them. There is one fifteen-inch gun south of Gris Nez and three eleven-inch guns at Gris Nez itself."

Lieutenant Reed asked, "Were you in that area, Harsker?"

"Yes, sir. There are cliffs there. Further south, towards Boulogne itself there are a few sandy coves and then there are some closer to Calais but Gris Nez is like the White Cliffs of Dover. The beaches and sand dunes are a mile or so away from the headland."

Captain Foster nodded, "That marries up with what we have seen on the aerial photographs. I am planning, if we have to go, on taking just two sections: Sergeant Johnson's and Sergeant Green's. I will lead one and Lieutenant Reed the second. These missions will require stealth and not numbers. I think one of the problems we had with Freya was too many cooks. I want those two sections to familiarise themselves with the terrain. The other four sections can come up with a plan to disrupt the railway guns. They are further inland. At the moment they are a nuisance but they could become a larger problem in the future.."

We discovered that the Captain would be leading our section. Sergeant Johnson said, "I am not sure we would need to spend too long over there, sir. They look to me to be on the coast. We nip in and nip out again."

"That is the plan but the MTBs cannot hang around. The Germans have radar there. We have to have a contingency plan in case they are delayed in getting back to us."

My heart sank. I had been lucky enough to escape once; a second time might be asking too much. The three of us went back to our digs. Daddy was an observant man. "You are worried about something aren't you, Tom?"

"We know that there are thousands of German troops in Boulogne and in camps behind the coast. It is an invasion army. It isn't as though they are a few tired old guards. If they find out we are there then they will be all over us like fleas on a dog. When I escaped the last time there were just a handful of Germans and even then we nearly didn't make it."

We locked the front door behind us. "Then we shall have to make sure they don't find us. I think that is why the Captain is just taking one section. This is one objective which has more chance of success with a tiny number of men and our section is the best."

The Wimpey bombers did not damage the concrete structures. We saw the aerial photographs and their bombs had pockmarked the grass and the land around them but the bombs had not been big enough and they hadn't even scratched the concrete. The barrels were still there and the guns were still firing. The two teams were separated from the rest so that we could share ideas. Lieutenant Commander Trimble joined us.

"The MTBs can drop you easily enough but you are quite right, Captain Foster, they cannot hang around. How long would it take you to do the job?"

"We would have to assume an hour, perhaps longer to reach the guns. Then we would have to overcome the guards and lay the charges."

"Sir, the moment we take out the guards then we will be on the clock. How can we damage the guns?"

"TNT in the breech block." They all looked at me. "It wouldn't have to be a big charge and a gun cannot fire if there is no breech block. We can delay their pursuit by laying booby traps." I nodded to the Captain, "They worked in the Low Countries, sir. It would buy us time to escape."

He nodded and said to the Lieutenant Commander, "Three hours, possibly four, that would be the time we needed."

"I can get Lieutenant Herd to return after three hours. It might be possible to hang around for a wee while if things are quiet." He paused, "If they are not then we cannot risk an MTB. You might be stuck there and that would mean, for the duration."

"I know. We will just have to get in and out silently then." The next two hours were spent in detailed planning. One of the unusual things about Commandos was that we were all involved in the planning process. When I had been in the 1st Loyals I just followed orders. When we became separated we were lost. That would not happen with the Commandos. The Captain was keen for us to share our ideas and to know what the overall plan would be. He knew we could find ourselves isolated. I showed all of the others how to rig booby traps using Mills Bombs. We had all had the same training on explosives but my background in engineering meant that they deferred to me in that area of expertise. All of the others could rig the TNT if anything happened to me. And this time I would need my Thompson machine gun. With just eleven of us, we needed every man and every gun we could take.

The RAF tried a second raid with the same results. That night we heard the sound of many German aeroplanes overhead. The air raid siren had gone but we had deigned the shelters. If it was our time then so be it. As it happened they carried on west. We later found out that the Germans had begun to bomb London. It was the beginning of what was termed the Blitz. The Germans would bomb London day and night for the next few weeks in an attempt to cow the capital into surrender. It would not work. The next day we were given our orders. Sergeant Johnson came in and he was beaming, "It is on. We go tonight. Get your gear aboard the MTB!"

We hurried down to the boat. Above us, more German aeroplanes were seen heading west. The port's anti-aircraft guns popped away at them. It seemed inconceivable that they could miss such a massed target but miss they did. Not one German aeroplane had to turn back.

As we lay in the sun waiting to leave, Corporal White said, "I reckon the Germans could come over any time. These big guns can defend the straits and make it impossible for our ships to sail between the Channel and the North Sea. If they stop our navy then we are lost."

Bill had his pipe going and he shook his head, "The Navy is here, Corp and we will stop them. We sank the Bismarck didn't we?"

"Aye but it took our biggest, best and newest ships to do that and we still lost the Hood. They have the Scharnhorst, Gneisenau not to mention the Bismarck's sister ship the Tirpitz."

"Oh, ye of little faith."

"Anyway, what I am saying is that our little effort here is important."

"I agree with you there Corporal. I wonder why your officer isn't taking more men?"

Daddy threw his cigarette stub over the side. "They would get in the way. If Tom here hadn't placed his charge the last time then we would have failed. There were three other sets of explosives but there were just too many men. Everyone thought everyone else was doing it. This way we are a tight team. I know your Navy is reliable well this section is too. We will get the job done."

"I hope so because those guns are making that part of the Channel into Hellfire Corner! It isn't safe for anyone."

As the afternoon drew on we set sail. This time we waited below decks as Captain Foster had more information to give us. "The Germans are building more of these emplacements. If we have time we are to find out where they are. Perhaps the bombers can do something while they are being constructed. Lieutenant Reed and his men will take the single gun and they should have time to search to the north. With three guns to deal with we may be pushed for time."

Once again we heard the drone of German aeroplanes as they continued to pound London into submission.

"Right lads black up."

The MTB's engines were slowed down to almost an idle and we knew that we were getting close to the French coast. "Lights out."

We turned off the lights so that our eyes would become accustomed to the dark and we would not give away our position when we went on deck. After five minutes the hatch opened and the bosun said, "Right sir, get your lads on deck. We are here. All ashore that's going ashore!"

Lieutenant Herd hissed, "Bosun!"

"Sorry, sir."

The tide times had been calculated and we were taken in by the tide. The barely throbbing engines just kept our way. Sean leapt into the water followed by the Sergeant and the Corporal. I was the fourth man to brave the choppy sea. I pushed against the surf and then dropped to one knee as soon as I reached the sand. I had the Thompson levelled in case of danger. We had landed just four hundred yards from the cliffs.

To our left was Wissant. Although we were on the opposite side of the port from the one where we had stolen the boat I recognised the land. I looked at the cape and saw that it would have been too difficult to scale. The inland route was safer. As we waited for the others to land I wondered why there were no beach defences. There was not even any barbed wire. Perhaps Herr Hitler thought it was unnecessary and that we were a beaten people. He was wrong.

Daddy tapped me on the back as he came past me and I ran after him, tapping Sean on the way. There were a number of deserted buildings on the shore. They had been part of the seaside attractions in happier days. One looked to be a bar while the other an ice cream parlour. We used them for cover. I turned, with my back to the former bar, and I could barely make out the MTB which was backing out to sea. We were on our own now. Just then I heard voices and I waved to the others. We scrambled around to the side of the bar. I took out my knife. If we used our guns then the mission would have failed before we had even started.

They were Germans, "Sepp, you are hearing things! Oberlieutenant Manstein will not be happy that we have left our post."

"I tell you I heard an engine!"

"And where is it?" I suddenly realised that our footprints were clearly visible in the wet sand. If they looked down our goose would be cooked. The two Germans walked towards the sea and the incoming tide. "Shit! Now I have wet trousers! Back to the guard hut, you idiot."

I heard their voices recede. Their voices were dimmed for the sound of the surf masked them. Percy slithered around to the end of the bar and then waved us forward. We had been lucky. We could have been seen. Although we could have taken out the two Germans sentries, the guns and their crews were just a few hundred yards away and the gunfire would have alerted them. We saw a flicker of light as they opened the door of the hut they were using as a guard room. It was at the end of the road which led to the beach. We ran silently past the hut. Our rubber-soled shoes made no sound on the sand-covered road.

Percy darted through the gap in the fence and we entered the field which lay below the cliff. The ground rose steadily and steeply up to the cliff. We could now see the glistening barbed wire which they had placed on the landward side of their gun emplacement. There must have been a barrier of some sort on the side of the emplacement which met the road but we had to cross the fields and negotiate the barbed wire. I hoped that it was not mined. The first two men used their wire clippers and took out a section of barbed wire ten feet across. It seemed to take forever and yet I know that it was moments only. It took four of us to shift it. We could not afford any noise at all.

We knew that the guns were ahead but the aerial photographs had not given us any idea of the other buildings. They had been well camouflaged. We moved cautiously. Sean tapped me on the shoulder and pointed to the cliff. There was a machine-gun post and I guessed sentries within. It was less than fifty yards from us and we could not risk them turning. Captain Foster pointed to Sean, Percy and Daddy. He pointed to the machine gun and drew his hand across his throat. They put their Thompsons down and moved towards the machine gun. It was tempting to watch them but we had to identify where the barracks was. There would be up to forty men operating the three guns and we could not afford a firefight. My eyes had adjusted to the dark and I saw the prefabricated barracks building. Suddenly there was a flash of light as one of the Germans came out. Their blackout curtains soon covered the light. I heard the sound of water and I knew what was happening. He could not be bothered to go to the toilet and was relieving himself outside. There was a brief flash of light again and then we heard the door slam. Percy and the others joined us and nodded. When I glanced over at the machine gun post I could still see the Germans. They had been killed and left in position. To a casual observer, they would appear to be on guard still.

Having identified the barracks and eliminated the clifftop threat we headed to the cliff. There had to be an entrance to the gun there. We moved quickly. Harold and Dick formed a rearguard to watch our backs Suddenly the first huge concrete gun emplacement was before us. There were two of them. One had one gun and the other two. We saw the massive barrels peeping out. Sean and I ran ahead and reached the concrete bunker while the others watched for danger. We moved to the rear of the emplacement. There was a metal door. We knew that it was a new structure and I hoped that the door would open smoothly.

I held the door and nodded to Sean. I flung it open and he raced inside. It was pitch black which I took to be a good sign. It meant that it was unoccupied. The only danger would be if someone was asleep within. We moved through the racks which were stacked with shells. Then I saw the two guns. They were huge. I left Sean to wave the others in. They would keep watch while I did my job. I took off my Bergen and began to take out the charges. I had four. I placed one in each of the two breeches and put the Cordtex and Safety fuse in the TNT. The timers were new ones. They looked like a rather large watch. They were battery operated. I hoped they worked as well here as they had during training. I did not attach the wires. That would be the last job I would do.

I tapped Daddy on the shoulder and he followed me back out of the emplacement. Sergeant Johnson and Percy were in the second emplacement. Here there was just one gun. I put the charge and fuses in the breech. Leaving the three of them I went back to the Captain. He would decide when we were to explode them. We had been in Occupied France for an hour and a half so far. It would take half an hour to return to the beach. We did not want to be waiting there when the guns were destroyed.

I nodded to the Captain. And we waited. While I waited I put my last charge next to the shells. That filled some time and then I joined the others and I watched the hands on my luminous dial move slowly around. Sean and the Captain were close to the shells. I went to the breech. We could not speak and we dared not move around too much. If a shell was knocked to the ground in the dark then it would be a disaster. We pressed as far back into the shadows as we could. It proved to be a wise move for the door suddenly opened and I heard a German voice, "Who is in here?"

I realised that there were two shadows. I heard a gun being cocked. "It is me, Sepp. Oberlieutenant Manstein thought he left his binoculars in here. Come and help me look."

I heard the German laugh, "You should have brought a torch, you idiot."

"I thought there was one in here but I can't find it."

The other German laughed, "It is in the locker under the barrel of the gun. I will show you."

The two sentries came towards me but they were both dead within five paces. The Captain and Sean saw to that. Their knives were sharp and we were well trained. We did not have the luxury now of time. The Captain held both his hands up three times, thirty minutes. It was the work of a moment to attach the timer and set them. I did the one by the shells and then returned to the single gun. As the four of us left the emplacement I estimated that we would be on the beach when the guns went off and the MTB would be twenty minutes away.

We had to move cautiously around the barracks and it took time to move the barbed wire back into place. I was acutely aware of the passage of time. We needed to be on the beach when the guns went off. We also had to move silently when we neared the beach. More German sentries might be on patrol. The tide was still high and we did not have as much beach. We waited. I gripped my Thompson tightly. I might have to use it in anger for the first time since we had fired on the E-Boat. The Captain also had a watch with a fluorescent dial. He kept glancing at it. Although the timers we had used were accurate I knew that, as I had set them in the dark, there was a risk that I could be out a minute or two either way.

The Captain waved us to our knees. Nothing happened. Every eye turned to me. Had I done something wrong? Had they discovered the charges and defused them? Suddenly there was a crump from above us. The cliffs hid the guns from us but a column of fire leapt out into the dark. A moment later there were another three crumps and then an explosion which announced that my charges had ignited the shells. We heard cracks and explosions as shells went off. Corporal White took out his Aldis lamp and began to flash out to sea. Lieutenant Herd had to have seen the explosion, surely he would be on his way to pick us up.

Two German sentries rushed from their hut. They must have seen the light of the lamp for they fired three hurried shots at the shape on the beach. Four Thompson machine guns barked and they retreated back up the hill. There was no need for silence any longer. "Well chaps, it's up to the Navy now. Just use short bursts."

I took out two Mills bombs and laid them next to me. In the dark, they were better weapons to use as they were invisible. The Germans, who I assumed would be racing from their barracks, would see our muzzle flashes. Explosions were still going off above us and I could hear whistles and shouts. They were coming. The Corporal shouted, "Sir, the MTB. It is on its way."

"Move back to the surf but keep watching Jerry!"

I didn't move immediately. It was a mistake, albeit a necessary one, for we could be seen against the sea. I saw the muzzle flashes from the Germans who were now at the end of the road. I heard a cry. They had hit one of us and then I heard the throb of the MTB and heard the reassuring chatter of the two Vickers. I picked up one of my two grenades and drew the pin from one of them. I hurled it as far to my right as I could and then repeated with the other. The second one I threw to the left. I turned and ran. My feet splashed in the sea and then I heard the two grenades as they went off in quick succession. I could not resist turning around and I saw the Germans had taken cover. They had, however, set up a heavy machine gun. I found myself up to my waist in the water but the bow of the MTB was just ahead. The heavy machine clattered away and I saw a line of holes stitched in the plywood hull of the boat. The Bosun shouted, "Get a bloody move on!"

Hands reached down and hauled me up. As I landed on the deck I heard Captain Foster shout, "That's it! Let's go."

Those of us at the bow emptied out magazines at the shore. I had no idea if we hit anything but having been on the receiving end of such fire I knew that it made people keep their heads down. As Lieutenant Herd threw the MTB around the Oerlikon began to pump out its shells. I lay on my back and closed my eyes. We had made it. I lay still for quite a while as the MTB put space between us and danger. I had no doubt that E-Boats would be scrambled from Wissant and Boulogne and they were much faster than we were.

Sergeant Johnson shouted. "Right lads, to the stern and keep a watch out for Jerry."

As I rose I noticed that there was a body covered in a blanket and Harry was being helped to the mess. I pulled back the blanket. It was Dick. We had lost our first man. I reloaded my Thomson and nestled next to the depth charges. Daddy was next to me. "That was bloody close!"

I nodded, "You are telling me. At least the explosives detonated."

He ruffled my head, "And none of us doubted it for a moment."

"How is Harry?"

"Dunno, the Corporal is with him. Shame about Dick. He was a nice bloke."

There was no more to say. Unlike the men I had lost in the retreat here, I would be able to talk with the others about his loss. And we would know where he would lie. The 1st Loyal Lancashires lay spread around Belgium and Northern France.

We raced across the dark Channel and I began to believe we had escaped until Bill Leslie shouted, "E-boats to starboard. Two of them and they are coming fast!"

We lay flat across the canting deck of the careering MTB. Lieutenant Herd turned slightly to port to take us away from their course. I glanced astern and saw the faint glow that heralded the dawn. There was no point looking to the west, it was too dark to see where the land lay. Our change of course also meant that the two E-Boats had to follow in line astern. Only one of them would be able to bring their guns to bear. The powerful diesels of the E-boats were steadily gaining on us. It was fortunate for us that it was a flat calm. Had there been waves of any sort then the Germans would have closed with us even faster.

Suddenly I heard the Bosun shout. "Leslie, go to the stern and be ready to release two depth charges on my command! Shallow settings."

Bill came by and I saw that he was grinning. "Never a dull moment eh, Tom!"

I saw him take a spanner and adjust the fuse on the depth charge. He then took four cork floatation devices from the locker close by and tied two of them to each of the charges. He saw my look. "It stops them from sinking too fast. Don't want our arses blowing off do we?"

The seaman was almost thrown from his feet as the MTB was hurled to starboard. The young lieutenant was doing all that he could to throw off the aim of the German gunners. After a minute or two on that course, he reverted to his original. The gunner on the leading E-Boat began to fire. He was using tracer and we watched it arc towards us. It missed but we knew he would be adjusting his aim. Our gunner waited for another heartbeat or two and then the cannon began to pump out shells. It made a reassuring sound as round after round was sent astern. We began to slow slightly and I wondered if there was something wrong. The leading E-boat almost leapt towards us.

"Release! Now!"

Bill let one depth charge go and then the second. "Depth charges away!"

Even as he spoke the Lieutenant gave full power and we surged ahead like a greyhound. Behind me, just forty feet from our stern twin geysers of water erupted in two huge columns. They were less than forty feet from the leading E-Boat and he swerved to starboard to avoid them. His consort had to do the same and we began to edge away. The ruse had bought us time but it had not saved us.

Bill ran back to his post on the bridge. The Oerlikon gunner took the opportunity of firing at them when they were beam on to us. The two E-Boats turned back to port and surged after us. The gunner was either lucky or good. His shells struck the hull of the leading E-Boat. It slowed slightly and the second E-Boat took the lead. The hit had bought us a few more minutes and every minute took us closer to England.

Astern of us I could see definite light as dawn broke. The second E-boat's guns began to fire. I felt the MTB judder as the shells hit the hull. It was now only a matter of time. Suddenly two more geysers of water erupted in front of the E-boat. I wondered how. Bill had only released two depth charges. The two E-boats turned as four more geysers erupted. Daddy was grinning and pointing west. There was a frigate and an armed trawler; they had opened fire and it was their fall of shell I saw. I could see the coastline ahead. We had made it. And then the engine stopped. The last shells from the E-boat had found their target.

The two coastal defence vessels fired another few rounds and then turned to come alongside us. The captain of the frigate shouted, "Do you need a tow?"

"Yes, please. A timely arrival!"

"Lucky there were just two of the buggers though, what?"

We were towed in to Southend on Sea. Captain Foster said, "Right lads, let's get ashore. The MTB will have to stay here for repairs I am afraid."

We carried Dick's body ashore and Harry was able to walk. He had taken a couple of bullets to the shoulder. He would be out of action for a while. I nodded to Bill as I stepped from the boat. "Take care."

"And you!"

A pair of medical orderlies raced over to us with a stretcher. Harry snapped, "I don't need that.," he pointed to the blanket-covered body. "Take my oppo though."

"You go with them, Golightly. You did well." He smiled at us all, "You all did well. Sergeant, take charge while I go and get some transport arranged."

The others all lit up. I noticed that the place bristled with guns. One of the gunners on the nearest battery warned, "You lads better put your tin lids on. The Germans have some new guns across there in France. They'll be laying a few eggs soon!"

We just laughed. I think they thought that we were mad. We knew that there were three guns which would not fire again; at least not until they had been either replaced or repaired.

Chapter 19

We sat in the back of the lorry. Captain Foster had refused the offer of a seat in the cab to stay with us in the back. "What did you say to that Jerry, Harsker, when we were in the emplacement?"

"He asked who I was and I said I was looking for an officer's binoculars. He believed me."

"That was quick thinking." He turned to the sergeant, "I think your section deserves some leave, Sergeant Johnson. When we get back have Sergeant Dean give each man a seven-day furlough."

"Right sir!"

"Thank you, sir."

"It will give us the chance to assess the success of this raid." He lit another cigarette. "I hope Mister Reed had the same success as we had."

An hour and a half later, as we pulled into the dock area we saw that the other MTB had also been damaged. It was with a sense of dread that we entered the meeting hall. The ladies had a pot of tea ready and were spreading what passed for margarine on to thin grey bread. Sergeant Dean came out of the back. He said, quietly to the Captain, "I am afraid Lieutenant Reed ran into a spot of bother. He and his lads were spotted before they reached the gun. Just three of them made it back and the MTB was damaged. He went to the hospital with the two wounded men." He seemed pleased to see us. "How did you get on sir?"

"We got the guns but we lost Kirton. Have leave chits made out for this section Sergeant, they deserve it." He shook his head, "Besides it seems we only have one landing craft now. We have had a bit of a setback."

"No sir, we haven't. You were trying to get rid of four guns. You got rid of three of them. In my book that is a success."

"Perhaps." He turned to us. "Leave your weapons here with the sergeant and enjoy your leave."

We lined up to receive our travel warrants and leave chits. All of us would have to go through London. That was a daunting prospect. The newspapers had been filled for days with news of fires raging all night and daily bombing raids by the Luftwaffe. We would be in as much danger in our own capital as we had been in France. It would be worth the danger to see our families. The last time I had seen Mum had been before the war. I had been a different person then.

We shared a third-class compartment. We had to wait just outside London for an hour while the track ahead was cleared. I could see teams working to repair rails. There were sandbagged anti-aircraft guns every half mile or so. When we disgorged it was into a city filled with broken buildings and cratered roads which was wreathed in smoke and smelled of death. It was like stepping into Dante's Inferno. Dazed people were staggering around, some of them clutching bags with what looked like the last of their possessions. I had seen this in France when the Stukas had bombed the refugees. It was hard to bear in my own capital city. The all-clear must have sounded some time before we reached the metropolis for people were busy clearing the streets.

"See you, lads."

Sean shook his head, "By the time I get home it will be time to come back again." He began to sing, "North of the border, down Glasgow way!" We all shook hands and went our separate ways.

I went in search of a working telephone box. It was not as easy as I had hoped. When I eventually found one and got through it was Mary who answered. I heard a squeal of delight which almost burst my eardrum, "It's Tom! Where are you?"

Before I could answer my mother's voice spoke as she came on the line, "Go and watch that pan, Mary, hello Tom."

"I have a leave. I am on my way home."

"Where are you now?"

"London."

I heard the catch in her voice as she said, "Is it bad there?"

"Yes Mum, it is a mess. I am glad that you and Mary are safe. I'll see you when I see you."

It was late afternoon by the time I managed to reach home. Navigating across London was a nightmare and the trains had to negotiate damage left by bombers who had released their bombs short of their targets. This was even more worrying than I had thought. Disruption was everywhere. In the old days, I would have got a taxi from the station but they were a peacetime luxury. I walked. It was just four miles. During the walk, I had the time to reflect that Mum and Dad had done the right thing to buy a place of their own. If Mum and Mary lived on an airbase as we had done for many years, then they would be in as much danger as I was.

Mum was waiting at the front door. She threw her arms around me and began crying. I had only seen her crying at funerals. I held her tightly, "It's all right Mum. I'm safe and I am home." Mary threw her arms around me and she, too, began to cry. "Anyone would think I was wounded or something!"

Mum held me at arm's length. "Don't even joke about that! It is a year since we saw you!" She began to recover and she dragged me inside. "Let's have a look at you." She frowned, "You are so thin! Don't they feed you?"

"They feed us, fine Mum. I have put weight on since I joined up."

"Well, I have done you a nice rabbit stew. I used the meat ration already but Mr Jones shot a couple of bunnies and he let me have one. Your sister here is a dab hand at growing veg too."

I looked at my little sister. She was rapidly becoming a woman. "Well done our kid! Grandad would have been proud of you. I'll just get washed up."

I went to the bathroom and stripped to the waist. There was, thankfully, hot water; Mum must have put the immersion heater on for me. Her voice came up the stairs, "You can have a bath if you want?"

"I'll have one after supper. I am starving."

When I got downstairs there was a steaming casserole in the middle of the table. I could not help the smile which went from ear to ear. "This is great, Mum."

She smiled, "I know your Gran did a good one, let's see how mine compares eh?"

It was just as good. After dinner, we sat and they asked me what it was like in the Commandos. "I thought you would have come home after Dunkirk. Your father rang and said he had seen you."

"I know, Mum, but Captain Foster wanted me to join and… well… you know…"

She laughed, "I do, you are just like your father! It is exactly what he would have done."

"Is he still in London then? I haven't had a letter from him for a while."

Her face darkened, "He is in the Middle East. Egypt I think or Crete, I can't be sure. All very secret. I thought we had finished with all of that after the Great War. Your father did his bit then."

"But he is Dad. That is the way he is."

She shook her head and she and Mary began to clear the table. "War to end all wars! Politicians! If they had to fight then I am certain we would have no more wars." That was the signal to talk of other things. She told of Auntie Alice and her war work. Mary was just about to finish school and she was planning on going to University too. It was harder for a girl to get to University but my little sister was heavily influenced by Auntie Alice and she knew her own mind.

Surprisingly enough I found it hard to adjust to the peace of the family home. The war seemed remote. Each night we listened to the radio and heard about the continuing raids in London and around the fighter bases and airfields. Once or twice the airfields nearby were bombed and we took shelter in the Anderson Shelter but the base was over five miles away. We seemed to be cocooned by trees and ripening crops. Flights of Hurricanes and Spitfires flew overhead each day but we were safe. I was grateful for my mother's sake. She had endured the Great War in London. She had had to suffer raids by Zeppelins and Gothas. It was not perfectly safe here but it was considerably safer than living in London or on an airbase. On September the third we realised that we had been at war for a whole year, yet there was no cause for celebration. We were in the darkest of hours. Mr Churchill's speech about fighting on the beaches was even more apposite now. In my case, it was a time for remembrance and all those I had lost in Belgium. They had slowed down the enemy advance. The Matildas had been sacrificed so that we could get an army back to England. Now we needed time. Our only allies were the Commonwealth. This was not the Great War; we were alone.

When it was time to leave I could see the pain on Mum's face. They had used their rations to make me a fruit cake. She had even used some whisky to soak the fruit. Dad would have called it a sacrilege. She had put it in an old biscuit tin. "This will keep for months. If you eke it out then you will have some left for Christmas." She hugged me, "Do you think you will be home for Christmas?" She shook her head and reprimanded herself, "Beattie Harsker, have you no sense?" She clasped me to her tightly, "You take care of yourself and don't try to be the hero. I want you to survive this war. I want you and Mary and your Dad to be safe. I want grandchildren. Remember that."

I felt myself filling up. I nodded and hugged Mary. I whispered in her ear, "Watch out for Mum eh?"

She nodded and I saw tears in her eyes, "I am proud of you, our Tom. Be safe." I looked over my shoulder as I headed down the lane and they stood waving in the doorway.

I walked to the station with leaden legs. You never missed what you never had. I had had a year without family. I had been home for a week and they filled both my head and my heart. I had to store them in a little room for I was going back to war.

Harwich had been bombed as had Felixstowe. All of the streets were filled with rubble. It was but a week since I had walked them and now it was as though a giant had torn through the town. Even the meeting hall had suffered some damage. I met Daddy, he was coming out of a tobacconist. I saw a pipe in his hand. "What happened to the cigarettes?"

"The wife reckoned I was smoking too much. I started coughing at night. I thought I'd try a pipe."

"How is the family?"

"Oh they are fine but they have had a few air raids too. I thought they would be safe up north but Jerry has taken this war everywhere. Her mam has come to live with us. Her dad died just a month ago. Heart attack. It's good for the wife. She has company now." He jammed the pipe in his battle dress and we headed towards our digs. "That's another reason I volunteered, the extra money comes in handy."

I realised how lucky I was. I didn't need to worry about money. We weren't rich but Dad was well paid and we had used some of the money Gran and Grandad had left him to buy the house. I knew now how fortunate I was. I tried to use my extra pay to help the lads out. It seemed fair somehow.

Sean was not yet back. I did not expect him until the last minute. We did not have to report until seven the next morning and so we went to the pub for a pint. We met Sergeant Dean there. He had an angry expression on his face and he was drinking alone; that was always a bad sign. However, when he saw us he brightened and came over. "Well lads, did you have a good leave?"

We both nodded. "I see the Germans raided here, did you and the other lads suffer Sergeant?"

"Not in the raid but…" He sat down, "You might as well know; Lieutenant Cole went over on your MTB and they went after the other gun. They found a minefield. Only two got back to the boat and the MTB was jumped in the Channel. The only survivors were your mate Bill Leslie and Lieutenant Herd. The Captain has gone to the depot to pick up the replacement Commandos. He'll be glad to see you two back. And when you turn up tomorrow you will see that half of the meeting hall has been blown up. There is still part of the roof left but I am afraid it all looks like it will fall down when the winter winds blow."

"I know Sergeant I saw the damage but in the dark, I couldn't see how severe it was."

"Well, we might well be homeless again!" He shook his head and then smiled, "Can I buy you, lads, a pint?"

"Yes Sergeant."

I enjoyed the evening. We chatted away to the Sergeant who now regarded us as veterans. We had come through much together and the bonds that were there were like those of a family. The losses just made us value the ones who still lived even more. The men of number four squad had trained with us at Oswestry. We had messed with them and we had laughed with them. It was probably just luck which had meant we survived and they did not. The sergeant was rueful. We discovered that the Germans had improved the beach defences; there were now mines and more wire. If we were to go back then it would not be as simple as it had been. Perhaps Hitler now knew he could not invade. Maybe he was shutting the stable door.

Sean awoke us at midnight as he blundered his way into the digs. His train had been held up north of London. The German air raids were now biting. He was also angry for the houses around his home had been destroyed. It was only by the grace of God that his family had been spared. "Bastard Germans! It's all very well killin' soldiers. We know what we are getting into but my ma is sixty!"

There was no point in telling him that we had bombed Germany too. He would not listen.

We reported to the hall with the rest of the squad the next morning. The Captain was not yet back. The hall was no longer suitable for the WI but we were used to hardships. Some engineers arrived later that morning to show us how to use pressure switches. It was a way of booby-trapping a large structure. The switch was attached to the explosives and when something touched the switch it sent an electrical impulse and the explosive would be detonated. It would be set off by the enemy themselves and meant we had more chance of escaping. We could not have used it on the guns but I knew there would be other structures where it would work perfectly. Lieutenant Reed was in command. Until the captain returned with our replacements then he would be the only officer. He insisted that everyone became competent with them.

"We can't leave it all to Harsker. What if he is down eh? Do we all toddle off home eh?"

We all smiled. He had a tendency to pronounce off as '*orf*'. He was posh but he was one of us. We had new explosives too. It was still TNT but this variant could be moulded. We could hide it better. We could do far more damage with our new weapons.

The Captain returned with twenty new men and two new officers two days later. He came with a grim face. "The Germans bombed East

London the other day. Over four hundred people died and fifteen hundred were injured." Those who had had no leave and were Londoners showed their anxiety. I was grateful, again, for the relative safety of my own family. Captain Foster also had some surprising news for us. "We will be moving out of Harwich, albeit temporarily. This structure has been deemed unsafe. We will be moving south, closer to Clacton. There is a manor house there and the owner, who has gone to Canada for the duration, has loaned it to the Army. We have it for the duration. I have acquired four lorries too. Get your stuff from your digs and be back here in an hour. We will be moving to our new home then."

Inevitably Sean grumbled, "I like our digs. I bet there is no pub close to this manor house."

"I am guessing that might be part of the reasoning, Sean. Take away a distraction."

"That's your trouble Tom; you don't have the thirst a Scotsman has!"

I smiled to myself when I saw the manor house. The officers and the sergeants would be comfortable but we would either have to be under canvas or in the rather dilapidated barn. As our lorry was the first to reach our new base Daddy and I decided to claim the barn. It would accommodate almost forty men but only twenty or so would have the shelter of a roof and two walls. We staked the best corner of it. We quickly organised it so that when the next lorries arrived we had our blankets laid out, kit bags stored and boundaries erected. Sean stood belligerently glowering at the other Commandos who looked enviously at it.

We were still supposed to fend for ourselves and so we set up our own kitchen. There was enough wood and trees around for fuel. Our only problem was getting food to cook. The manor house was close to a tiny village which had no shops. The nearest place was Clacton and that was almost deserted since the war had begun. It was a problem we would have to overcome.

One advantage we had was that we no longer had the ladies of the Women's Institute to worry about. Captain Foster gathered us together. Reg Dean had a big box and a grin on his face.

"Right lads gather around, Major Foster has some information to give out!"

Those of us who had been with Major Foster for some time gave a cheer. His promotion was good news. "Settle down! You don’t want to incur the wrath of your new Sergeant Major do you?" Again we cheered. Another promotion. We must have done something right.

Major Foster indulged us. "It seems we have done well. This part of Number Four Commando has a good reputation. The Sergeant Major will hand out your new green berets and your new shoulder insignia. You can sew them on later." He waved forward our two new Lieutenants. "This is Lieutenant Holmes and Lieutenant Fletcher. We now have four officers and with the replacements, we are up to our complement of eighty. However, we have lost non commissioned officers. Private Grant you are hereby promoted to Sergeant and Private Harsker to Corporal."

I was somewhat embarrassed at the cheers and applause I received. Although flattered I suddenly realised it would mean moving from my section. I wondered if I could refuse.

The Major continued, "I want to spend the next three days training. The new men and newly promoted officers will need to get to know their sections. Reveille will be at six in the morning. Until then get to know your surroundings and your new billets. We will be here for some time."

Sean and Percy almost knocked me over with their slaps on the back. "Bloody hell, you are going to give me orders! Who'd have believed it?"

"Sorry to disappoint you Sean but you already have a Corporal. I guess Daddy and I will be going with the new lads."

Sean's face fell, "But we are oppos!"

Daddy said, "We have to follow orders. They couldn't leave us with you lads. Too much familiarity. You will have to get yourself promoted."

Sergeant Major Dean waved us over. "I knew about this when we were in the pub the other day but I couldn't tell you. I think you are both sound appointments. You will take over the new lads in number eight squad." He handed us our new stripes.

Daddy nodded, "Do we need to know anything about any of them?"

He shook his head, "The Major handpicked them. They'll be sound as a pound believe you me."

"You two had better get your stuff in the manor house."

"Could we spend the last night with the lads, Sergeant Major?"

He smiled, "You know for a posh bloke you have some funny ways. Aye, of course, you can. But tomorrow you make that leap and you can never go back." He nodded to me, "Your dad knew that."

"I know, Sergeant Major."

We were ribbed, in a good-natured fashion, by the rest of the section. I knew they were pleased for us but, equally a little sad at our departure.

As Percy said, "With Dick's replacement and you two that means we have three new lads to break in."

Marty Murphy said, "Now I know why they had us all learning how to lay charges!"

I found it hard to sleep and I was awake by five. I silently packed my kitbag and took it to the manor. I carefully sewed my new badge and my stripes on to my battledress. I made sure that I was well presented. I was a corporal; Daddy, Sergeant Grant, and I had to set a standard for the others. I went back and made a pot of tea for Sean and the rest of the section. I buttered the shared loaf we had and spread it with the last of the homemade jam Mum had given to me. Daddy and I would have to get our new section organised. I wondered if the promotion was a poisoned chalice. Would I have been better off remaining a private?

Daddy was up before reveille too and he joined me with his mug. "Nice touch," he paused, "Corporal."

I smiled, "Thanks, Sergeant. This will take some getting used to."

"You will manage." We ate our share of the sandwiches and left the huge pile for the others.

We waited outside the manor house until the bugler came out and sounded reveille. Sergeant Major Dean nodded as he came out, "First things first; now that I am Sergeant Major we have a headquarters section. That should make it easier for all of us. This morning we take everyone on a ten-mile run. Push them; they are new lads and we want to see when they break." He handed Daddy a map. "This is the route we are taking. We leave with a five-minute gap between each section. The route is flat and it should not be too taxing." He leaned in, "Between the three of us I think we will be having another raid soon. The loss of the last one left a bad taste in the Major's mouth. So let's get the lads to a fighting peak again eh?"

We stood with arms behind our backs and legs spread as the troop assembled. Sergeant Major Dean roared, "Attention!"

Major Foster had his new insignia sewn on too. "This morning we will have a little run to warm us up. Hand to hand combat when we get back and then explosives training. We have some Engineers coming this morning to set something up for us. Sergeant Major Dean!"

"Number One Squad! Go!"

We knew that we had thirty-five minutes before we went off. We marched to our section. Daddy looked them up and down. "I am Sergeant Grant and this is Corporal Harsker. For the moment that is all, you need to know about us. We will find out your names when we get back. If you are clever then you will work out that the Major wants to know how good you are. If you are not clever then you are in for a rude awakening and soon. I will be leading this run. If anyone falls behind then Corporal Harsker here will have some interesting punishments lined up for you. Don't fall behind. Nor will you overtake me. Do not let these grey hairs fool you! I have earned every one of them!"

We turned as Sergeant Johnson led our old section out. The new boys stood out like sore thumbs. One ran next to Sean. My old oppo would not like that! We were the last squad to leave. At least we could not be overtaken. The section all looked the same to me. I couldn't have differentiated between any of them. We were all carrying our Bergens and Thompson machine guns. We all wore our helmets. Normally we would wear just comforters but the Major was making a point. Daddy set off at a steady pace. He was a good runner and I knew that he was letting them relax into the run before he increased the pace.

I saw that one of the lads in front of me was out of step. We were not marching but running was better if you were in time with the others. "Keep the same pace eh lads. Look at the ones in front."

"Sorry Corp."

"Don't worry, you will learn." I had discussed, with Daddy, what he wanted to do. I watched the eight men before me. "They are ready Sergeant!"

He began to lengthen his stride. It was the easiest way to increase the pace. I saw a couple of them as they struggled. "Open your legs and stride further." Soon we were all running just that little bit faster and I saw, ahead, Sergeant Ramsden's section. We were gaining on them. "Just keep the same pace lads and you will be fine."

Now that they were running faster they found it easier. As soon as we began to overtake the next section number seven squad tried to respond. They got into a tangle and two stumbled. I heard Corporal Harris shout, "You dozy buggers!"

Then we had passed them. I nodded to Sergeant Ramsden as we overtook them. He did not look happy. We were not on an out and back route. It was a circular. The flat ground meant it was hard to see beyond the next section. Soon, however, we began to catch them. Daddy raised his arm and I said, "Watch for the increase in pace." He dropped it and began to run faster. "Here we go again!"

This time we could not lengthen our stride anymore and we had to run a little faster. Daddy and I knew that there was no way we could make up thirty-five minutes but we hoped to improve our position as much as possible. The two new lieutenants were running with Sergeant Major

Dean and the Headquarters squad just behind number four section. They were our target.

We powered along the slightly downhill section and caught number six section unawares. We were now travelling as fast as was comfortable. We were like my Dad's Alvis. The only gear left was top gear and that would have to wait until we were within sight of the camp before we used it.

I glanced at my watch. By my reckoning, we had run four of the ten miles. Number five squad was struggling ahead of us. They too had a couple of new men and I saw that they were not running evenly. As we reached the halfway mark we overtook them. Ahead I could see Sergeant Dean and the officers. He would not be caught quite so easily. I could feel my chest aching and my shoulders were feeling the Bergen and the gun. Our new men would be finding it even harder and they all went up in my estimation for none of them had complained.

It was harder to reel in the officers and the Sergeant Major. We were gaining but it was not as obvious. I saw a couple of heads droop a little. "Come on lads, we are more than halfway home and won't it be a good feeling to beat the Sergeant Major, not to mention the officers."

I began to sing:

Kiss me goodnight, Sergeant-Major
Tuck me in my little wooden bed
We all love you, Sergeant-Major,
When we hear you bawling, "Show a leg!"
Don't forget to wake me in the morning
And bring me 'round a nice hot cup of tea
Kiss me goodnight Sergeant-Major
Sergeant-Major, be a mother to me
Kiss me goodnight, Sergeant-Major
Tuck me in my little wooden bed
We all love you, Sergeant-Major
Even when your neck grows rather red
Don't forget to wake me in the morning
And bring me 'round a nice hot cup of tea
Kiss me goodnight, Sergeant-Major
Sergeant-Major, be a mother to me

The rest of the section joined in at the second line. The singing, I soon discovered, helped with my breathing and I noticed that our pace began to pick up along with the rhythm of the song. I saw a sign for the Manor. It was an old wooden one and no one had thought to remove it.

It showed that we had one mile to go and our target was just a hundred yards ahead.

We had finished the song and Daddy shouted, "One more time!" This time, as we sang he increased the pace. We were approaching top gear. I could see the gap diminish step by step. As we overtook them I saw the officers struggling a little. The Major had made them run with the same equipment as we had and they were unused to it. The Sergeant Major could have matched us but he had to keep pace with the officers. I saw the entrance to the manor and number four section had just entered. I saw Sergeant Johnson and our old section. They were cheering and clapping us. We found extra speed in our legs when the applause started and we sailed through the entrance.

Daddy stopped and turned to face the section. He winked at me, "And next time we beat them all back!"

To our combined delight they all chorused, somewhat out of breath, "Yes Sergeant!"

Chapter 20

Our success was not done to show we were better than the rest but to make the new men feel part of the team. We had worked together and, as a result, had had success. Dad had told me that in the dark days of the Great War when he and his fellow pilots had been suffering from the Fokker Scourge of the Fokker monoplane even though they had been flying an inferior and slower aeroplane they had prevailed. They had done so because they had not fought as individuals but as a team. The fact that Dad shot down more German aeroplanes than anyone else was irrelevant. He would not have shot them down without the others and they all knew it.

After we had spent an hour or so with them, getting to know them, showing them the ropes about the new style camp life we left them and went to meet our new team, the officers, sergeants and corporals. The nod from Sean as we left the barn told us that our old section would keep an eye on the new lads. All of the beds in the manor house had been commandeered already, as had the bedrooms. That did not bother Daddy and me. There was a sitting room in the back of the house. We took the four cushions from the sofa and the armchair and made two beds which were as comfortable as a bed.

We discovered that there was a more formal cooking arrangement here than in our sections. We saw that it was our duty to wash and dry the pans after the meal. As with the section every man looked after his own mess tin and mug; even the officers. Here there were no servants as Dad had had in the Great War. There was no John to keep Major Foster looking smart. That was his own responsibility. The handful of officers ate in what had been the dining room. We ate in a crowded kitchen. It reminded me of the *'Big House'* in Burscough. Auntie Sarah had given me a tour once. There the servants had their own hierarchy she as a housekeeper, and Cedric, her husband, had been the senior servants and the others had deferred to them. Here it was the same and Reg Dean and Jack Johnson, as the longest-serving non-coms, were in charge.

We were made to feel welcome. "In here, lads, we are all the same, no rank." Reg waved his knife around, "Out there we keep the ranks. It is how we maintain discipline. We are a smaller team than in the regular army." He nodded towards Daddy and me. "You two will know that more than most." He put a forkful of food in his mouth and chewed. We all ate in a business-like way. The food had little to commend it save that it kept us alive and no more. We ate to live and not the other way around. "You two lads did well today."

Joe Ramsden laughed, "I couldn't believe when you sailed past us. How did you come up with that song?"

Daddy had finished and was lighting his pipe, "That was Tom here. It worked though."

"Aye, it did. Well young 'un, where did it come from?"

"I just remembered reading that when sailors, from the time of the Vikings to Nelson, were working, they found they worked better with a rhythm and a song. The slaves in the cotton fields of America worked better with a song." I shrugged, "It just came to me."

Reg had finished and he lit a cigarette up. "You are a clever lad and quick thinking. Jack told me about that gun emplacement when you pretended to be German."

"I am just lucky; Dad made me learn German and I could already speak French, I pick up languages quickly."

"It wasn't the language that saved the section, Tom, it was your quick thinking. Even Captain, Er Major Foster, couldn't think that quickly."

The senior sergeants gave us the secrets of command. Many of them I knew for Dad had told me but some were new. We also discovered the other side of command; the paperwork. It appeared to be an anathema to most of them. As we cleared the table and Daddy and I washed the pots and pans Reg said. "Major Foster gave me the nod today. We have another raid coming up. This time it will be something different. Keep the lads on their toes."

The Royal Engineers who arrived brought with them some damaged railway lines and railway sleepers. They made a two hundred yard length of railway line in the field. It was not particularly straight because the rails were bent but it would serve a purpose. We could blow it up. It only took them a morning and then they were off. I guessed what we would be doing with that. They also left rolls of barbed wire. Sergeant Major Dean gathered the sections around him. "As Sergeant Johnson's section discovered we have to contend with this stuff. Each section will be given thirty feet of barbed wire. We want you to use it to protect part of the perimeter."

Sean said, "Sarn't Major, where are the gloves and the tools?"

He grinned, "You have them already." Sean looked confused. "Your hands and whatever you have in your Bergen!"

It had sounded daunting but we had a lot of equipment. Our section looked to Daddy and me. "Open your Bergens and let's see what we have."

The new section spread what they had before them. Private Paul Poulson, we learned his nickname was Polly, said, "There's nowt here, Sergeant."

I held up the toggle rope. "What about this?" It was still not clear to them. I shook my head I held up the commando knife. "And this?" Daddy nodded to me. "Ford and Poulson bring your knives and your toggle ropes and come with me."

I led them to the wire. Jack Johnson's section had taken their length. "Right, the two of you use your two knives like a pair of scissors and cut the wire. If the knives are sharp enough it will work."

"Like scissors, Corp?"

"Yes. Work as a team."

They quickly worked out how to do it but it cost them a few cuts. They cut one end.

I pulled a pair of homemade wire cutters out of my battle dress. "Of course if you have made yourself a pair of these then it is even easier." I snipped the wire.

"That's cheating, Corporal.!

"No it isn't, Polly, it is called using my head. Now how can you use the toggle ropes to move the wire?"

This was easier and they managed to put one end through the loop and carry the wire back to the rest without injury. They looked pleased with themselves. We spent the morning placing the wire across an open part of the perimeter. Once we had them thinking then they soon adapted what they had. We had our brew when we had finished. The newly formed WVS helped out; each day four of them would come and make tea during the day.

We took our mugs and found a quiet corner of the camp. "The thing is, lads, that this isn't like fighting in a regular unit We will be behind enemy lines and we will only have what we carry. There are no stores to go and get something we need. Half the time we will not even know what we need. That's why Corporal Harsker here made those wire cutters. He is handy with his hands and he made smaller ones than those you might have used in your battalions. He has to carry them and we need to have as light a weight as we can." He began to fill his pipe, "Show them what you carry, Corporal."

I laid out my treasures: my wire cutters, penknife, my pull cord torch, flint, cigarette lighter and finally, my Luger. Ken Curtis pointed to the pull cord torch, "What's that Corp?"

"It is a torch which works by pulling this cord. It illuminates the light for a few minutes. If you want the light for longer you keep pulling the cord. This one is from the Great War. They have wind up ones now but I managed to get this one from one of my Uncles who fought in the war."

"Why the flint Corporal? You have a lighter."

"And if I run out of petrol, Griffiths? What then?" I saw all of their eyes drawn to my Luger. I picked it up. "And this just gives me extra firepower. I have one spare magazine and although it is hard to get the ammunition here, when we are in Europe I have more chance of getting 9 mm than .45, haven't I?"

"Where did you get it, Corporal?"

"In Belgium off a dead officer." I saw the looks on their faces. They were bright lads and they joined up the dots.

The afternoon was spent learning how to demolish railway lines. I had to force myself to stand back. I was the Corporal now. Private Griffiths, Ian, and Bill Beckett would have the initial responsibility for demolition although we used every Commando that afternoon. Only one charge was actually ignited using the new pressure switches. We rigged up an old railway bogey and just used a one-pound charge. It proved effective enough. The pressure switches worked and although the line was not wrecked we all saw the potential.

On the thirteenth of September, we heard that the Italians had invaded Egypt. It meant little to the rest; Egypt was a world away but to me, it was a worry. Dad was over there. He would be in danger again. Mum had not been sure if it was Crete ort Egypt. Both were problematic. Two days later we watched as German bombers tried to finally destroy London and our will to win. We later discovered that over five hundred bombers were sent by Goering. It would be the climax of the battle of Britain. We did not know that at the time but we knew that it did not bode well for London.

We also heard the sound of the German guns which were bombarding not only Dover now but also Southend just a few miles to the south of us. The work we had done had merely slowed down the Germans. They now had enormous eleven one inch railway guns. They did not have a great rate of fire but one of them managed to fire a shell fifty-five miles. They terrified the civilian population for there was no warning for an attack.

There may well have been some high up official who decided that enough was enough. Perhaps some relative had lost something. Who knew? Whatever the reason they decided to send in the Commandos. Three days after the German railway guns shelled Chatham in Kent,

Major Foster came back from London with a series of aerial photographs. We were being sent back to France.

This time I was briefed along with Daddy and the officers. "When we go over on this raid we will be attacking multiple targets. We will have three raiding parties and three targets. For that reason, each section will only know its own target. We do not want to run the risk of one section being captured and revealing information."

Corporal White said, "I am sure none of our lads would do that, sir."

"There are Waffen SS in the Pas de Calais now. Corporal Harsker will tell you about them."

I nodded, "They are ruthless, Wally. If the lads know nothing then they can reveal nothing."

"Two sections will be in France for a whole day. Number eight and number three sections will land and then make their way inland to the railway lines. Their task will be to sabotage the railway line. Hopefully, the new pressure switches will work and derail the guns."

Sergeant Johnson asked, "How many railway guns are there, sir?"

"Two but they are a little further inland than the coastal batteries and they have concrete emplacements to protect them from bombing raids. The RAF has bombed them but they are repairing them as fast as we damage them. The bombsights aren't accurate enough at the moment. It has been decided to make a ground attack. You will have to place two charges a hundred yards apart. They will be linked by wire so that when the pressure switch on one goes off it sets the other one off too. Repairing that much line takes time." He pointed to the map. "Section 8, under the command of Lieutenant Lloyd, will land from a Motor Launch here and Section 3, under the Command of Lieutenant Reed, will land here. They will also use a Motor Launch. Lieutenant Reed and Corporal Harsker both speak French which may come in handy but you will have to lie up during the day. You won't be able to get back to the MLs in daylight. You will have to wait until night."

Lieutenant Lloyd asked, "Where do we hide?"

The Major smiled, "Wherever you can. But I should warn you that the Germans will be looking for you. The rest of us will be using the LCA and we will be assaulting the guns on the cliffs and then withdrawing the same night. We have the advantage that we have been there once and know the layout. We should be able to do a better job this time. Hopefully, they will think we were the only raid as we will have the bulk of the raiders."

As we were taken through the logistics of the raid I couldn't help wondering about the logic of this. The rails could be repaired and the guns would be better protected. We were like a burglar returning to rob a house less than a week after we had done so. The Germans would be prepared and would be wary.

"You tell your men in detail about your target and no other. They will all know that the entire troop is taking part but they should not know everything. It would not help them in any case. If you are wondering, as I did, about the wisdom of this act then all I can say is that it will hurt the Germans and it will show our people that we can strike back. London has been badly hurt by the German bombers. Now Kent is being shelled too. This has come from the Prime Minister. It is deemed to be a risk worth taking." He paused and sighed, "One more thing, when we leave we will be photographed. They will be army photographers but the photographs will be shown in newspapers after the event. You know the sort of headline, **'PLUCKY SOLDIERS SHOW HERR HITLER THAT WE CAN FIGHT BACK'** that sort of thing."

I knew it was the sort of thing Dad hated but I also knew that the top brass now appreciated good propaganda like this.

"When do we leave, sir?"

"Tomorrow night, Sergeant Major Dean. We have today to brief and to practise and tomorrow to be ready. We go to Harwich to embark in the afternoon and sail at dusk."

The new men were as keen as mustard. The Lieutenant let Daddy brief them. I think he was as nervous as anyone about the daunting prospect of spending a night in Occupied France.

"Four of you will carry and be responsible for setting the explosives. That is in case anything goes wrong. Those four will lay the charges while the rest of us stand guard. That part should be a cakewalk. The gun will be guarded but we hope that the railway is not." He looked pointedly at the four men. "You have one job to do. Destroy the rails. The rest of us will stop you from being bothered and then deal with any sentries. Once it is done we head back to the coast and lay up until night time."

Private Griffiths asked, "You mean behind enemy lines?"

"That is exactly what we mean and we will have to trek five miles from the coast to reach the railway line too."

That night, after we had practised what we would do on the dummy lines the Royal Engineers had built we all checked our gear. We would need to do so again in the morning before we left for Harwich. I wrote a letter home, just in case, I didn't get back. We all did. The letters were left on the top of our beds. Those who did return would ensure they were posted. It was a reminder of our own mortality. I said what I needed to say. Dad would understand my words; as for my Mum…

The next morning everyone was up early. Daddy and I paraded our men. I held a cardboard box. Daddy said, "Right lads I want everything with writing on it in here. You just want your equipment and your identity tags. There should be nothing to identify where you are from. If you have a letter for home then leave it on your bed. If the worst comes to the worst then one of us will post it for you with a letter saying… well, you get the picture."

I saw the reality sinking in. Notes, letters, similar to the one I had written, and photographs were dropped in. I smiled, "You will get them back after we return. It's less for you to carry."

When we reached Harwich it was just after one. I saw the two motor launches and Lieutenant Commander Trimble on the LCA. We put our gear below decks on the ML we would be using and then went back to the jetty. Since we had last been here they had erected a corrugated iron wall around the port. This was partly for security and partly to prevent damage from bombs. Our old meeting hall had been totally demolished by either bombs or shells.

I saw one of the ratings I recognised from the LCA, "What happened to the survivors of the MTB which was sunk?"

"You mean Bill?" I nodded, "He was a lucky bugger and no mistake. He was made up to leading seaman and he is on a Motor Gun Boat. He is still attached to Combined Operations, he is just with another troop from Number four Commando."

I nodded, "If you see him tell him I was asking after him."

"You are as likely to see him as I am, matey."

It was sad, the bosun, Bill and the rest of the crew of the MTB had been part of our unit and we would no longer serve with them.

For the rest of the afternoon we went through all the hand signals we would be using when we were ashore. The times we could speak would be few and far between. The new boys were keen to learn.

Major Foster came aboard just before sunset. "You chaps have a hard job and I know that you are new but Sergeant Grant and Corporal Harsker are the most experienced Commandos in the troop. Do your job, obey orders and you will all get back safe. God speed."

He gestured for myself, the Lieutenant and Daddy to follow him to the gangplank. "The launch will return at midnight tomorrow. They have orders to wait for an hour but if the Germans come…"

Lieutenant Lloyd shook the Major's hand, "I know sir. We shall be there."

It was a confident call but this would be the Lieutenant's first foray into France.

We slipped silently into the dark just before dusk. The motor launch was a sleeker vessel than the MTB and was longer. We all had more room but there was just a Hotchkiss 3 pounder and two Vickers. Sadly she was still slower than the E-Boats. I knew that to the south of us were the LCA and the other ML. We had the northernmost landing zone. We were using a small beach which was close to Calais. It was a risk and it meant we had the longest journey to our target but the maps showed plenty of cover. This time the RAF was putting on a raid by Wellington bombers. They would bomb our targets. It was hoped that this would distract the German defenders and act as a double bluff. They would not think we would raid them from the ground and the air. In hindsight I can see that the thinking was flawed but, as we sneaked across a choppy Channel, we were hopeful.

We heard the drone of the bombers as they headed east. The lookout waved to show that he had seen the coast and we prepared to disembark. We saw the searchlights further south and heard the anti-aircraft batteries as they pumped 88 mm shells into the air. We were almost at the beach when we heard the first of the explosions. The Wimpeys were dropping their bombs. Putting all that from our minds we leapt ashore. I was the first one in the surf and I raced towards the low dunes. I threw myself to the ground as I heard a vehicle on the coast road. I waved my arm behind me and hoped that the others would hit the sand. The Thompson was cocked and aimed ahead in case it was danger.

The sky to the south of us was lit up by the ordnance going off. It would take a strong-minded sentry or driver not to look south. I lifted my head and saw that the road was clear of vehicles but half a mile down the road was a German roadblock. We were close to Sangatte and perhaps this was a new security measure. I half crouched and, keeping my eye on the backs of the two Germans at the roadblock, I waved my left arm to send the section across the road. The bombers must have struck something close to the guns for a column of flame rose in the distance. Daddy tapped the back of my head as he passed me and I ran across the road. I took the rear and he led us off to the next waypoint.

We were heading for Saint-Inglevert. The railway line was half a mile to the east of it. It would have been but an hour along the road, perhaps less, but we had to use the fields, woods and small villages. It would take us much longer but would be safer. We reached the road close to Peuplingues. Daddy and the Lieutenant were waiting. It had been decided that I would go first whenever we were near French houses. My French might help us. I peered down the darkened lane. The huddle of houses looked quiet and I darted across the road. I waved the others across one by one. We had to move half a mile down the lane before we could seek the safety and security of the fields once more. I took us down a route which paralleled the road, the D243. It would guarantee that we found our objective.

I saw the next village in the distance and knew that we had to keep that half a mile to the east of it. We headed across the field and I discovered it was open and had no cover whatsoever. I felt exposed; it was like the nightmare when you walk down a street in your underwear. In the distance, I could hear the receding sound of the Wellingtons' engines and the glow which marked where they had hit some guns. Major Foster was landing to the north of the battery the Wellington bombers had attacked. I hoped they had landed successfully back at their base. The RAF held a special place in my heart. I began to slow down when I saw, in the distance, the large shadow which appeared. It looked to be a building of some description. From its size, it looked to be our target. I dropped to one knee. The Lieutenant patted me on the head as he passed me. He and Gordy Barker would get a little closer to identify the building. If my navigation had been good then that would be the bunker where they housed the gun. I say bunker but we guessed it must have been made of concrete. The RAF bombs had done no damage to it at all.

I heard the sound of small arms fire in the distance. It was hard to estimate the direction. It was idle to speculate. It might be the other Commandos but it could equally be the French resistance. I turned back to my task. The Major had sent three teams in so that we would not have to worry about the others. I returned to the job in hand and I scanned the field before us.

Once the two had trotted off to check the perimeter Daddy led us to the edge of the road where we waited. It seemed to take the two of them an inordinate amount of time to reach the perimeter and be able to identify the structure but, in reality, it could only have been a few minutes. They returned and the grin on the young lieutenant's face told its own story. He pointed to the right and we followed. After half a mile or so we saw that the ground had been cleared. There was a ring of barbed wire. We set to and cut it. I smiled for all of the men had their own crude cutters. We were through in no time. Once through we peered ahead. I saw a glint and knew that it was a rail. We had found the railway line. Daddy was about to wave us forward when he held his hand up. He pointed ahead to the sign with the skull and crossbones and the single word, '**MINEN**.'

I took out my Commando knife and nodded to Daddy. He nodded back. He waved his arm for the section to spread out and I dropped to the ground. The railway line was a hundred yards away but, with a minefield before us, it might as well have been a hundred miles. The sign had been invisible from the aerial photographs. There was no way we could have known that they had put a minefield in so quickly. I began to crawl forward. We had had training in mine disposal. I was looking for freshly turned earth. The guns had only been here for a couple of weeks and they could only have put the minefield in after they had finished the railway line. I knew that, behind me, Daddy would have assigned someone to mark my route.

I edged forward over ground which looked undisturbed. Ahead, and to my right, I saw some disturbed earth and I thought I could see the small metal pressure plate which would mark a mine. I moved over to it and put my knife into the ground. It slid in easily until it touched metal. I tensed as I did so. The instructor had told us that the Germans were developing mines which could be exploded from the side as well as the top. This was not one. I was still alive! I dug around and cleared the soil away. In six months time, the ground would be too hard to do this. I carefully lifted the mine and placed it to my right. I turned and pointed. It was Ken Curtis behind me and he nodded. He had seen it. He repeated the signal for the others so that they would know there was mine. I was lucky. I only had to move three mines and then I reached the railway line. I crouched next to the metal rail and peered to the east and west. I saw no one.

I turned and saw the line of Commandos snaking across the minefield. Bert Smith was at the back and he was laying a thin rope to give us a quick and safe escape route. When they all reached us Lieutenant Lloyd patted me on the back. I nodded and signalled for Gordy to follow me. We headed down the line to the shed which housed the mighty gun. I was confident that there would be no mines within three yards of the line and so we moved quickly and confidently. I was fifty yards from the entrance when I smelled cigarette smoke. I recognised the smell; it was the same as the cigarette I had given the dying Scouser. I dropped to the ground as did Gordy. I saw, ahead, a German smoking by the shed. I rolled to the side and waved Gordy to the other. The German threw the cigarette away and began to walk towards us. This was the disaster we had hoped we could avoid. If he came close to me then I would have to kill him… silently. That would not be the disaster that would come when he was missed and they searched his patrol area. They would find the charges and then search for us. We had to remain hidden for another twenty hours! We could not afford a hue and cry.

He came closer and closer. I kept my face pressed to the ground and hoped that Gordy would do the same. He was almost within six feet of me when I heard a noise from the bunker, "Heinz, coffee!"

He turned and I heard his footsteps on the gravel between the ties as he walked back east. I waited a moment or two and then lifted my head. I saw him heading towards the door. Our Sergeant Major would have had a fit at the light which shone from it. When it went dark I rose and waved Gordy to follow me. We reached Connor and Poulson who were laying the first charges. The Lieutenant cocked his head to one side. I gave the sign for Germans and he nodded. He made the 'hurry up' sign to the two men. Gordy and I turned and faced east. Our job was to stop any Germans who tried to interfere.

Daddy tapped me on the shoulder and I turned. I could see that the charges had been laid but, alarmingly, I could see the pressure switch. I picked up a handful of soil and spread it across the switches. We moved down the line to the other charges. They had been hidden. The Lieutenant waved us back across the minefield. I went last and rolled up the rope to hide our escape route. The first light of dawn was peering from the east and its rays flashed from one of the mines. I would have to bury them again! I reached the first one and scraped the soil from the bottom of the hole. I laid it in and then covered it again. The mine still stood a little proud but I hoped that it would be hard to spot. It seemed to take forever and I was aware that I was alone in the field now and dawn was breaking. If the German sentries had binoculars they might see me. The one thing I could not do was to rush. When I had buried the last mine I picked up the rope and moved quickly to the hedge.

"What the hell kept you, Harsker?"

"I had to rebury the mines sir or they would have been seen."

Realisation flooded his face. "Well spotted. We have to find somewhere to hide and quickly."

"There was a wood in the middle of that field on the other side of the road sir. It isn't perfect and it is a little close to the line but …"

"Any port in a storm. Lead on."

I ran across the road and, quite literally, dived through the hedge on the other side. Once clear I began to run at the crouch towards the tiny wood which looked like an oasis in the ploughed field. I was just grateful that it had not rained recently or our footprints would have been clear for all to see. There was a farmhouse just a quarter of a mile to the right of us and I kept half an eye on that one. The stand of trees was more of a copse than a wood. There were just fifteen or so trees and bushes but it was cover. I collapsed into it. I saw that there was a small pond in the middle which explained why the farmer had left this anomaly in the middle of his field.

The last one through was Daddy. He grinned and, putting his head close to me whispered, "Well done, Tom, that was quick thinking." He made a circle with his hand; the signal to spread out. We had already made sure that they were in four pairs and I saw that they had followed our orders. The pairs looked north, south, east and west. They were our sentries. One would watch while the other rested and then they would switch.

Daddy and I slithered down to the pond with the Lieutenant. "Well done, Corporal but this hiding place is just too close to the gun. They will search here."

"They may not, sir. Besides, it couldn't be helped. We didn't know that Tom would have to clear the minefield, did we? Let's just see which way the dice falls eh? " Daddy opened his bag and took out his water bottle. He poured some into his mug and mixed it with some porridge and some salt. It was a disgusting concoction but the powers that be had told us that this would give us energy and stop us from becoming dehydrated. I did the same. I could see the frown on the Lieutenant's face as he swallowed the gloop. I reached into my Bergen and unwrapped the greaseproof paper. I broke off two squares of fruit cake and handed them to the other two. It was little enough but it would take away the taste of the salt. They nodded gratefully and we all ate the little luxury slowly to savour the taste. Mum would have approved. I savoured every morsel.

Dawn broke fully and we heard vehicles moving down the road. Then we heard the sound of an engine getting up steam. A cloud of black smoke appeared above the hedge line. At eight o'clock we heard the sound of doors being opened and we moved back to the edge of the wood so that we could see. Only half of the huge bunker was visible but we saw the steam from the train as it moved the huge gun into position. I was picturing where it would be. I saw the very top of the barrel above the distant hedgerow. It was almost an anti-climax when we heard the double explosions and the barrel jumped in the air and then disappeared. There was no flash of fire and the explosion seemed almost muted. The klaxon we heard, however, was a joyous sound. We had succeeded. We had not destroyed the gun but that day in September and the next were two days when they would not terrorise the civilians across the Channel. We now had to stay alive and that would not be easy.

Chapter 21

It was as though an ant's nest had been disturbed. We heard the sound of vehicles as they raced down the road from distant checkpoints and barracks. The noise from the smoking field grew. We could hear orders being barked out. We could not, however, see anything. It was our minds which saw what we had done and that was only guesswork. And then the rain started. I had been so concerned about the gun that, once the sun had risen, I had blocked the sky from my mind. As the first drop fell, however, I looked up and saw the heavy rainclouds rolling in from behind me. I pressed myself into the bole of a tree to escape the worst of the rain. It soon became apparent that the rain was not just a passing shower. The sky was rain-filled. It bounced down. I was grateful that I had managed to choose an old tree with big branches and I remained mercifully dry.

The Lieutenant crawled to the edge of the woods. Visibility had been diminished but we could still see as far as the hedge. He crawled back, "I can't see anything. What do you think, Sergeant?"

"I think we are nice and safe here for the moment." Sergeant Grant pointed to the pairs of men and added, "The lads will watch. You get your head down Lieutenant. We will keep an eye on things. This suits me. It means Jerry can't see us as well and it will slow down their repairs."

He pointed up, "Sleep? In this?"

Daddy laughed, "Don't worry, you close your eyes, sir and you will be asleep before you know it."

He reluctantly crawled back to join us beneath the tree. There were still plenty of leaves on the tree above us and we had a dry spot. He was soon breathing heavily; Daddy had been right. We moved a little way away so that we could talk. "The rain is a Godsend, Sarge."

"How's that?"

"If we did leave any tracks then the rain will hide them and it will make the ground around those mines that I moved muddy. They will not know how we got there. If they had seen the disturbed soil around the mines they would have known."

"I know but it makes moving harder when we do leave the safety of this wood."

I shrugged, "We have got until midnight. That means we have four hours of darkness to reach the rendezvous point. We can do it in an hour at the most."

"Perhaps. The roads will be crawling with Germans."

"Germans who have been working all day and will be tired. Besides they will think we are long gone."

"I suppose. Best go round and see how the lads are, eh Tom?"

I crawled to the bush under which Polly and Ken sheltered. "How are things? See anything?"

"Not certain, Corp. I thought I heard the sound of an engine but I can't be sure."

"They would be using the engine to pull the gun back on to the rails. That won't be easy. If you see anyone appear then give a whistle. That means civilian or German."

I turned to go and Ken asked, "Do you think we got it, Corp?"

"The charges went off and the gun isn't firing." I looked at my watch, "It is ten o'clock now and we were told that the gun normally fired its first round at nine o'clock. I think we have stopped it firing."

"But they can repair the line."

"Of course they can, Poulson, and the gun will fire again but that won't be for two or three days. They also have to pull the derailed gun back on to the track. That may take them as long, if not longer than repairing the rails. Even then they will have to check the damage on the gun too. When the skies clear the RAF will send over reconnaissance aeroplanes and, later, bombers. It is easier to slow down building than bomb railway lines."

They nodded, "I wonder how the other teams got on?"

"We will have to wait until we get home to discover that."

"But we will get home, Corp."There was nervousness in Curtis' voice. He was like a child seeking reassurance from a parent.

"You are a Commando, Curtis; you always get home!"

I left them but the confidence I had to try to imbue was not within me. The coast would be alive with angry Germans seeking us. We had one chance to get off on a Motor Launch and that was all. It took me fifteen minutes to get around the others. By then the rain had slackened to a drizzle. By eleven it had stopped.

"What worries me, Tom is that we haven't heard any other explosions. How did the others get on? I would have expected the guns the major was attacking to have made a bit of a noise."

"I know. The railway track explosion was not loud. I didn't necessarily expect to hear the sound of the other railway gun being sabotaged but the guns on the cliffs is a different matter. I wonder now about that small arms fire."

I crawled to the western edge and saw the sky lightening over England. There was a whistle and I scurried, along with Daddy, over to Poulson and Curtis. They pointed towards four Germans, with machine pistols who had entered the field. I slithered down to the Lieutenant, "Germans sir, in the field."

I went back to the other three and armed the Thompson. I saw them scanning the wood with binoculars. It looked as though they were staring at us but I knew that was an illusion. We were blacked up and not moving. One of the exercises back in England we did was an adult game of hide and seek. It was a game at which we excelled. All of us of could remain still for hours at a time. It was movement which gave you away. I breathed a sigh of relief as they put their glasses away. I felt a movement close to my leg and I cautioned the Lieutenant with my hand. He moved imperceptibly until he was between Daddy and me.

The Germans began examining the ground and then they began to move towards us. If they reached the woods then they would see us. I began to calculate if we could escape from the wood and make the next road to the west without being seen. The Germans had vehicles. It was unlikely. Just then we heard, as did the Germans, the sound of a Merlin engine. I glanced up and saw the Spitfire zoom from the west. It was only armed with a camera but it made the Germans scurry back to the safety of the field boundary. They raised their guns and popped away ineffectually at the fast-moving fighter. Other guns and anti-aircraft joined in the welcome. The Spitfire circled and then spiralled up before heading back west.

The three of us moved back down as the Germans left the field. "Is that it do you think, Sergeant?"

"Dunno sir, but it has given us a little more time. The Spit will report back and then, who knows?"

A short while later we all heard the unmistakable sound of small arms fire to the south and east. That was worrying for this time it would not be the resistance. It had to be Commandos. That meant it was either the other team who were waiting like us for night to fall or some of the major's men had not made it back home. Worry and concern for Sean and the others nagged in the back of my mind.

At one o'clock we heard the distant drone of engines. It grew closer. Through the foliage, I saw to the west fifteen Blenheims. Six of them peeled off and headed in our direction while the other nine continued east. We heard the German siren sound and then the flak as they fired at the bombers. This time we felt the ground shake as the bombs from the Blenheim bombers fell. Some of the bombs had to be incendiary for flames shot up in the air. It was either that or the bombers had hit some vehicles. After their bombing run, the six turned and headed west. A pall of smoke covered the field with the railway gun but I saw two of the Blenheims smoking. They had not escaped unscathed.

The bombing raid must have had an effect for we heard more vehicles arriving at the field and more noise of repair. It was as we had speculated our work had enabled the bombers to damage the gun when it was vulnerable and in the open. We had lured the beast from the safety of its cave. During the afternoon Daddy and I took the opportunity for an hour of sleep. Daddy shook me awake at five in the afternoon. "It's all quiet but we need to get some food and be ready to move soon." I nodded, "When you have eaten you had better check the map for the best way back to the rendezvous."

The first thing I noticed, when I looked up was that I could see the top of a crane which had a cable dangling. They had brought heavy equipment in to right the wrecked railway gun. If the bombers came back now then they could do even more damage. The sky was still filled with rainclouds and the bombers might not be able to take off. I ate more of the dried rations and drank some water. I would not risk refilling with water from the pond. There was no need. I still had a few mouthfuls in the canteen. We tried to use moving water to refill whenever possible. It was healthier. I crawled to the western end of the wood. Our route back would be the reverse of the previous night. The difference was that the Germans would be on the alert now. The empty roads of the previous night might be just a little busier,

As soon as darkness fell I slipped from the woods, leading the others. I had confirmed the route on the map. It would be the reverse of our outward route. The danger this time would be checkpoints which had not been there the previous night. I felt terribly exposed but I knew that was an illusion. It was pitch black. We would be almost impossible to see. The rain might have gone but it had left cloudy skies behind. We were approaching the road on the far side of the field when I heard a vehicle. I waved my hand and dropped down on the muddy field. The sound moved from the north and then disappeared south. I reached the hedge and, after peering through clambered on the road. There appeared to be no one and I waved the others through. I crossed the road and disappeared into the hedge on the other side.

All went well until we neared Peuplingues. I heard voices and, peering down the road, I saw a German vehicle. It was a checkpoint. That way was out. We could not go back the way we had come. I waved the others to my left. I had the map in my head. There was another route. We would have to head for the coast and the village of Escalles. It was close to one of the gun emplacements and there would be Germans there but it could not be helped; the roadblock showed that they were seeking us at Peuplingues.

We crossed fields which had not been ploughed. There had been animals in these fields before the war. Now there were craters. This area had either been shelled or bombed. It was handy as we would have somewhere to shelter if we saw anyone. We heard traffic on the road ahead and I waved the men to the ground. Khaki was as good as black at night time in a field; especially one which was as uneven as this.

I bellied up to the hedge which was next to the road. The farmer who had planted it had wanted to stop the withering winds from the sea. It was only a low one. It suited us for the rest of the section all made the safety of the hedge and had somewhere to hide. I waited until the road was quiet. I was about to move across when I heard two vehicles approach. I took shelter once more. This time they stopped and the drivers turned off their engines. I heard a match strike and then smelled German cigarette smoke.

I glanced at my watch; it had a luminous dial. It was ten o'clock. We had two hours to get to the beach which was now less than a mile away. There were Germans to the east and north of us and now to the west. I wondered if we should head for the other rendezvous point. I turned and looked at the Lieutenant and Daddy. I pointed through the hedge and shrugged. The Lieutenant pointed to his gun. Daddy shook his head and made the sign for '*patience*'.

Then the Germans spoke. "Are you certain the radio message said that the Englanders were coming this way?"

"Yes, Feldwebel. The Oberlieutenant said that they were Commandos and they had automatic weapons."

"Well, I can see no sign of them. If it was the same Commandos who blew up the gun they must be lost for they are moving in circles. We will wait another half hour and then backtrack to see if we can find them."

I was the only one who would have understood the words. Perhaps that was a good thing. The others would be terrified if they knew that we had been seen. I wondered where and when. Ten minutes later I had my answer.

"There they are! Open fire!"

There was a sudden rattle of rifle and machine pistol fire and then the heavy bark of an MG 42. They were not firing at us. I cocked my gun anyway and then took out a grenade. I saw the others do the same.

"Cease fire!" I could smell the cordite in the air and I heard the moan of a wounded or perhaps dying, man. The Feldwebel spoke again but this time it was in English. "Hands up!"

I heard a voice that I recognised, it was Sergeant Jack Johnson. This was the other team. It was our old section. "All right Fritz, we have a wounded man with us!"

I turned to the others. They too had heard the sergeant. I decided to risk rising. I needed to know how many we faced. I did it slowly. As my head cleared the hedge I saw that there were two Kübelwagen. They were on the other side of the road, about twenty feet away and the Waffen SS were looking towards the clifftop. One Kübelwagen had an MG 42 attached to a metal pole next to the driver. There were four Germans that I could see. I turned and made the sign for two vehicles and four men. The Lieutenant waved the men to their feet and, like me, they peered over the top. I could not see Sergeant Johnson and his men. I had no idea how many there were. From Jack's words at least one was wounded.

Just then I heard the Feldwebel say, "Shoot them they are not in uniform!"

I threw my grenade at the machine gun, fired my Thompson and shouted, "Down lads, they are going to shoot you!" The Feldwebel turned at the English voice behind him. Every gun in our section opened fire and tore into the Germans. I saw my bullets strike the Waffen SS Feldwebel. His body danced as tough a puppeteer was working him. There was a crump and a wall of air knocked us to the ground as the Kübelwagen was struck by my grenade. I lay for a moment, winded. I had been lucky. Shrapnel did not care who it struck. I rose to my feet and, groggily, clambered on to the road. The Germans were all dead. One had been torn in two by the combined fire of two Thompson machine guns. Daddy joined me as we searched for our friends. We found Sean and Sergeant Johnson. They were bandaging Corporal White and Percy Cunningham. Wally looked to have injured his arm but Percy's left leg appeared to have taken a number of bullets. I left the Lieutenant to ask the inevitable questions and to administer first aid.

I grabbed Poulson and Barker. "Find any German stick grenades and bring them to me. We are going to leave some booby traps." While they searched I went to the body of the machine gunner. He was slumped forward in his seat which had survived the impact. After taking the maps and papers from the well of the vehicle I took the pin from my Mills bomb and then carefully jammed it beneath his bloody body. The deadweight held the handle in place. When they came to move it they would get a nasty surprise but, more importantly, we would have a warning that they had discovered the ambush.

The two men came back with four stick grenades. This would be a rapid lesson in sabotage. "Watch me and then do the same on the other one." I broke the porcelain safety device and then carefully laid the grenade across the seat. I leaned in and tied the cord to the inside handle. "When Jerry pulls the door open it will yank the cord and the grenade will go up. They nodded and left. I took the last two and repeated the same but this time I put them underneath the body of the Feldwebel and the wheel of the Kübelwagen.

I saw that the others were still tending to the wounded. "Sir, I don't want to rush you but we have a boat to catch and I can hear more vehicles coming."

He nodded. "Right lads, back to the rendezvous point."

Daddy joined me, "Harsker and I will be rearguard, sir."

"Righto. Don't be too long." Carrying a wounded man would slow them down and we needed to see how many came to find us. I guessed that the vehicles came from the checkpoint at Peuplingues. I had seen at least ten men there.

The others hurried down towards the sea; Percy and Wally would slow them down. We were close enough to the beach for us to make the boat if it arrived on time. The question remained, would the Germans allow us the time? We stopped just a hundred yards from the wrecked vehicles and lay down in the sand. The distance was far enough away for us to be both hidden from sight and far enough away to avoid injury when the booby traps went off. Equally, we were close enough to hurl grenades and to fire at them.

Suddenly Sean appeared at our side and cocked his Thompson, "Can't let you two get all the glory can I?"

It was pointless reprimanding him and besides, I could hear trucks coming from the direction of Peuplingues. I had already changed my magazine and I took out my last two grenades. I laid them before me. The three of us were spread out and our frontage was just twelve feet. The first truck had dimmed headlights and he came cautiously. He stopped thirty feet from the Kübelwagen. An officer waved his men forward. There were twenty of them. Another truck came from the direction of Boulogne. There were more Germans than I had anticipated.

The officer shouted, "Anyone alive?" The silence was only broken by the surf below us. "Spread out and look for the Englanders."

I was on the left and I tracked the five men who came to my side of the Kübelwagen. One of them pulled open the door and the grenade went off. The others dived to the floor but the explosion made the Kübelwagen roll back a little and the second grenade went off and scythed through the Germans who were sheltering beneath. The Kübelwagen kept rolling down the slight slope and bumped into the other one. The impact must have knocked the German grenade and that too went off.

The second truck disgorged its men and then they ran to tend the wounded. A few men came around the vehicles and headed towards the tops of the dunes. Daddy whispered, "Grenades. They will think it is more booby traps."

We hurled the three grenades and then buried our faces in the sand. The shrapnel whistled over our heads. The screams and shouts in German told their own tale. They were confused. "Back down to the beach."

We slid backwards for thirty yards until we could risk standing and we moved slowly down the slope. Above us the leaderless Germans, for the officer had been killed, were milling around. They would take some time to continue their search. We reached the beach and I checked my watch. It was just ten to midnight. With luck, we would only have minutes to wait. I glanced up at the road and saw more dimmed headlights appear. They were being reinforced. The exploding vehicles had alerted the enemy. I tapped Daddy on the shoulder and pointed. He nodded and, turning to the Lieutenant said, "I reckon we have fifteen minutes at the most, sir."

Just then a Very pistol was fired and a flare went into the air. We were all frozen like a tableau as the slowly descending light illuminated the whole of the beach. A second flare followed. I heard a German voice order them down to the beach and then machine guns sounded. Their tracer arced towards us.

Sean said, "Make that five minutes, sir! Unless Navy gets his finger out we will be up shit creek without a paddle!"

We had two wounded, one of them seriously and we had at least twenty odd Germans coming for us. I saw the Lieutenant looking indecisive. "Sir, like Dunkirk eh? Take the wounded out into the water to meet the ML. Navy won't let us down."

"Good idea. Smith and Ford, take Cunningham and Corporal White out to sea. Just leave your heads showing above the water."

"Sir, I can make it on my own."

"Just do it, Corporal. The rest of you back to the water and lie in the surf. The foam may hide us."

It was a good idea and we backed into the water and then lay down. I had one grenade left and, before I left the dry sand I took out the pin and placed it underneath a flat rock. "Get a move on Tom!"

"Coming, Sarge." I hit the water none too soon for there was a rattle of machine gunfire. They had aimed at where we had been stood and the bullets whistled harmlessly overhead.

"Hold your fire. Keep them confused!"

I heard Norman shout, "Sir, I can hear the ML!"

The Germans must have realised we were lying down for they began to aim at the edge of the sea. Their first volley hit nothing but a shout from Gordy told me that they had adjusted their sights. He had been hit.

"Open fire."

We had the advantage of the light from the burning vehicles behind them and we let loose with our Thompsons. The .45 bullet is a man stopper and the line of advancing Germans was forced to lie down too. One must have disturbed the rock covered grenade and I saw his body flung into the air as shrapnel hit the men on either side.

"Into the sea, while they are recovering." As we crouched to retreat we fired again and then moved west. There were more volleys from the Germans.

I saw Ken Curtis fall into the water and, firing one handed I ran to him. "Leave me, Corp, I'll slow you down!"

"We leave no one behind. " I slung my Thompson and hoisted him over my shoulder in a fireman's lift. I drew my Browning and aimed at the three men who ran at me. I fired as though I was on the range. I fired four shots and three fell. I turned and began to wade out into the blackness. I saw a lightening of the dark and I knew it was the ML.

Bullets zipped into the water behind me. I was nearly deafened as Curtis emptied his magazine from over my shoulder, "Got you, you bugger!"

We were the last two and I heard the others urging us on while emptying the last of their magazines at the Germans. I was chest-deep in the sea when I reached the bow. I had no strength left to lift Curtis but the others hauled him up and, as the ML reversed I was pulled to safety by Sean and Daddy. Daddy shook his head, "Always the bloody hero eh?"

If we thought we were out of the woods we were wrong. We had certainly disturbed the wasps' nest. The young lieutenant who commanded the Motor Launch tried everything he could to extricate us from our predicament. While Percy and Wally were taken below decks he gave full power as he thundered west. There were too many Germans who knew of our presence for us to escape without pursuit. We all changed our magazines; we only had one left each and I had no grenades.

I sat amidships with Daddy and Sergeant Johnson. Daddy asked as we checked our guns. "What happened?"

He shook his head, "A cock-up from start to finish. We found a minefield and Davis set one off and blew himself up. It wasn't the Lieutenant's fault, Davis was just clumsy. He rushed it. We headed south, to take attention away from the guns and from you lads. We were lucky at first and we hid up during the day in a little wood. Then we headed towards the rendezvous. That was when we hit trouble. The Germans were all over the roads like fleas on a dog. The Lieutenant did well until we ran into a large patrol. He and Golightly took the two new lads and headed inland to draw them off and we headed for the beach. They were waiting for us. That was where Wally got it. McKinley was good. He should be corporal after this. He was rearguard all the way. We managed to avoid trouble and we decided to head for your rendezvous point. We had almost made it when we ran into those Krauts. If Tom hadn't shouted then we would have been dead."

Daddy nodded, "What do you reckon happened to the others?"

He shook his head, "Only two outcomes, dead or in the bag. He was a good lad was the Lieutenant. He just didn't have Tom's luck."

The first light of dawn was appearing over the French coast. We were halfway across and began to believe that we would survive. I had read, at school, of the Vikings who believed in these three sisters called the Norns who spent each day weaving webs of deceit and confusion so that man would be forever trapped in their plans and plots. That night I began to believe in them. As dawn broke the lookout shouted, "Stuka!"

A line of six Stukas appeared in the east. They were not the fastest of aeroplanes but they were faster than the ML. I remembered the retreat and how we had fought them off before. "Sir, I have fought these before. We need to send up a solid wall of fire."

He shouted, "Thanks, Harsker, but there are six of them and we are short of ammo. Sarn't Johnson, your lads fire at the first one, Sarn't Grant you, Smith and Poulson fire at the second, Harsker, Barker and Griffiths at the third and we will all fire at the fourth."

Sean mumbled, "And then we are out of bullets!"

"What about the ammunition from the wounded lads?"

The Lieutenant was no slouch, "I'll get them. Johnson, take charge!"

We braced ourselves against whatever we could find. The first Stuka began its attack. The scream of the siren no longer worried us but the machine guns and the bombs it carried did. The Hotchkiss sounded powerful but it was no use against a diving Stuka. It was made to fire at slow-moving ships and not diving bombers. The two Vickers, however, could fire five hundred rounds per minute and were belt-fed. The two machine guns converged their fire and the three Tommy guns added to the wall of lead. The leading pilot was the commander and he was determined to carry out his orders. It cost him his life. The bullets of five machine guns tore through the propeller, engine, cockpit, pilot and gunner. It never pulled out of its dive. It hit the sea and disappeared from sight. The second pilot was also brave and he managed to drop his bomb before his wheel was shot away and his gull-wing damaged. He headed home. His bomb hit twenty yards astern. Had we had depth charges then our stern might have been blown off.

Then it was my turn. "Wait for my command, lads." I did not want to risk missing and so I waited and when we did fire we could not miss. The Vickers' gunners had their eye in and we were bolstered by the success of the others. Like his leader, we destroyed the aircraft. The remaining three were more cautious. They circled and tried to use their rear gunner to fire at us. It was not successful. They tried another attack but the heart had gone from them along with their leader. Each Stuka dropped his bombs from too great a height and they exploded noisily but harmless astern. We were still nervous and watched to the east for either more aeroplanes or the dreaded E-Boats, until the lieutenant who commanded the boat shouted, "We are under an air force umbrella lads, we have made it." I looked up and saw the Hurricanes as they came to follow the departing Stukas.

I stood and saw the thin line that was the coastline of England. We were almost home.

Epilogue

Harwich had been bombed again. Even as we came ashore the hard-worked firemen were still dousing the fires. As we approached the dock I saw the other ML. That was undamaged and the LCA. Welders were already at work repairing the damage.

Captain Foster awaited us, his arm in a sling. He shook Lieutenant Lloyd by the hand. "Well done Roger, you were the only section who completed their mission." Behind the Major, I saw Sergeant Major Dean. He was smiling. He touched his beret with his swagger stick. It was a salute.

I looked at Daddy in surprise. He shrugged.

"Really sir? We know about Lieutenant Reed's problems. What happened to you?"

"They had strengthened their beach defences. We never even got ashore. They had machine guns, barbed wire and mines. There looked to be a company. We lost ten men and didn't hit a single German. We were lucky to get away without losing the landing craft. We had to head back home." He held up his arm. "I was lucky. We waited at Headquarters. We heard from the Spitfire reconnaissance aeroplane that you had damaged the rail and derailed the gun. It enabled the Blenheims to put the line out of action for at least a week. The gun was on its side and we will send another Spit over tomorrow to see the effect of the Blenheims. Well done. You succeeded in your mission. You prevented a mishap from becoming a disaster but, even so, we have lost Algie and some good men."

The Lieutenant nodded towards us, "My success is down to you, sir. You gave me the best section in the whole troop. A man would have to be a complete idiot not to succeed with those men. They worked as a team and never panicked once. I would like to recommend Corporal Harsker for the Military Cross, sir. He saved not only his own section but also the men of Sergeant Johnson's too."

Sergeant Johnson said, "And that is right sir! We would all be dead but for Tom sir."

Captain Foster turned to me, "You are a constant surprise Corporal, and yet you should not be. You are your father in every way shape and form. You may not be a fighter ace but you are something just as good, you are a Commando!"

I nodded; I had tried to escape my name and escape my past but I could not. My father's blood coursed through my veins too. I had been a fool to think I could avoid a comparison. This was not a competition. I was a Harsker and I was just doing what my Dad had done and my grandfather too. I daresay if I had gone back in time I would have found Harskers doing the same thing at the Alma, Waterloo, Blenheim; probably back to Agincourt and Crecy. You don't change your blood.

"Thank you, sir, I take that as a compliment." I took out the papers I had recovered from the Kübelwagen. "I found these too sir. I thought they might have some useful information in them. "

He nodded, "And I am glad that you decided to join us. The 1st Loyals' loss is our gain."

As I trudged towards the waiting lorries I was happy that I had left the OTC and University. That had led me to the 1st Loyals and that in turn had taken me here. I was only a corporal but I was a corporal in the Commandos and it did not get any better than that.

The End

Glossary

Butties- sandwiches (slang)
Chah- tea (slang)
Comforter- the lining for the helmet; a sort of woollen hat
Corned dog- Corned Beef (slang)
Fruit salad- medal ribbons (slang)
MTB- Motor Torpedo Boat
Oik- worthless person (slang)
Oppo/oppos- pals/comrades (slang)
Potato mashers- German Hand Grenades (slang)
Schnellboote -German for E-boat (literally fast boat)
Scragging - roughing someone up (slang)
Scrumpy- farm cider
Stag- sentry duty (slang)
squaddy- ordinary soldier (slang)
Tommy (Atkins)- Ordinary British soldier
Two penn'orth- two pennies worth (slang for opinion)
WVS- Women's Voluntary Service

Historical note

The first person I would like to thank for this particular book and series is my Dad. He was in the Royal Navy but served in Combined Operations. He was at Dieppe, D-Day and Walcheren. His boat: LCA 523 was the one which took in the French Commandos on D-Day. He was proud that his ships had taken in Bill Millens and Lord Lovat. I wish that, before he died I had learned more in detail about life in Combined Operations but like many heroes, he was reluctant to speak of the war. He is the character in the book called Bill Leslie. I went back in 1994 with my Dad to Sword beach and he took me through that day on June 6th 1944. We even found the grave of his cousin George Hogan who died on D-Day. As far as I know, we were the only members of the family ever to do so. Sadly, that was Dad's only visit but we planted forget-me-nots on the grave of George.

I would also like to thank Roger who is my railway expert. The train Tom and the Major catch from Paddington to Oswestry ran until 1961. The details of the livery, the compartments and the engine are all, hopefully accurate. I would certainly not argue with Roger!

I used a number of books in the research. The list is at the end of this historical section. However, the best book, by far, was the actual Commando handbook which was reprinted in 2012. All of the details about hand to hand, explosives, esprit de corps etc were taken directly from it. The advice about salt, oatmeal and water is taken from the book. It even says that taking too much salt is not a bad thing! I shall use the book as a Bible for the rest of the series. The Commandos were expected to find their own accommodation. Some even saved the money for lodgings and slept rough. That did not mean that standards of discipline and presentation were neglected; they were not.

The 1st Loyal Lancashire existed as a regiment. They were in the BEF and they were the rearguard. All the rest is the work of the author's imagination. The use of booby traps using grenades was common. The details of the German potato masher grenade are also accurate. The Germans used the grenade as an early warning system by hanging them from fences so that an intruder would move the grenade and it would explode.

During the retreat the British tank, the Matilda was superior to the German Panzer. It was slow but it was so heavily armoured that it could only be stopped by using the 88 anti-aircraft guns. Had there been more of them and had they been used in greater numbers then who knows what the outcome might have been. What they did succeed in doing, however, was making the German High Command believe that we had more tanks than they actually encountered. The Germans thought that they had many more times the 17 Matildas who actually held them up. They halted at Arras for reinforcements. That enabled the Navy to take off over 300,000 men from the beaches.

Although we view Dunkirk as a disaster now, at the time it was seen as a setback. An invasion force set off to reinforce the French a week after Dunkirk. It was recalled. Equally, there were many units cut off behind enemy lines. The Highland Division was one such force. 10,000 men were captured. The fate of many of those captured in the early days of the war was to be sent to work in factories making weapons which would be used against England.

The Germans had radar stations and they were accurate. They also had large naval guns at Cape Gris Nez as well as railway guns. They made the Channel dangerous although they only actually sank a handful of ships during the whole of the war. They did, however, make Southend and Kent dangerous places to live.

The E-Boats were far superior to the early MTBS and Motor Launches. It was not until the Fairmile boats were developed that the tide swung in the favour of the Royal Navy. Some MTBs were fitted with depth charges. Bill's improvisation is the sort of thing Combined Operations did. It could have ended in disaster but in this case, it did not.

The first Commando raids were a shambles. Churchill himself took action and appointed Sir Roger Keyes to bring some order to what the Germans called thugs and killers. Major Foster and his troop reflect that change.

The details about the Commando equipment are also accurate. They were issued with American weapons although some did use the Lee Enfield. When large numbers attacked the Lofoten Islands they used regular army issue. The Commandos appeared in dribs and drabs but 1940 was the year when they began their training. It was Lord Lovat who gave them a home in Scotland but that was not until 1941. I wanted my hero, Tom, to begin to fight early. His adventures will continue throughout the war.

Reference Books used

- The Commandos Pocket Manual 1949-45: Christopher Westhorp
- The Second World War Miscellany: Norman Ferguson

Commando

- Army Commandos 1940-45: Mike Chappell
- World War II: Donald Sommerville
- The Historical Atlas of World War II: Swanst
  Swanston

Griff Hos* ... 1915

Other books by Griff Hosker

If you enjoyed reading this book, then why not read another one by the author?

Ancient History

The Sword of Cartimandua Series
(Germania and Britannia 50 A.D. – 128 A.D.)
Ulpius Felix- Roman Warrior (prequel)
The Sword of Cartimandua
The Horse Warriors
Invasion Caledonia
Roman Retreat
Revolt of the Red Witch
Druid's Gold
Trajan's Hunters
The Last Frontier
Hero of Rome
Roman Hawk
Roman Treachery
Roman Wall
Roman Courage

The Wolf Warrior series
(Britain in the late 6th Century)
Saxon Dawn
Saxon Revenge
Saxon England
Saxon Blood
Saxon Slayer
Saxon Slaughter
Saxon Bane
Saxon Fall: Rise of the Warlord
Saxon Throne
Saxon Sword

Commando

Medieval History

The Dragon Heart Series
Viking Slave
Viking Warrior
Viking Jarl
Viking Kingdom
Viking Wolf
Viking War
Viking Sword
Viking Wrath
Viking Raid
Viking Legend
Viking Vengeance
Viking Dragon
Viking Treasure
Viking Enemy
Viking Witch
Viking Blood
Viking Weregeld
Viking Storm
Viking Warband
Viking Shadow
Viking Legacy
Viking Clan
Viking Bravery

The Norman Genesis Series
Hrolf the Viking
Horseman
The Battle for a Home
Revenge of the Franks
The Land of the Northmen
Ragnvald Hrolfsson
Brothers in Blood
Lord of Rouen
Drekar in the Seine
Duke of Normandy
The Duke and the King

Danelaw

Commando

(England and Denmark in the 11th Century)
Dragon Sword
Oathsword

New World Series
Blood on the Blade
Across the Seas
The Savage Wilderness
The Bear and the Wolf
Erik The Navigator
Erik's Clan

The Vengeance Trail

The Reconquista Chronicles
Castilian Knight
El Campeador
The Lord of Valencia

The Aelfraed Series
(Britain and Byzantium 1050 A.D. - 1085 A.D.)
Housecarl
Outlaw
Varangian

The Anarchy Series England 1120-1180
English Knight
Knight of the Empress
Northern Knight
Baron of the North
Earl
King Henry's Champion
The King is Dead
Warlord of the North
Enemy at the Gate
The Fallen Crown
Warlord's War
Kingmaker
Henry II
Crusader

Commando

The Welsh Marches
Irish War
Poisonous Plots
The Princes' Revolt
Earl Marshal
The Perfect Knight

Border Knight
1182-1300
Sword for Hire
Return of the Knight
Baron's War
Magna Carta
Welsh Wars
Henry III
The Bloody Border
Baron's Crusade
Sentinel of the North
War in the West
Debt of Honour
The Blood of the Warlord
The Fettered King

Sir John Hawkwood Series
France and Italy 1339- 1387
Crécy: The Age of the Archer
Man At Arms
The White Company
Leader of Men
Tuscan Warloed

Lord Edward's Archer
Lord Edward's Archer
King in Waiting
An Archer's Crusade
Targets of Treachery
The Great Cause
Wallace's War
Struggle for a Crown
1360- 1485
Blood on the Crown

Commando

To Murder A King
The Throne
King Henry IV
The Road to Agincourt
St Crispin's Day
The Battle For France
The Last Knight

Tales from the Sword I
(Short stories from the Medieval period)

Tudor Warrior series
England and Scotland in the late 145th and early 15th century
Tudor Warrior
Tudor Spy
Flodden

Conquistador
England and America in the 16th Century
Conquistador

Modern History

The Napoleonic Horseman Series
Chasseur à Cheval
Napoleon's Guard
British Light Dragoon
Soldier Spy
1808: The Road to Coruña
Talavera
The Lines of Torres Vedras
Bloody Badajoz
The Road to France
Waterloo

The Lucky Jack American Civil War series
Rebel Raiders
Confederate Rangers
The Road to Gettysburg

The Soldier of the Queen Series

Commando

Soldier of the Queen
Redcoat's Rifle

The British Ace Series
1914
1915 Fokker Scourge
1916 Angels over the Somme
1917 Eagles Fall
1918 We will remember them
From Arctic Snow to Desert Sand
Wings over Persia

Combined Operations series
1940-1945
Commando
Raider
Behind Enemy Lines
Dieppe
Toehold in Europe
Sword Beach
Breakout
The Battle for Antwerp
King Tiger
Beyond the Rhine
Korea
Korean Winter

Tales from the Sword II
(Short stories from the Modern period)

Other Books
Great Granny's Ghost (Aimed at 9-14-year-old young people)

For more information on all of the books then please visit the author's website at www.griffhosker.com where there is a link to contact him or visit his Facebook page: GriffHosker at Sword Books

Made in United States
North Haven, CT
18 April 2024

51512313R00117